*The world's most powerful toxin is now
a weapon of mass destruction—
and a madman is ready to use it!*

OVERKILL

Robert Stark: He walked out on the CIA and its murderous games. Now he's in the protection racket—and his client is the woman everyone wants dead . . .

Sultana Mirnov: In the U.S.S.R. sh[e] who pursued biological research. Bu[t] brought in the KGB. And she di[d] ran . . .

Les Halliwell: Ex–Secret Service with White House experience. He's Stark's partner in hostage rescue—but he drops out when the game heats up . . .

Benedict MacMillan: His father made billions trading between East and West. Now Benedict will deploy the company's deadliest asset—biological killer that can wipe out millions . . .

Peter Hornaday: He's deputy to the National Security Adviser. But when MacMillan threatens blackmail, he's trapped—and sends the CIA after Sultana and Stark . . .

Charon: The CIA's top assassin, he thwarted Stark years before. Stark knows he's out there, hunting him down . . .

OVERKILL

MARK SCHORR

POCKET BOOKS
New York   London   Toronto   Sydney   Tokyo

Another *Original* publication of POCKET BOOKS

POCKET BOOKS, a division of Simon & Schuster Inc.
1230 Avenue of the Americas, New York, N.Y. 10020

ISBN: 978-1-451-67237-4

First Pocket Books printing July 1988

10 9 8 7 6 5 4 3 2 1

POCKET and colophon are trademarks of Simon & Schuster Inc.

Printed in the U.S.A.

To Hastings House, Ltd.:
Ida, Paul, Miriam,
Michael, David & Rachael

ACKNOWLEDGMENTS

I wish to thank David Keene, M.D., in Los Angeles and officials at the Atlanta Centers for Disease Control for their advice on the thousands of shocks flesh is heir to.

I also appreciate the time and advice given me by the former FBI counterintelligence agent and the CIA case officer who assisted in my research. They, as well as the three Russian émigrés I consulted with, have requested anonymity.

Any errors which have crept into the work are mine alone.

PROLOGUE

The American army surplus Huey helicopter with *federales* markings traveled low over the trees. The pilot—who had been a dope smuggler before he was recruited by the mercenary he knew as Jefe—could avoid radar with ease.

The chopper passed over a large rocky field where seraped men worked with short hoes on the corn crop. Corn, beans, and squash provided ninety percent of their diet. Chicken or goat meat was reserved for a once-a-week treat.

As the chopper reached the dirt square at the center of the village, the four boys kicking a peeling soccer ball back and forth stopped and waved. Women, working at their outdoor looms and gossiping, barely bothered to look up. But their young daughters, who were supposed to be learning the craft of weaving, were distracted. The girls, too, waved excitedly.

The Indians weren't frightened by the helicopter. They had been visited several times by government officials in such noisy beasts. The officials brought vaccines, food (during a famine), and lots of promises. It was fun to listen to the promises and pretend they would come to pass.

"We will be building a road here . . . a school is going up . . . more money will be paid for crops next year . . . a land reform program is being started."

The helicopter had hovered over the village the day be-

1

fore. The people on the ground had been barely able to make out the figure of a man in a strange outfit by the door, manipulating some sort of sprayer.

The man had been wearing a plastic decontamination suit and a gas mask. To the villagers, he had looked vaguely like an Aztec god. There had been a long discussion of which deity the figure represented.

Now the helicopter was back. The more superstitious argued whether it was a good or evil omen.

The chopper passed over the village and headed for the clearing a half kilometer away. When it reached the landing zone, Jefe signaled for the drop to begin.

He and three of his men were lowered to the ground. Wearing treated, semipermeable jumpsuits, their bodies were trapped in individual saunas. The rubber of their activated charcoal Whetherlite gas masks stuck to their faces. They checked each other over, making sure all the protective gear was in place, then set out.

Jefe and his men found the narrow dirt roadway that served as the major thoroughfare into town. They followed it, escorted by skinny mutts and wide-eyed children.

The men of the village had gathered. They knew an event was about to happen. They did not know what, but it was important that such meetings not be left to the women. The town elder, a sixty-year-old with painful arthritis, was helped out of his small adobe house by his grandson.

"We have reports of a fugitive in the area. Is everyone from the village here?" Jefe asked crisply.

One of the more adventurous boys snuck over, touched Jefe's strange garment, and ran away. His peers cheered him for his bravery and demanded to know what it felt like.

The head man looked around and sucked on his few good teeth. The visitor was hard to understand through the gas mask, and his Spanish didn't sound like the other government officials who had come in the past. The elder couldn't recognize a Cuban accent.

"There is no one here who has not been since they were born," the old man said. "Why do you wear those masks?"

Several of the women giggled. Jefe was soaked with sweat. He wished he could take the mask off and gulp fresh air. His discomfort made the task easier. He desperately wanted to get it done.

An old woman was the first to cough. Her coughing got worse and she fell. Several of the younger women hurried over. Others began to pick up the cough. Jefe gazed at his wristwatch.

Some of the young men guessed that their intruders were behind the illness. Lifting their machetes, they charged.

Jefe's men—Sánchez, Oroszco and Hernández—cut them down with a few bursts from their automatic weapons.

Men, women, and children were coughing convulsively, bent double, spitting up blood, and gasping for air between coughs. A man staggered into a cooking pot fire, and his white pants ignited. He screamed, a human torch. The other villagers were too caught up in their own suffering to help him. Bodies spasmed like fish out of water.

"It's for a good cause," Jefe muttered, as much to reassure himself as his men.

Jefe was used to death. Death was part of his life as a soldier. But it was a horrible sight.

Old bones snapped from the violent spasms. Young bodies twisted in agony. The dirt was flecked with coughed blood. The man who had staggered into the fire stopped screaming only after the flames reached his head. The gasps and agonized shouts merged into one cacophony of pain.

There were seventy Indians in various stages of the illness, and nine who were healthy. Jefe had been briefed about biologic variability—that some people might take longer to be affected and that some might be lucky enough to be immune. The horrified expressions on the faces of those who were yet untouched were nearly as pathetic as the bodies writhing from the disease. Some watched, immobile, unable to grasp the horror. A few tried to run and were gunned down.

Jefe marched among the sick, his men trailing him like goslings. Dying men and women clutched their ankles.

I'm a soldier, a good soldier, Jefe kept repeating to himself. I have my mission.

After another half hour, he could take it no longer. "Basta!"

He and his men sent from person to person, firing a few shots into each head. The horrid coughs, gasps, and screams subsided. They executed the healthy ones, who accepted their fate as numbly as Jonestown residents had.

3

Even with the special filters in place, Jefe smelled death. Cordite mixed with blood, and the odors of excretion as the Indians died, voiding themselves.

"Gather the bodies. Make a fire," Jefe ordered. His men began piling the corpses.

Sánchez retrieved two jerry cans of gasoline and poured them over the bodies in the square.

The goats, chickens, and dogs wandered amid the carnage. Their health beside the human holocaust added a grim touch.

Jefe watched as his men continued to haul bodies into a heap. Hernández lit the bodies. The stink of burning meat filled the air. Jefe checked his watch. The germ should no longer be infectious. He gave the "okay" signal, but none of his men removed their decontamination suits. Only after he had peeled his off did they do the same. The outfits were tossed into the fire.

Jefe radioed up. The helicopter lowered to twenty feet above the ground and began lifting the men. As they got into the helicopter, they sprayed each other with a solution that smelled of isopropyl alcohol.

The helicopter rose to two hundred feet. Jefe took out a metal object the size of a wine crate. He pulled a pin, threw a switch, and dropped it from the copter into the middle of the square.

The helicopter flew off. Two minutes later, the delayed fuse on the bomb ignited.

The shockwave shook the helicopter.

Hernández looked back to the village and crossed himself. Sánchez stared straight ahead. Orozsco muttered a curse.

"It works," Jefe said.

PART
I

CHAPTER
1

Hokkaido—1975

Kenji Matsumoto cupped his hand around the match and tried to light a Peace cigarette. The cold wind whipping off the Pacific made him waste a half-dozen matches before the tobacco caught fire.

It would've been much easier if Matsumoto had stepped inside the concealed bunker just a few meters behind him. But he wanted to absorb the scene with all his senses. Standing on Nemuro Peninsula—on the northernmost edge of Japan—chilled and excited him.

His title translated roughly to investigator for the deputy minister of defense. The lean fifty-year-old spent most of his time traveling the four main islands of Japan, inspecting and evaluating the Japanese Self-defense Forces. It grieved him that his country did not have a larger military. Japan was too dependent on the United States for protection. How long would it take the U.S. Seventh Fleet to respond? How sure could the Japanese people be that the U.S. would support them? The foolish politicians insisted they depend on the United States. At least the Americans were better than the barbarians to the north.

He puffed on the cigarette as it caught fire and inhaled a lungful of sharp smoke.

The snow-capped peaks of Soviet-controlled Kunashiri Island were as clear and clean as a Hiroshige painting. A

7

beautiful reminder of just how close Japan was to the Russian bear. Matsumoto could see bobbing Japanese fishing boats plying the slate blue waters. There was also an ugly Soviet gunboat, with 50mm cannon fore and aft, and numerous antennae poking from her bridge. The Russian sailors sometimes swamped the fishing craft to relieve their boredom.

Hokkaido Island, from which Nemuro Peninsula jutted, was barely two miles from the tip of the Soviet Union. Though Hokkaido had only one twentieth of Japan's population, one third of her self-defense forces, including four infantry divisions, and one brigade each of artillery, antiaircraft missiles, engineers, and tanks were stationed there.

Matsumoto had spent a week inspecting them. Morale was high, the *bushido* spirit. But of the sixty tanks, seventeen were virtually useless. There were critical shortages of spare parts for the M-16s they had gotten from the United States. A radar station had been destroyed by a recent storm. They had a stockpile of only thirty SAMs.

He had written reports before, emphasizing how crucial the base was. The Sea of Japan had as many Russian submarines as the emperor's garden had *koi*. For Red navy subs to get into the Pacific, without taking the long way around, they would pass dangerously close to Japan.

The balance of power in Asia was shifting. Just two months ago, the United States had abandoned South Vietnam. The television pictures of the fall of Saigon, the helicopters leaving the embassy compound, the desperation, the terror, the humiliation, burned into Matsumoto's mind. He was convinced the Japanese would not cave in so easily. But how long could they last?

He shook his head in a nervous twitch. His tic had gotten worse recently. He prided himself on his stoic samurai heritage, and here he was, a warrior with a nervous tic. The stresses on him were building.

Matsumoto had started feeding information to the CIA a year earlier. It was a way to manipulate the Americans for the good of his country. Divulging his country's secrets violated everything he believed in, and yet it was his duty. His selective leaking could persuade the Americans to buttress Japan's defenses.

He thought about this CIA handler. Robert Stark didn't

push, but he drew out the information. Matsumoto was convinced that Stark genuinely cared about Japan, and Matsumoto. Several times Matsumoto had nearly backed out but Stark had helped him through the difficult periods, convincing him he was a patriot and not a traitor.

Matsumoto ground out and field-stripped the cigarette.

He had never trusted another man with his life. Only his confidence in Stark kept him going.

Toyko—One Week Later

The *marunouchi* line train roared into Shinjuku station. More than a million passengers a day passed through the turnstiles. Tokyoites put aside the polite conventions, and survival of the fittest ruled in the clean, brightly lit corridors and on the packed platforms. During rush hours, white-gloved pushers shoved people into the color-coded trains like cannery workers packing sardine cans.

Robert Stark let the crowd surge past him onto the train. The gleaming silver tube disgorged passengers, absorbed passengers, and sped away. Women's skirts blew as it created a vacuum.

Within minutes, the platform refilled with a fresh cast of travelers. Stark was one of a few *gaijin* on the platform. The others looked like typical foreign businessmen, overwhelmed by the hustle and bustle, the burly delicacy, that came from doing business in the capital of Japan.

Stark's cover assignment was cultural affairs liaison for the American embassy; his actual job was running five operatives for the Central Intelligence Agency.

At age thirty-four, Stark had nine years with the CIA. For the past five, he had been a case officer assigned to the Far Eastern Division of Clandestine Services. He had worked out of field stations in Thailand, Hong Kong, and Tokyo. The latter city was far and away his favorite. He had even begun to lose the awkward feeling that being a *gaijin* in Japan produced; the sense of being too big, too clumsy, too insensitive, of missing nuances and subtleties, and just not belonging.

He walked up the stairs and then down a nearby flight. Clear. Stark had spent the past two hours dry-cleaning himself, making sure that he was not being followed. All for a brief brush contact with Matsumoto. The man would bump into him and slip him a copy of a report.

Stark edged through the crowd, bobbing along with the flow of Japanese businessmen in suits, women in conservative dresses, sometimes kimonos, and teenagers wearing western T-shirts and jeans.

A train roared in, and the exchange of passengers occurred again. He scanned the crowd. The asset he was waiting for was accused of being a triple agent—secretly working for the Russians and feeding the CIA disinformation. Stark was supposed to accept the report and pass him a note arranging a clandestine meeting.

At the meeting, Matsumoto would be doped and interrogated. Squeezed, tried, and convicted all within a few hours. Then, most likely, he would be disposed of. A car accident. Even if he was innocent of what he was accused of, it was usually necessary to terminate him.

No one trusted an agent who had been tortured. Some spy masters insisted they would be so fearful of being tortured again, they would spill anything at the sight of a cattle prod. Others believed that having survived the torture, they would be fearless, and defy the rules of the game. A third school felt they would be so embittered, they could do anything.

Kenji Matsumoto had picked a bad time to come under suspicion. Stark believed the order to extract Matsumoto had been an outgrowth of CIA paranoia. The fall of Saigon had been a debacle. Copies of confidential reports, lists of agents in place, agents of influence, were left lying on desks as the Americans pulled out. Entire networks were rolled up, sentenced to death, or worse fates in "rehabilitation camps." The panic had spread throughout Asia. Maybe as far as Langley. It had brought out the hardball players, the act-first-and-ask-questions-later gang, looking for scapegoats.

There was a wet work specialist in town. Stark had caught a glimpse of him at the embassy. The only reason Stark knew the man was a hired killer was they had been in the same class together at the CIA's academy, the Farm, near Williamsburg, Virginia. They had used aliases in the class. The man had been known as Charon. Stark didn't remember his first name. It was possible he had never heard it.

10

Charon had excelled in what was nicknamed the "boom boom course": paramilitary operations. The beefy, black-haired Charon was an unerring marksman, could shimmy under a barbed wire fence faster than a terrier, and had a ruthless knack for winning the war games.

Far down on the platform, Stark saw his contact. The deputy defense minister's investigator looked even more nervous than usual.

The two men worked their way toward each other, slowly, casually.

Stark unbuttoned his suit. He was adept at sleight of hand and could pocket the report and pass the note undetected. He fingered the note, Matsumoto's death sentence.

They moved closer. Another train roared in and out, and the momentary flow of humanity prevented their forward progress.

Stark didn't believe the minister's investigator was working for the Russians. Like any good handler, he prided himself on knowing as much about the agent-in-place as the man's wife did. Maybe more. Stark had never had an agent betray him.

He could see his man clearly now. Matsumoto's head was shaking so much, it was like he was palsied.

They bumped into each other. Stark took the report.

"I must see you," Matsumoto whispered. "There is a traitor in my department."

"Excuse me," Stark said.

"Excuse *me*," Matsumoto said, bobbing his head.

Stark kept the note in his pocket. He had to trust his perceptions. He'd delay the extraction until Matsumoto had a chance to explain.

Although he was jeopardizing his career, Stark felt relieved. Falling into an "I-just-follow-orders" mentality was too common throughout the intelligence community.

Stark nodded to Matsumoto. They would arrange a meeting later, using proper tradecraft, going through the usual precautions.

Matsumoto continued down the platform toward the stairs. Stark prepared to board the next train in. There wouldn't be a very long wait. The report was under his suit jacket. He casually rolled it up, tucked it into an inside pocket, and buttoned his jacket. He watched Matsumoto edge through the crowd.

Stark saw Charon less than a dozen yards away. The wet work man had tinted his skin yellow and was slightly stooped to better fit in with the Japanese. He was a few paces from Matsumoto, and moving toward him like a shark slicing through the water toward a wounded fish.

Stark tried shoving his way through the densely packed crowd, but there were too many people. He only progressed a few feet.

A train was barreling into the station.

"Kenji!" Stark shouted.

The subway drowned out Stark's words.

Kenji Matsumoto suddenly toppled onto the tracks. There were no screams from the passengers, only a massive collective gasp. The brakes of the train did the screaming, but it was too late. The first two cars passed over Matsumoto before the juggernaut halted.

The wet work man had it timed perfectly. Charon moved smoothly through the crowd, disappearing up an escalator while Stark thrashed and struggled against the bodies around him.

In the locker room of the *jiujitsu dojo,* Stark pulled on his white *gi,* the white cotton uniform the students wore. *Jiujitsu* was the art from which *aikido* and judo were developed, and karate related. It included aspects of all three: arm locks, throws, and blows. Stark had studied the spiritually oriented martial art for four years, trying to find *dojos* wherever he was posted.

Stark knotted the black belt around his waist and walked out to the main room. A twenty-by-fifty-foot mat was surrounded by pale pine wainscoted walls. He slid his sandals off, and left them by the long row of similar footwear at the edge of the mat. Stepping onto the padded white canvas, he bowed to the photo of the school's founder.

The murder of Kenji Matsumoto kept replaying in his mind. And murder it was, despite the doubletalk the CIA Tokyo station chief had given when Stark confronted him. The station chief said it had been decided to terminate Matsumoto forthwith. Stark had been used to set his asset up to be executed. The bosses had agreed that Stark would probably not cooperate and had left him uninformed.

"It was done to make things easier on you," the station chief said. "You should be grateful. Quick and painless, for you and Matsumoto."

In the corner of the mat, Stark stretched, and then quickly found a partner. The man was a foot shorter than Stark and about twenty pounds heavier. A fellow black belt, he was hostile toward the *gaijin*. Just what Stark wanted.

Usually practice was friendly, throwee helping thrower, both learning. But now Stark wanted someone to let off tension.

Rather than smooth movements, it began to look like judo, more strength than style. His opponent threw Stark and twisted his wrist further then necessary during a *kote gashi*.

Pain shot up Stark's arm. He was ready now. It was his turn.

"Stark-san, would you have the time to talk with me?"

The voice belonged to a *sensei,* one of the senior teachers. He was a man of unguessable age, probably in his mid-sixties. His voice was soft, but somehow louder than the yells and thumps coming from other students in the *dojo*.

The teacher walked to the small office at the edge of the mat. Stark, his arm hurting, his rage boiling, longed to continue with the stocky student. But he bowed perfunctorily to his adversary and followed the *sensei* into the office. There were no chairs. The teacher folded his legs under himself and sat on the tatami mat floor.

The only furnishing in the room was a black lacquer desk that looked like it could have sat in a *shogun*'s antechamber. The walls were white, bare, with a scroll hanging in a corner. The scroll bore a *sumi-e* ink drawing of Daruma, Zen's first patriarch. The scowling image of a pudgy, bearded man leaped off the rice paper.

"It is not often we have the honor of your presence here on Tuesday nights," the teacher said in formal Japanese. The *sensei* stared at him with his usual half-smile on his gentle face. The sounds of the *dojo* drifted in.

As time passed, Stark felt the pain and the rage subside. He was depleted, emptied, and the words spilled out.

"I saw a man killed today, *sensei*. Maybe I could have saved him, warned him. I used to believe in what I did, but

13

lately . . ." There was silence again. The teacher let Stark's momentum carry him on.

"When I was in Cambodia, I saw atrocities by the Khmer Rouge," the American continued. "I didn't feel bad about what I did back. They were like animals, worse than animals. As if a teenage gang had taken over a country. They beat old women to death, they . . ." Again Stark trailed off.

"I felt I was doing the right thing. Now, I don't know. I was in Vietnam. Did we serve the Vietnamese people, or the American people? Or did we protect a bunch of scummy pimps and dope dealers who were looting their own country while young soldiers on both sides died?

"I've corrupted good men, and helped people who made my skin crawl. I guess it's been building to this, I mean, there were things in Thailand that, that, that . . ."

The *sensei* reached into the desk and took out a piece of paper, a brush, and an ink bottle. Stark thought he was being dismissed, his rambling monologue an embarrassment to the teacher's reserved Japanese spirit.

The small hand moved, the brush danced across the paper. A minimum of movement and ink. The teacher affixed his seal to the corner.

He handed Stark the paper like a doctor proffering a prescription. It bore an address in Kamakura.

Now a Tokyo suburb famous for its statue of the Daibutsu Buddha, Kamakura had been the center of power from 1192 to 1333. The *shoguns* then had been Zen adherents, and a number of prestigious and powerful temples were founded that remain to this day.

"*Arigato gozai mashita*," Stark began, and continued to thank the *sensei* profusely until the older man waved his hand and got up slowly. The teacher bowed and walked back to the mat.

Stark folded the paper carefully. Although his professionalism had prevented him from divulging any specifics, he had just blurted out classified details of his life. His tours of duty were regarded as national security information. He could be suspended, fined, or booted out of the agency.

It didn't matter anyway. From the moment the *sensei* had led him into the office, he knew his CIA days were over.

* * *

The first few weeks were exhausting. Four hours of sleep a night. Meditation six hours a day, with a smack from the monk's stick if there was any sign of dozing. Hours spent doing menial labor, scrubbing the wooden bowls in icy water, raking the garden, mopping the stone floors.

He was cut off from the occidental world, even from the Japanese world of the twentieth century.

"If you do not get it from yourself, where will you go for it?"

"Your mind is like an undisciplined monkey, running through the house, tearing things apart," one of the senior monks said. "You must learn to discipline it, or live in chaos all your life. The focused mind can pierce stone."

Stark's head was shaved and he was given a gray robe. Just like military training, all recruits were treated the same. But he was the only non-Japanese.

"If you do not get it from yourself, where will you go for it?"

After a couple of months, it was revealed to Stark that the head monk was also a *jiujitsu shihan*, a master instructor in *jiujitsu*.

Stark was granted permission to work out at the nearby *dojo* and plunged into the lengthy sessions with vigor. In Japan, where the threat of street crime is minimal, the martial arts are a way of focusing oneself, like flower arrangement or ink drawing. For Stark, the clarity came from coordinating mind and body in combat, a form of moving meditation.

Stark savored his walks between the monastery and the *dojo*, his limited contact with the modern world. He would sneak a peak at a newspaper, buy a sweet bean pastry, or follow the graceful passage of a pretty woman. Then it would be back to the harsh discipline and pain of either the temple or the training hall.

The interludes made his physical and mental workouts all the more special. The hustle-bustle of modern Japan contrasted with the tradition, the order, the serenity of the *dojo*.

"When you stand, stand. When you sit, sit. Don't wobble."

While meditating, he visualized throws he had practiced, coordinating his legs and arms, not anticipating, learning to react without conscious thought. Then the thwack of the

15

monk's stick would bring him back to trying to empty his mind.

"Expect nothing, be prepared for anything."

In audiences with the head monk he would be challenged with *koans*. They sounded like silly riddles, surreal jokes, yet they could be frustrating mind-binders.

"Does a dog have Buddha nature? What is the sound of one hand clapping? If a tree falls in a forest and there's no one there, does it make a noise? What was your face before you were born?"

In the *dojo,* his legs aching from the long hours spent in meditation, he would repeat the same simple moves over and over, until the *shihan* would nod approval. A slightly different twist could mean the difference between a beautifully executed throw or a clumsy assault.

During one of his trips between temple and *dojo,* the newspapers headlined stories of a major spy case. The deputy minister who had been Kenji Matsumoto's boss had defected to the Soviet Union. Newspaper accounts told how he had tried to create dissension in his bureau, make loyal staff members come into suspicion. He had been the double agent working for the KGB.

The Japanese newspaper carried a statement from the traitorous deputy minister. He spoke of Matsumoto and how he was sorry to have dishonored him. The traitor revealed Stark's failing to set up Matsumoto, and how the CIA killed the Japanese anyway. The deputy minister couldn't have known about Stark and Charon unless he'd been briefed. Obviously a KGB full-court press.

There were angry denials from American officials and demands from Japanese authorities for a full investigation.

Stark crumpled the newspaper and dropped it into a garbage can.

On subsequent trips into the city, he didn't bother buying a paper. He didn't stop for sweet pastries, and didn't notice pretty women.

Three years after he first entered the monastery, he was ready to leave.

CHAPTER
2

New York—1987

Calvin MacMillan leaned forward in his high-backed Italian leather swivel chair. He peered through the telescope behind his antique Louis XIV desk at a skyscraper a mile or so away. He could almost see the man he was talking to on the phone.

Actually, he wasn't talking. He was allowing the silence to grow more and more oppressive. He enjoyed letting the man squirm.

The man at the other end of the line wasn't used to squirming. He was the head of a major airline, who sat on a half-dozen corporate boards, including those of a bank, an insurance company, and a car rental agency.

"C'mon, Cal," the man said. "I just can't make it that night. You already hit me up a few months ago."

"I understand," MacMillan said in his croaky voice, his tone making it clear he didn't. "Take care."

"My daughter's getting married on Saturday," the man said.

"Sure, sure. Good-bye."

Just before the airline president hung up, MacMillan said, "Oh, by the way, the head of the FAA is going to be there. I thought you might want to talk to him about your new Washington-to-Sacramento route. I heard American is planning on expanding."

17

"Son of a bitch," the airline president muttered.

"What? I missed that," MacMillan said. "These old ears aren't what they used to be." At eighty-two, MacMillan was as sharp as a man thirty years younger.

"Nothing."

"You know, the FAA chief graduated from NYU. He's going to miss your being there. I'll tell him you were just too busy. Anyway, take it easy."

"Okay, you got me. How many should I buy?"

"I was thinking a table would be nice. Forty grand."

"I'll messenger over the check."

They exchanged insincere pleasantries and hung up. MacMillan grinned. Until the age of seventy-five, he had been a ruthless businessman, dubbed a modern-day robber baron in the press. At seventy-five, when he suffered a heart attack, his outlook changed. He discovered he could get as much satisfaction bulldozing people in the name of charity as he had gotten bulldozing them for his own profit. He had become a philanthropist, giving away millions, and inducing fellow captains of industry to do the same. Like Japanese industrialist Ryoichi Sasakawa, or American corporate giant Armand Hammer, MacMillan was frequently written about as an elderly successful businessman who craved the Nobel Peace Prize as recognition for his good works.

MacMillan, the son of a Scottish laborer who had emigrated to America at the turn of the century, was working as a cab driver when Prohibition started. He quadrupled his income by ferrying customers to speakeasies and smuggling drums of bootleg whiskey for illegal distilleries. By the end of the Roaring Twenties, he had a small cab fleet. Always distrustful of banks, he invested heavily in real estate.

When the Depression struck, his fortune was virtually untouched. He was able to buy up more property and expand his fleet. Then he bought a few gas stations, to supply his vehicles. A tire company. An auto parts firm. A restaurant where his drivers always ate. A small motel chain. An insurance company.

He was a workaholic, a ruthless negotiator, with an intuitive knack for buying, or selling, at just the right moment. He pioneered the "in-house market," integration and reciprocity among various businesses that he owned. He would use his insurance company to cover his cars and real estate.

His auto parts firm supplied his taxis, his taxis had corporate accounts from his other firms. Traveling executives from any of his companies stayed at his hotels.

It allowed him to shuffle money back and forth among his companies and keep outsiders from selling to his markets. The small, wiry MacMillan had built a multimillion-dollar corporation and then gone public. He diversified more, getting into heavy industry. A truck manufacturing company, an aircraft supply firm. A munitions firm.

His International Sales and Service became one of the first multinational corporations. MacMillan never felt restricted by national boundaries. He had plants in Hitler's Germany and swapped dirty jokes with Stalin. Winston Churchill and MacMillan enjoyed smoking cigars together, and MacMillan had twice beaten Eisenhower at golf. *Forbes* had described him as a "cross between Harry Geneen (of ITT) and Armand Hammer (of Occidental Petroleum)." The *Village Voice* had likened him to mobsters Meyer Lansky and Lucky Luciano.

Influenced in part by a discussion he had had with Hitler over the importance of good genes, MacMillan had married a healthy, big-boned woman with an IQ of 140. His wife was not as striking as other corporate wives, but she was far more astute than ninety percent of the people MacMillan dealt with, including the world leaders. When he wanted a good-looking woman to screw, there was always one available. He kept mistresses in three cities, and Elizabeth Mac-Millan knew to keep her mouth shut.

In 1943 she bore him a son, Benedict. The child was tended by a top-notch governess, tutored from an early age, provided with every luxury.

When Elizabeth learned that her husband was selling arms to both the Allied and Axis powers, she demanded he stop or she would leave him. He laughed at her. She filed for divorce. He spent close to one hundred thousand dollars on the case, but succeeded in making sure she got nothing. Including Benedict.

MacMillan had few paternal urges, but he'd be damned if he'd let that woman take the boy from him. From the moment she filed for divorce, she was referred to as "that woman."

When she had died of cirrhosis, ten years after their

divorce, he had sent a twenty-dollar floral arrangement. He had forbidden his son to attend the funeral. Benedict had obeyed him, as he always did.

Benedict had gone to medical school, but shortly before he took the boards, MacMillan had ordered him to leave.

"You'll make more, and be of better use to me, as a shyster more than a pissant sawbones," MacMillan had said.

Benedict had obediently gone to law shool. He'd graduated with honors, and came to work for ISS. MacMillan had him work in various divisions, learning different aspects of the huge corporation, which by the 1970s had over ninety companies and holding companies, in twenty-one countries, under its corporate umbrella.

Benedict's official title was senior in-house counsel. He was now a general corporate troubleshooter, who would deliver cash payments to balky government officials in Turkey, or supervise the construction of a new plant in Mexico, or play hardball with tough guy union leaders at his father's behest.

"Send Benedict in," MacMillan croaked into his intercom.

The corporate president put his fingers on his carotid artery and felt for his pulse. He monitored it for a minute, grunted when he found it was close to one hundred, and tapped his fingers on his desk.

He toyed with the report the MacMillan Foundation, a Connecticut-based think tank, had prepared on his orders. The fifty-page report detailed the leading methods of destruction stockpiled by the major powers. "Nuclear, Chemical, and Biological Warfare: Strategies, Tactics, and Options," it was titled.

Benedict MacMillan was a hulking six-footer, who regularly competed in triathalons and had won the Iron Man competition in Hawaii when he was thirty-five. He was known as a company hatchet man, and his presence in a division made senior vice-presidents cringe.

Yet as he hurried toward his father's office, he felt the butterflies in his stomach that he always got on seeing his father. He bumped a secretary as he got into the elevator and glared at her so ferociously she got off to wait for the next car up.

He strode down the carpeted corridor on the fifty-seventh floor of the MacMillan building, indifferent to the nervous greetings of the executives he passed.

His father's secretary nodded that it was okay to enter and he hurried to the large oaken door. He knocked meekly.

"Come in."

The old man was hidden in his chair, his back to the door. He was peering out the telescope. Sometimes Benedict thought his father had gotten senile. But then the old man would engineer a deal that Benedict would wish he could've done.

"Hello, sir," Benedict said to his father's back. He never knew how to address him. "Dad" seemed too informal.

"Did you read the report?" MacMillan asked.

"Yes. It was interesting, but I don't understand . . ."

"Of course you don't understand. I haven't explained why yet." MacMillan was looking through the telescope at a young woman sunbathing topless on a rooftop. He wished he'd feel the throb in his groin he used to. But no such luck. He spun in his chair.

"Of the three options discussed, which seems the most viable as a global threat from a nongovernmental source?" MacMillan snapped.

"Uh, uh, BW. Biological warfare, I guess."

"Why?"

"Nuclear warfare is too well regulated by governments and limited to the area where the bomb is detonated. Chemical warfare also has a limited area. But biological agents can spread by themselves."

"Go on," MacMillan commanded.

"Well, a Third World power might not have the industry to create fissionable material or enough chemical agents. But they have bacteria, viruses, and fungi in abundance. The biggest problem would be safe handling. During my time at our plant in India, I was amazed at the unsanitary conditions. The vermin, the proximity to animal life, which is the host for many infections, the . . ."

"Yes, yes, yes. Fine. I want you to look into BW specifically. When can you have your analysis ready?"

What did his father want, Benedict wondered, but dared

not ask. Why didn't his father just have the MacMillan Foundation do a more focused study? How extensive should the report be? Whom should he speak with first? "A month?"

"Fine." As he watched his son leave, MacMillan wished he could say something kind to the boy. It was nearly time to pass on the reins, and they had never been as close as a father and son should be.

He knew he was tough on the boy. He had to be. It was a tough world. Benedict had to be ready to handle it.

After running a Nexus search on the office computer, and reading a dozen or so articles on biological warfare, Benedict had his staff research personnel records on ISS personnel in their biotechnology division. He found a scientist in their San Mateo plant who had worked for the U.S. Army BW Center at Fort Detrick. At the two-billion-dollar Maryland facility, forty-five miles from Washington, more than 2,600 army personnel, and five hundred civilians strove to build a better bug.

Benedict MacMillan took the company jet out to San Mateo. This was obviously important to his father. He'd prove that he was a competent and capable executive, a worthy heir to the MacMillan name.

Dr. Henry Crenshaw pushed his glasses back up onto the bridge of his nose. He adjusted his papers for the tenth time, fiddled with the pens in his pocket, tugged at his tie. He wiped the sweat from his brow.

The hatchet man was coming. He wondered what he had done wrong. There had been no explanation in the message from New York, just a time to expect Benedict MacMillan.

A limousine had been dispatched to pick him up from the airport. Crenshaw prayed that the driver had performed properly, that traffic was light, that the bar in the limo was well stocked.

The car pulled up. Black, like a Mafia hit car. Benedict MacMillan strode up the walkway. God, he was big. His shoulders taut against his custom-tailored suit, he radiated power, confidence.

"Welcome to our plant, Mr. MacMillan," Crenshaw said,

offering his hand. "I'm Doctor Crenshaw. I'd like to show you around."

"I supervised the building of this facility, Crenshaw. I probably know more about it than you do."

"Well, maybe we've made some changes since you were involved."

"Send me a memo. I want to talk to you."

Crenshaw felt weak in the knees. He was nearing sixty. If he lost this job, he had no idea where he'd go. Finding it had been hard enough. Most of his experience was with biological warfare. There wasn't much call for that in the private sector. He and his family didn't want to live solely on the pension from the military.

"Yes?"

"I want to talk with you about biological warfare," Mac-Millan said.

Crenshaw felt a warm, soothing rush wash over him. He wasn't in trouble. In fact, they'd be talking about something he knew he was an expert in.

"What do you want to know?"

They sat in the small park in the atrium of the building. Word had spread that Benedict MacMillan was talking to the boss, and everyone avoided the area. A few people peeked out of their offices, eager to see what was going on. Judging by Crenshaw's body language, the meeting was going well. The doctor talked with animated gestures, smiling, enthusiastic. The rumor that the San Mateo plant was about to be shut died. Several employees broke out bottles of champagne.

"There are 160 catalogued infectious diseases that are considered useful for biological warfare. Virulence, infectivity, shelf life, means of dispersal, period of contamination, are the factors which must be considered," Crenshaw was saying. "Only thirty-two diseases are actually viable. For example, anthrax, particularly pulmonary anthrax, is favorably regarded in the BW, that's biological warfare, community.

"Anthrax is spread by a bacterium which forms spores which can be inhaled into the lungs. First the disease seems like a common cold or flu. Then the cough gets worse and a

23

high fever develops. Then breathing gets difficult, the victim becomes cyanotic, and death occurs within eighteen to twenty-four hours."

"I know about anthrax, Crenshaw," Benedict said. "I have a medical degree."

"Oh. I didn't know that." Despite MacMillan's abrupt tone, Crenshaw didn't get flustered. He was on his own turf and felt safe. He decided to offer more of an overview.

"BW goes way back in history. Tartar invaders used to catapult diseased corpses into cities they were besieging. Later, conquistadors and some American colonists used it against the Indians. For example, Jeffrey Amherst, for whom Amherst College was named, gave fomites, in the form of smallpox-tainted blankets, to the Indians."

"This was all long before germ theory."

"True, true. No doubt it was motivated by superstition. But it proved entirely effective."

"I'm more interested in current affairs," MacMillan said. His tone had softened as he was caught up in Crenshaw's enthusiasm and breadth of knowledge.

"During World War II, quite a lot of work was done. The Japanese found out that BW was specifically prohibited by the Geneva Convention. They assumed that the only reason for the prohibition was that we and the Russians were doing it covertly.

"The Japanese set up the world's first BW installation at Pingfan in 1939. They did pioneering work with typhus, anthrax, cholera, botulism, bubonic plague, and a dozen other incapacitating or deadly diseases. Reverse public health, we call it."

Benedict MacMillan laughed. Loud and hard, almost out of control. Crenshaw had grinned at first, then realized what he was talking about and resumed his serious expression. MacMillan gestured for him to continue.

"Chinese prisoners were used as guinea pigs. After the war, there was a push to prosecute several officials as war criminals," Crenshaw continued. "But we decided their knowledge would be of use to us, and they were never tried.

"The Germans also did work, as you might imagine. Auschwitz and Dachau both had BW labs. Melioidosis, brucellosis, blastomycosis. We seized several of their top BW people. Right out from under the Russians' noses.

"The Russians concentrated on fungi. They're big on mushroom picking over there, you know."

"Yes."

"The British also had a BW program. They did experiments on an island in Gruinard Bay during World War II. Dropped a few small anthrax bombs in 1943. To this day, there are signs on the island warning the ground is contaminated and landing is prohibited."

"What about here? What sort of program did we have?"

"Better than everyone but the Germans, I'd say. George Merck, of Merck Pharmaceuticals, was one of the top Americans. Of course, we were only studying it on a defensive basis, in case the other side started it.

"There are four primary ways of disseminating a BW agent: sexually; by insects; by food or water; and by aerosol. For you to remember it, think of the four Bs. Bedroom, bugs, belly, or breathe. An STD, or sexually transmitted disease, is not practical. Fornication is unpredictable."

Benedict guffawed again. Crenshaw waited for him to stop, then said, "Insects are undependable as a vector. If some escape the target areas, well, you are no doubt aware of the problem with the killer bees.

"As far as gastrointestinal introduction of the agent, there have been effective programs. In Brazil in the 1960s, for example, Indians were given free sugar laced with toxins. This helped the government acquire lands. However, making sure that the subjects eat the proper amount, at the proper time, creates a problem."

"Airborne is the best," Benedict said.

"Generally, yes. Most of the research has been done in that area and bears out that conclusion. For example, the army tried spreading a harmless germ in New York subways in the 1960s."

"How?" asked a fascinated MacMillan.

"Using sprayers concealed in attaché cases. It worked remarkably well. The army has done some interesting work. They developed an inhaled vaccine. Soldiers are marched through a room with droplets of tularemia in the air to build immunity. Tularemia bacteria are considered an excellent BW agent, aside from their instability."

"All this talk about airborne microbes is well and good, but wind currents are unpredictable in the real world,"

25

MacMillan said. "The active agent could be blown out of the target area, dispersing harmlessly over the sea or adversely impacting on a neighboring area. What about the possibility of epidemic?"

"That's always been a problem in the past. But I've heard rumors about pioneering work being done with phage. Bacteriophage."

"The viruses that prey on bacteria. What about them?"

Crenshaw hesitated. How much of what he knew was classified? What could he tell MacMillan? Why did he want to know?

"Don't hold back on me, Crenshaw. Either you're a team player, or you're benched."

"What, what exactly do you want to know?" Crenshaw asked, hating his weakness.

"Pull!" Benedict barked, and the groundsman fired a clay pigeon into the air. Benedict blasted it out of the sky.

"You won," Peter Hornaday said. "You're quite a shot."

"You gave me a run for my money," Benedict said. With a wave of his hand, he signaled for the groundsman to leave. The groundsman took his time emptying the machine.

"Damn it, I told you to get out of here," Benedict said. He leveled the shotgun at the groundsman, who scuttled away.

Hornaday eyed him. Benedict opened his shotgun and showed Hornaday both chambers were empty. Then MacMillan laughed until he had to fight for air. Hornaday smiled politely, warily.

They were on the grounds of an exclusive country club on the north shore of Long Island. Hornaday—a dapper dresser with a bit of a weak chin and an impressive shock of blow-dried graying hair—had been flown up from his Virginia home in the MacMillan jet.

The fifty-five-year-old career bureaucrat had risen to become the deputy to the National Security Advisor.

He had started in the Senate, as a staff assistant to the Joint Committee on Intelligence, switched to the State Department, where he served as a liaison with Defense. He had a three-year stint on staff with the Joint Chiefs of Staff before rising to the National Security Council. During his two dozen years in the seat of government, he had developed contacts at every juncture. Through Restricted Interagency Groups, social contacts, and ad hoc committees, there wasn't a major agency that he couldn't put a call in to and find an acquaintance. He owed few people favors, but many of his contacts were indebted to him. He tended to vote Republican but was bipartisan in his machinations, and whichever party was in power had little effect on his career.

The flexibility of the day-to-day agenda at the NSC allowed Hornaday a wide area of operation. Like the other staffers, one day he might be playing diplomat, meeting with foreign ambassadors, the next he would act as a protocol officer, handling Presidential correspondence. He would supervise the preparation of reports, or sit in on meetings with the President. Hornaday was known to have had as many private meetings with the President as most Cabinet members.

Hornaday was acknowledged as the real power at the NSC. His boss, a borderline alcoholic, had run the President's election campaign and been given the advisor post as a reward. He had turned out to be a major disappointment to the Administration, but Hornaday had more than made up for his ineptitude. Hornaday didn't make that much money and didn't have the most impressive title, but he had as much power as all but a handful of men in Washington.

One of the early lessons Calvin MacMillan had taught his son was the importance of having government contacts.

"Regulatory agencies can be either a pain in the ass or a way to keep the competition in check," MacMillan had lectured his son. "Throughout the government there are fat-ass bureaucrats who slow things down, and manipulators who can get things done. You've got to find the movers and shakers. Build their egos, fill their wallets. Whatever it takes."

"You know, I'm thinking of retiring," Hornaday said as they walked toward the lounge, the shotguns open and hanging at their sides.

"Really. I hope you're not going to work for the competition."

"I doubt it."

"Job offers?"

"A couple. The hallowed halls of academia beckon."

27

"Well, I trust you'll consider coming to ISS. A man with your expertise could be invaluable."

"Thanks. I'll keep that in mind. Now what did you want to talk about?"

"Biological warfare."

Hornaday kept a poker face. "Why?"

"My father's developed an interest in it. I think he wants to help the U.S. government. We've got some facilities that could be of use."

"What's the quid pro quo?"

"I'm not sure. Maybe he's just feeling patriotic."

"Or maybe he wants to get licensed for recombinant DNA work?" Hornaday asked cynically.

The men chuckled.

"This is a nice gun," Hornaday said, hefting the Browning Presentation shotgun. The weapon was hand-oiled, with French walnut stock. It had a five-eighths-inch-wide vent, premium tolerance machining, and gold trim.

"It's a limited edition Broadway Trap 12. As you said, a nice gun. I hope you'd accept it as a little souvenir of your visit here."

"I couldn't."

"Please. Take a look at the underside."

Hornaday turned it over. His name was engraved near the trigger guard.

"Thank you. This really is wonderful," Hornaday said. "Now, how can I help you with this biological warfare research?"

Exactly one month after his meeting with his father, Benedict MacMillan completed his two-hundred-page report. His father had him sit in a chair while he read it, making occasional grunts and notations.

"This historical stuff is a waste of time, but otherwise, a competent job," MacMillan said in conclusion.

"Thank you, thank you very much."

"After all this study, which one do you think the government is most scared of?"

"It depends on the purpose. For example, if you want to incapacitate as many soldiers as possible, cholera is effective. Not only do you make the enemy sick, but each affected individual requires two support personnel to care for him."

"What's the most lethal?"

"Botulism. Maybe shellfish toxin. That's the poison the CIA issues to its operatives to kill themselves in the event of capture."

"I know. Ike told me he wished Francis Gary Powers had taken his. I believe it was concealed in a coin." MacMillan tapped his fingers on his desk. "Time to make sense out of this data you collected."

"Perhaps it's best if you look at the chart I prepared. It points out the pros and the cons of each. For example, anthrax spores can ruin an area for decades. Like Gruinard Island, which the Brits used for testing."

"I remember Winnie's misgivings," the elder MacMillan mused. "This material on bacteriophage is fascinating. Crenshaw seemed sincere?"

"Very."

"Who's the leading BW person currently?"

"There are a few. But they're all in top secret government programs. The Russians are actually running a bit ahead of us there, according to my intelligence community contact."

"Is that Hornaday?"

Benedict had never told his father who his contact was. Somehow, the old man knew everything. It made Benedict feel like a child.

"I have a Russian. KGB, works out of the U.N. He'll get the inside word on what they're up to," Calvin MacMillan said after a long pause. "His name's Zabotin. He's listed as a cultural attaché."

It was the first time his father had ever given him the name of one of his elusive inside contacts. Benedict knew he'd just gotten a pat on the head. He beamed.

"Would you mind my asking why you're interested in BW?" Benedict asked.

"All in good time. All in good time."

29

CHAPTER
3

Vladivostock—1987

The two-hundred-acre Lenin Polyclinic Institute for the Advancement of the Biologic Sciences is located fourteen kilometers north of Vladivostock—a city bleak even by Soviet standards, and closed to foreigners because it is the Red Navy's Pacific headquarters.

The institute is one of the most secure facilities in an area considered by the Kremlin to be a heartland of national security. The external Cyclone fence is razor-wire topped. A second internal perimeter has electrified wire, as well as a pressure-sensitive alarm. In the no-man's-land between the two fences, AK-47-toting guards with vicious Alsatians patrol. There are machine-gun equipped guard towers every hundred meters.

The first three checkpoints—with heavy metal doors, code-key entries that are changed daily and guards with Stechkin machine pistols—are to keep intruders out.

The latter three checkpoints are to keep the experimental material in. In April 1979, Military Compound #19, near Sverdlovsky, had an accident with anthrax. The area was closed off and Red Army TMS-65 mobile decontamination units rushed in. The number of people and livestock killed was hushed up, but it was rumored to be in the hundreds.

At the Lenin Polyclinic Institute, they were very, very careful.

Past the third checkpoint, researchers wore pale blue protective gowns, caps, and shoe guards, which were taken off and dropped into a chute for sterilization on exiting. At each sallyport there was a negative pressure air curtain. Air pressure in the small foyer was kept lower than the outside. In the event of a leak, the airborne microbes would flow into the contained space, rather than escaping into the environment.

There were numerous signs prohibiting eating or working in the room if one had an open cut. The scientists wore surgical gloves, goggles, and gauze masks, and worked at hooded laboratory benches. The clean-up crews were specially trained and equipped. The safety director made sure vaccination cards were up to date.

Dr. Sultana Mirnov had never caught so much as a cold from her research. Her title was deputy director of the department of viral studies, but her work cut across the disciplines of epidemiology, immunology, molecular biology, and oncology.

Her main interest was exploring the relationship between viruses and cancer. Scientists had established a statistical association between several viruses and cancer. Epstein-Barr, hepatitis B, herpes simplex, HIV and HTLV-III viruses are linked to specific cancers, and Dr. Mirnov searched for the reason why. She analyzed tissue cultures, explored the chemistry of diseased cells, and examined through an electron microscope particles so small scientists debated whether they could be called alive.

Because of her broad range of knowledge, she had been granted permission for several trips out of the country: on equipment buying expeditions to Japan; and to deliver speeches at major scientific conventions in Prague, Vienna, and Frankfurt. Fluent in English and German, she had been a keynote speaker. While Western scientific journals praised her pioneering work, the lay press gave her extensive coverage because of her looks.

Sultana was tall and buxom, with lustrous brown hair that she wore in a bun. Her green-gray eyes were alert and challenging, yet sensual and seductive. Commissars, generals, leading scientists had wooed her. At age thirty-eight, however, she remained unmarried and quite happy about it.

She immersed herself in her work, often staying through

31

the night. She enjoyed the privacy, the quiet. The only sounds came from refrigerators and incubators humming, the fans sucking air to be filtered, and guards padding about making sure no imperialist spies had sneaked in. She didn't think that very realistic. From her brief exposure to the West and the trade journals she was allowed to see, the Americans seemed far ahead of them.

It was not the fault of her fellow scientists. The fault lay with the government, the Soviets. Their restrictive practices on the dissemination of information, the wasteful and incompetent manufacturing methods that made much of her equipment outdated or inoperative, these were the things that kept her from making more breakthroughs.

Like with her project on liver cancer. She had become interested in aflatoxins, which took her into the area of mycology. Produced by aspergillus, a fast-reproducing fungus, aflatoxins are a major problem in Southeast Asia. Hundreds of Thai children had been poisoned because the popular "sticky rice" was a particularly fine way of growing aspergillus. And there was an alarmingly high liver cancer rate among adults from the same population group, which tied into her work with the hepatitis B virus.

Such toxins had been a problem in the Soviet Union as well. Sometimes a wheat crop would be warmed by the sun, frozen in a sudden storm, and then rewarmed. The pattern was particularly conducive to the formation of fungi which would ruin the crop, or poison livestock and humans.

She had reviewed the extensive studies of ergot, rye fungus, which caused the disease known as St. Anthony's Fire. The toxins produced by the fungus turned fingers and toes black and caused insanity and death. There were documented cases of entire villages going berserk.

In 1944, for example, there was an outbreak of mycotoxin poisoning around Orenburg in southern Russia. Thousands died. It was traced to eating contaminated grain products. There had been smaller outbreaks every few years. She could prevent so much misery, if the bureaucrats just let her work.

She had been doing an electron-microscopic analysis of an aspergillus spore when its peculiar shape had sparked an idea regarding the viral origins of cancer. That was the way her mind worked, jumping from one idea to another, spurts of insight. It was a process ill-suited to the Soviet system, where it was more important to fulfill the five-year plan than to pioneer a new approach.

There was an oft-quoted saying in Soviet science, though it was never said loud enough for the First Department *stukachi,* the KGB stoolies, to hear: "The Soviet scientist does what he can in the way he should; the American scientist does what he should in the way he can."

Her after-hours research in the lab had yielded interesting results, but nothing definitive. With the hard-drinking Russian people, information gathered from alcoholics in hospitals would help her liver work. She wanted to do comparative work of the cellular damage caused by the fungus, viruses, and alcohol.

But the State Committee for Science and Technology was hindering her. She needed autopsy results and tissue cultures from alcoholics' livers. People were dying, she had a theory, and her government would not let her prove or disprove it. The war against alcoholism was faltering, and anything to do with the crisis had been classified a state secret.

There were in-house politics involved, too. Rivals in other departments said she knew little about mycology. So she devoured texts until she could back her arguments with the latest research. Her being right made them dislike her even more.

But she had found a way around the system. The clerks who worked at the Lenin Polyclinic might never get a chance to leave the Soviet Union. During her trips to Japan, she was able to buy quality Western goods. Radios, televisions, toaster ovens, high fashion clothing. Sultana started her own black market. In return for a sleek dress, or a compact microwave, all Mirnov asked for was access to files. The clerks would give her a copy of a key, and let her pour through files at night. She could learn what was being done in other departments, progress being made, failures being suppressed. It had helped more than once with her own work.

Tonight, she was particularly eager to get to the files. Her time was limited. Now they wanted her to do fungal work full time, on a relatively rare disease. Why was it important for her to work on blastomycosis? There were so many more important diseases to be tackled. Which pompous bureaucrat on the council of ministers had decided to shift her?

Could it be her boyfriend? She was being switched to his department. Did he have the clout to do such a thing? He had chuckled when she had asked him. Dr. Boris Arkov had a secretive nature. Perhaps that's why he had risen high up so young.

Barely forty, already the head of a department, with rumors that he had a shot at heading the whole institute. He was tall, with close-cut, prematurely gray hair. A striking man with almost military, almost regal, bearing. Coldly effective in the lab and in the bedroom.

Mirnov worked late, on her own time, to try out an idea she had regarding the hepatitis B virus. Using the thin glass pipette like a soda straw, Dr. Mirnov sucked out growth fluid from several bottles. There was no danger from swallowing the mixture—there were no viruses in the fluid. Yet.

A thin layer of cells composed primarily of mouse fibroblasts adhered to the bottle wall. She added vitamins, fetal bovine serum, Orlov's balanced salt solution, Kolenko's basal medium, streptomycin, and penicillin. The antibiotics would make sure that no bacteria would contaminate the experiment. Antibiotics worked on bacteria, but had no effect on viruses.

Where the cell carpet fell apart, with gaps appearing that looked like moth holes, it meant that viruses were growing.

She added some of the fluid taken from several deliberately infected mice. Now she had to wait for the microbes to reproduce. If the plaques, the name for the gaps, appeared in the carpet, she knew she was heading in the right direction.

Mirnov peeled off her gown and threw it down the sterilizing chute. She removed cap, surgical mask, shoe shields, and gloves in the prescribed order and dropped them in the proper containers for sterilizing. She pushed through the doors and walked down the long cinder-block halls, enjoying the solitude and the space. The government had furnished her with an apartment near the facility, but it was typical Russian housing—cramped, no privacy, shoddy construction.

She thought of the liver cancer virus. The peculiar shape

and behavior haunted her. She would dream of it, see viruses boring through cell and nuclear walls, patching into the DNA, altering, and then blowing apart the cell, spreading the new virus-dictated genetic structure. Mirnov glanced at her watch. She could go home. Or give Arkov a call. But she preferred to continue her work, and to sneak a peek at some files.

Sultana toyed with the four illegal keys in her pocket. Possession of any one of them could earn her a few years in a labor camp. No prosecutor would understand that she was only curious, infected with a desire for answers.

Her parents hadn't even been members of the Communist Party, but she had scored so well on the tests given in her third year of school that the Soviets had allowed her to enter the science program. Despite pressure to go into physics—a favored Soviet science—she had pursued biology. Relieving suffering had an obsessive appeal for her, a result of watching her father devoured by cancer while Soviet doctors fumbled about.

While going for her *kanditat* (the equivalent of a Ph.D.), she had come under the sway of Dorokhov, a brilliant microbiologist. She worshipped him, and spent happy hours watching his long, delicate fingers play the microscope like a concert pianist rendering Rachmaninoff.

He became her mentor, and when he became the head of the Lenin Polyclinic Institute, she gladly moved from Moscow to that bleak city to work under him. Now he was retired, living in nearby Nakhodka, and she would visit him once a week to discuss her projects. He was in his eighties, nearly blind from inoperable cataracts, but as sharp as ever. He was one of the few people who could keep up with her fast-moving train of thought.

She reached the office of the director of the central department of records. His secretary was an attractive twenty-five-year-old, with a taste for silk blouses. Dr. Mirnov had given her three in return for the key she now used to open the door. The combination to the director's safe had cost her a clock radio and a miniskirt.

Dr. Mirnov took the penlight flashlight from her pocket and shut the door behind her. She knew the guard's schedule. He wasn't due to pass by for another half hour.

She moved to the safe, opened it, and took out a stack of

35

papers. She sat on the floor, back against the safe, and began to read. Requisition requests, routine reports. Nothing very exciting.

Twenty minutes into her reading, she came upon an autopsy report that made her frown. Six cases of Lassa fever. Named after the city in Nigeria where it was first discovered in 1969. Characterized by abrupt, high fever, agonizing pain in the muscles, chest and abdomen, coughing, vomiting, diarrhea. Mortality over fifty percent. No known treatment. Caused by an arenavirus, its vector a rat known as *Mastomys natalensis*.

Patients must be isolated in a special room with air filtration and negative pressure to prevent airborne spread. All bodily fluids and objects that the patients touch are considered contaminants. She should have been informed if there was an outbreak of such a virulent, lethal disease.

Lassa fever was virtually unheard of in the Soviet Union. There was no indication that the subjects had visited Africa. In fact there was no indication of the etiology.

She heard footsteps and glanced at her watch. She had overstayed her time. She closed the safe, scuttled behind the desk and switched off the flashlight. The guard's footsteps drew closer.

He tried the doorknob and opened the door.

"Who's there?" he asked. She could see his high black boots from under the bottom of the desk. He turned on the light and walked around the room, gun drawn. "Who's there?" he repeated. He was young, his voice high, nervous. He tried the safe. Fortunately, Sultana had shut it.

He finally left. He'd be filing a report. The director of the department would be punished for having left the office door unlocked. A breach of security. She didn't care. He was a pompous twit who made speeches that hinted that Stalin was the best thing that ever happened to the Soviet Union.

She reopened the safe, returned the papers, and sneaked out of the room back to her section of the building.

She tried catching up on her paperwork, but her mind wasn't on it. Lassa fever?

"Hello, Dr. Mirnov."

She jumped.

It was a guard, in his mid-twenties, with flat, Mongolian features.

"Hello," she responded.

"I stopped by before and didn't see you," he said. The guard had a crush on her and made a point of visiting.

"I'm running an experiment," she said. "I must keep going back and forth."

"Can I help you?"

"No," she said, too harshly. She smiled. "That's very nice, but no thank you."

"You seem tense. Having trouble?"

"Everything's fine. Please excuse me, my mind is on the experiment."

He nodded, smiled, and saluted her. She saluted back, and he marched away. A boy dressed like a man.

When he was gone from the corridor, she shut the door and hustled down the hall the other way. Another guard was seated in front of the locked door to the autopsy room. He stared at her, openly eyeing her legs.

"Let me see your identification," he demanded, though she knew he recognized her.

She produced her internal passport and identification from the institute.

"What are you doing here?" he demanded, stepping in close, trying to gaze down her cleavage. His breath smelled of liquor.

"You do not have the clearance to know. And you are drunk," she snapped. The only way to deal with a bully was to bully him back.

He retreated. She advanced. "What would your supervisor say if he heard of this?"

"I just had a taste."

"You are charged by the people with guarding this important facility, and you get drunk."

"Don't tell anyone. It's the first time. Honest."

"You promise you won't do it again?"

He shook his head emphatically.

"Okay. Our secret. You don't even need to put down I was here. Now open that door."

She entered the room with the guard still repeating his thanks.

Stainless-steel tables and gurneys gleamed under the fluorescent lights. The tables had drains which led to gutters in the floor where bodily fluids would drain off. Above each

37

table hung a microphone, for the pathologist to dictate his findings, and a scale, to weigh the various organs removed.

The autopsies had been done that day, and so the bodies of the Lassa fever victims should be in the bottom row. She went through all the drawers. Empty.

Impossible. It was strict procedure that a body be held for at least two weeks after autopsy, in case additional tissue cultures were needed. Thinking perhaps there had been a paperwork foul-up, she opened all sixty drawers in the room. The bodies that she found clearly had not died of Lassa fever.

What had happened to the Lassa fever victims?

CHAPTER
4

Dr. Boris Arkov sent for her the next morning.

"I called your apartment last night and there was no answer."

"I worked through the night," she said. "I got a few hours sleep on the cot in my office."

"Still with the virus-cancer studies?"

"Yes."

"Next week, when you get back from Japan, you come work for me," he said. "I want you to come to my house tonight. We have work to discuss."

"But I was hoping to run a few more tests."

"Tonight. At seven o'clock."

She nodded. He got up from behind his massive desk and took her in his arms. "It won't be all business, my sweet *kotiki*." He took her face in his hands and kissed her, forcing her mouth open and probing with his tongue.

"What is it? You are thinking of someone else?" he asked.

"Just my research. There's so much to do."

"Your seriousness is a commendable trait. But sometimes a little break is in order. Tonight, you'll relax."

He gave her a swat on the rump and sent her on her way.

She didn't want to go to his house but knew there was no way she could defy his order.

On the way back to the lab she stopped at the office of the

chief of pathology. The secretary's name was Tania, a lipped blonde with a surly expression. They had met times, but never really talked.

Dr. Mirnov pretended she was looking for the though she knew he was back in Moscow.

"I understand you have a big family," Mirnov said.

"Four children."

"Your husband help you?"

"Hah."

"It must be hard cooking and cleaning for all of ther

"Hard isn't the word for it. All boys. None of thei lift a finger."

"Have you ever thought about a microwave oven?"

"Thought about it? I fantasize about it."

"I'm going to Tokyo in a couple of days. Suppose I arrange to pick one up for you?"

The secretary got cagey. "In return for what?"

Negotiations took fifteen minutes. In the end, Sultai a key and a combination. The secretary had the pron a microwave and a vacuum cleaner.

"There is something strange going on at the lab," sł Boris Arkov as they sat across the dinner table fron other.

"Like what?" He gnawed at a chicken bone. Sh made chicken Kiev, his favorite, named after the city birth.

"Procedures not being followed. Unusual diseases not sure exactly what just yet."

"Woman's intuition?"

"For now. Have you heard of anything?"

"I have heard many things. But none of them are fo ears." He set the bone down. "You know what happ the head of wheat that stands above the others?"

"It gets cut down first," she said.

"Correct. Like with your persistence on the alcol question. As is well known, the research will be auth when it is time. For now, it is more important to conti spread of distortions and inaccuracy."

"All I want is material for my research."

"There are too many ways that facts can be interp

There is plenty of work for you to do in other areas. Now eat. Enjoy."

She finished her rice. Their plates were empty. She had encouraged him to finish the bottle of Pertsovka lemon vodka, but it seemed to have little effect on him. She'd hoped that he would open up.

"There was no dessert in the refrigerator," she said.

He pushed himself back from the table. "You are my dessert."

They kissed, his lips still scented with the spices she'd used, still greasy from the chicken. Although she was not a small woman, he lifted her easily and carried her up the stairs.

He undressed her, and then she him. His powerful hands alternately squeezed and caressed, pain and pleasure. She did the same for him, her nails either moving in delicate tracing, or digging deep into his lean, muscular frame.

"You never told me how you got this," she said, a finger running along the scar that ran from his waist to hipbone.

"An operation."

"The surgeon must have been a butcher. It's so ragged."

"Not that kind of operation. I am, I was in the military."

"Tell me about it," she said.

He answered by pressing his lips to hers. She tried to wriggle free, but he was too strong. Then he was in her, and she could think of nothing else.

He puffed on one of the American cigarettes he favored. As she lay in bed, her head on his shoulder, she made a mental note to pick him up a few cartons during her electronics buying trip. She'd only have two days, and most of her time would be spent in the Akihabara section of Tokyo, browsing crowded and noisy electronics stores for the latest technology that might be usable in the lab.

"What did you do in the army?" she asked Arkov.

"Many things."

"Like what?"

He ground out his cigarette and sat up. "You ask too many questions. I have heard criticism of you in the lab for the same problem. When you work for me, you mind your own business. If I catch you snooping where you don't belong, I will show you no special favor."

He got out of bed and strode to the bathroom. "After my shower, we'll talk about the project I have in mind for you. Blastomycosis."

"But that's not a problem. There're so many—"

"I'll decide what is a problem," he said, interrupting. "You get results. Don't ask questions."

He slammed the door to the bathroom.

She got up quickly, still naked, and hurried to the dresser. She rooted through his belongings. Underwear, shirts, socks. She touched hard metal. A Tokarev 7.62mm. Why would Dr. Arkov need a gun?

She listened. He was still in the shower, singing "Moscow Nights."

There was a small desk in the corner of the room. She pulled open drawers. Papers, pens, stamps. She opened a badge case.

Glavnoye Razvedyvatelnoye Upravleniye, the Chief Intelligence Directorate of the Soviet General Staff, known by the letters GRU. Her lover was a colonel in Soviet military intelligence.

It explained his arrogance, his confidence, even with the KGB creeps in the First Department. No wonder his division always had the first crack at the latest centrifuge or electron microscope.

But what was he doing at the Lenin Polyclinic Institute?

The singing stopped. She dropped the ID card back into the desk and raced back toward the bed.

"What are you doing?" he asked, when she didn't quite make it back to the bed in time.

"Where do you have your cigarettes?" she asked.

"In the night table. But you don't smoke."

"Sometimes I do. There's a lot you don't know about me. I have secrets, too."

"What does that mean?"

"Uh, nothing. Just you seem secretive sometimes."

He grunted. She took one from the pack, hoping that he didn't see her hand shaking. She lit it and inhaled, nearly coughing. After a few puffs, she put it out.

"Too strong," she said in response to his questioning gaze.

"Come, towel me dry," he ordered.

As she wiped him down, he toyed with her breasts, rolling

her nipples between his fingers. He grew hard as she dried him between his legs.

He pulled her to him.

"We have work to do," she said. "Blastomycosis."

"It can wait."

She had trouble concentrating on her work the next day. She accidentally knocked over a beaker containing live viruses. It was a major incident that required shutting down the lab and scrubbing under a painful chemical shower.

A KGB toady snooped and took notes, to assure that it was not a case of deliberate sabotage. Mirnov's colleagues and staff vouched for her and her long hours of hard work. She wasn't getting enough sleep was the general consensus.

"My report will not call for a disciplinary proceeding," the KGBer said. "Not this time. But you must prove your loyalty to the Motherland by working ever more diligently."

Although everyone urged her to go home, that night Mirnov sneaked into the chief pathologist's office. She had trouble with the key and had to jiggle it several times to open the door. She didn't know the guard's schedule in that part of the building and was so nervous that it took her two minutes to get the combination right.

What she found in the safe made the risk worthwhile.

She came across a report of a Q fever outbreak. Caused by the *Coxiella rickettsia*. Another rare disease. It was highly infectious, but only fatal in less than one percent of the cases. Again six cases. Etiology unknown. And again the report did not say where the six cases were but had a detailed account of the course of the disease.

She noticed a mark on the paper that indicated a copy had been made. The photocopying machine was located in the First Department office, and guarded as zealously as a nuclear plant.

She checked the cross-referencing and routing forms. It had been sent to a Yuri Zabotin at the Soviet mission to the United Nations in New York. Why?

Mirnov glanced at her watch. She could only risk staying a few more minutes. She was about to put the papers away when she took a look at the report on the bottom. She gasped. It detailed six fatal cases of blastomycosis. No wonder they want me to study it, she thought.

She read the reports. Ulcerated sores on the skin, dry hacking cough, invasion of the internal organs by the *Blastomyces dermatiditis*. There was a ninety percent fatality rate for the systemic variety.

But it didn't make sense. The report seemed to indicate that the patients had been under medical supervision from the onset of the disease, and yet they were untreated. The effects could be mitigated with intravenous amphotericin B. They could've been given painkillers.

She flipped back to the Q fever report. It was as detailed an account of the course of the disease, yet there was also no sign of any treatment. Tetracycline had reduced Q fever mortality to barely one percent.

Thinking back, there hadn't been any reports of treatment on the Lassa fever patients. That had a fifty percent mortality rate, but with antibiotics to prevent secondary infections, IV colloids, painkillers, and antifever drugs, previously healthy patients had a good chance of survival.

She flipped back to the blastomycosis study to look for any signs of treatment once again. What she saw made her sag against the wall. She felt weak, on the verge of collapse.

Her signature was forged on the bottom.

CHAPTER
5

"Calm down, calm down, child," Dr. Dorokhov said, patting her head. "Have tea and we'll talk."

Dr. Mirnov was nearly in tears as she sat in the small living room of her mentor's *dacha*.

"Who would do such a thing?" she asked. "Who would forge my name on a report? Why was the disease allowed to run its course without intervention? Why was a copy sent to New York?"

Dorokhov's movements were slow, careful. He used his finely tapered fingertips to guide the kettle to the cup. "You shouldn't ask these questions." He poured, and despite nearly sightless eyes, didn't spill a drop.

"That's what Colonel Arkov said," Sultana responded.

"Colonel?"

And she told him what she had discovered. She expected him to be outraged. Instead, he was patronizing.

He made a clucking noise and took her soft hand in his brittle one. "You don't know what is going on, do you?"

They sat and stared at each other.

"What interest would the military have in such medicine?" As she said the words, she knew. "But only the United States would do that. The possibilities of biological warfare are too horrible. Our peace-loving peoples would never allow such a thing to happen."

45

"You are a naive, sweet child," he said.

"I must do something. I will go to *Pravda*."

"Don't be foolish."

"The Central Committee must be told."

"They know."

"Impossible," she insisted. "The untreated patients. Watching them grow sick. Someone is doing live experiments. Live human experiments. It violates the Nuremberg Code. The Geneva Protocol. It's unbelievable!"

"Calm down, calm down," her mentor said.

She got up. "I'll go to the Council of Ministers. I'll tell everyone. Science cannot be used like this."

"Don't do it," he said, with a hint of the old power in his tone.

"I have to."

"These studies must be done. For defensive purposes."

She stared at him. "How long have they been going on?"

He didn't answer.

"Good-bye," she said with a note of finality.

She stormed out of the *dacha*.

Dr. Dorokhov had a grandson who was trying to get into the Communist Party. If anyone had seen Sultana coming into his house, and a scandal broke, his grandson's life would be ruined. He knew her well enough to know how strong-willed she was, and that the possibility existed that she would embarrass the powers that be.

His eyes were moist as he picked up the phone and called the local office of the Komitet Gosudarstvennoi Bezopastnosti.

Why couldn't Dorokhov help her? How much more did he know? Why was he unconcerned about this perversion of their work? Was it possible that the Politburo knew, too, and didn't care?

She was due to go to Japan the next day. Did she dare go to the international authorities? The United Nations was a toy of the United States, but still, maybe there was a chance she could stop the experiments.

She couldn't fall asleep as she lay in bed that night. She tossed and turned, dozed off, and awoke with a start. Finally, at about three A.M., sleep overcame her.

46

An hour later, there was a pounding at the door.

She stumbled out of bed. "Who is it?"

"Open the door," a man's voice bellowed.

"Who's there?"

The door rocked in its frame and the old wood gave way. Two big men entered the apartment. They wore hats pulled low, bulky trench coats, black leather gloves on their hands. They didn't need to identify themselves. It was clear who they were.

"You're coming with us," the one with a broken nose ordered.

"What—what's going on?"

"No questions."

"What do you want?"

Broken Nose slapped her face, hard enough to stagger her.

The other one, who had thick hair across his brow and coming out of his ears, stared at her. She realized she was wearing a flimsy gown, a gift from Arkov. She put her arms across her chest.

"Get dressed," Broken Nose ordered.

"I'll make sure she doesn't try anything," the hairy one said.

He put his arm around her and led her to the bedroom, one hand pawing her breast. She tried to escape.

"Maybe I'll begin the questioning here," Hairy One said.

"Don't take long," Broken Nose answered. "I'll look around."

Sultana struggled but he was too strong. He shoved her onto the bed and undid his trousers. "Traitorous cunt," he said, falling upon her.

She fought back. He slapped her so hard she felt dizzy. His hands reached between her thighs. He tried to kiss her. His breath smelled of dried fish and vodka. She turned her face away, bucking and writhing beneath him.

He hit her again and again.

"Don't break anything," Broken Nose shouted from the other room.

"Just her cherry," Hairy One said, laughing.

She felt his probing at the entrance to her body. On the night table a big wooden clock ticked off the seconds.

Both hands were busy parting her. She reached over,

47

grabbed the clock, and smashed it on his head with all her strength. His eyes rolled, and he collapsed on her.

Mirnov pushed him off. There was no way she could climb out the bedroom window. She was on the sixth floor of the walk-up.

Sultana moved to her small closet and dumped clothes off the rack. She pulled the bar out of the wall.

"What's going on in there?" Broken Nose asked.

She made a passionate moan.

Broken Nose laughed lewdly. "Leave some for me, comrade," he shouted to his unconscious buddy.

Mirnov hurried to the side of the door. The metal bar nearly slid from her slippery palm.

"Tovarich," she shouted as coyly as possible.

"Huh?"

"Come join us," she said.

Broken Nose stepped into the room. He saw her a second before she swung the bar and lifted his arm to block it.

She brought it down, shattering his arm. He yowled and lunged at her. He grabbed her throat. She poked at him with the end of the bar. He jerked it from her hands and threw it down.

They fell to the floor. He tried to reach under his coat for his gun, but she clawed at his face every time he lowered his hands. He got an arm around her neck, but she was able to bash his broken arm and force him to let up the pressure. She kneed him in the groin.

As he gasped, she grabbed the bar, and brought it down on his skull. It made a sickly, meaty noise.

She dropped the bar. She reached inside the coat and took out his gun. She pointed it at the unconscious figure, dreading that he would move. But he didn't.

She looked around the apartment. It was a wreck. Broken Nose had sliced open her couch, smashed the lithographs of Russian winter scenes she'd had on the wall, even torn up the old carpet.

She reached again under his coat. Komitet Gosudarstvennoi Bezopastnosti. Committee for State Security. A KGB captain. What she didn't expect to see was that he was assigned to the Nakhodka branch.

She took his identification and stuffed it into her purse.

She had nothing to lose. No one assaulted an officer of the KGB. She was already a dead person.

She ripped electric cords from the lamps and used them to tie up the KGB men. She taped their mouths.

She dressed quickly. Checking her watch, she saw she had two hours until she was due at the airport. She grabbed a quick change of clothes.

What would happen if there was any delay at the airport? The plane fogged in or her being bumped for some member of the *nomenklatura* who had more clout than her. It had happened more than once. How long before they discovered her assailants? She looked at the KGB captain's red ID case and then her own.

She hurried down to her Zhiguli and drove toward the lab. A cold, damp fog chilled her. The few street lights did little to pierce the gloom. The headlights of her Zhiguli were weak.

At the lab, the guards checked her ID several times, though they were used to seeing her at unusual hours. They could never know if it was a KGB test of their diligence. The First Department was everywhere.

It was quiet inside the building, the old familiar quiet. She knew it was the last time she would ever walk the corridors.

In her office, she opened her personal supply cabinet and took out a scalpel. She clamped her internal passport to a stand and carefully removed her picture. It was slow, meticulous work. Then she repeated the surgery on the KGB captain's photo.

She checked her watch. She had an hour to get to the airport.

She dabbed glue on the back of her photo and affixed it to the KGB ID card. It looked glued on. It wouldn't fool a school child.

She practically ran down the corridor to the megabar press. The study of high pressure physics had always been a priority, and the Lenin Polyclinic Institute had a press, which reportedly had cost twenty million roubles and could generate a half million kilograms of pressure.

The massive machine—as big as a locomotive engine—had its own room. She had seen it operated several times, and read the instructions and warnings posted near the control panel. She put the KGB ID in the receptacle and turned the machine on. There was a loud humming noise and a soft hiss. After ten seconds, she turned it off.

Perfect. The laminated photo was squashed into the page.

She ran to her car and drove to the airport.

The guard at Passport Control said a senior scientist from the lab had bumped her. She got haughty, flashed her KGB ID, and demanded to speak to a supervisor. After fifteen minutes of back and forth, she was allowed on board.

Nakhodka is a city of 125,000, about one quarter the size of Vladivostock. The head of the Nakhodka KGB office was jealous of his rival in the big city and had hoped to scoop Sultana Mirnov up and achieve a coup.

Instead, the two men he'd dispatched were long overdue. He had a choice. He could call his rival in Vladivostock and tell him, or send a few more men.

He decided to send in a second wave.

Mirnov fidgeted in her seat. What would it be like? Would they accept her? Would they believe her? What could they do? What would happen if the KGB caught up with her? Who had sicced them on her?

It had to be Arkov. Who else could know?

But, the KGB agents had come from the Nakhodka office, not Vladivostock. They must've learned about her outrage from Dorokhov. Her mentor had betrayed her. She felt nauseated. She grabbed an air sickness bag and dry heaved into it. Passengers around her moved away.

The Aeroflot Ilyushin jet touched down at Narita Airport and the passengers disgorged. She passed through Immigration in a daze, answering the inspector's question in a barely audible mumble.

"What did you say?" he demanded, studying her face for signs of illness or drug use.

She forced herself to snap to. "I'm sorry. I'm just here for a few days," she said, beaming him her most engaging smile.

He nodded and stamped her passport.

Who was watching her? she wondered as she walked

through the crowded terminal. She had vital secrets of state security in her head and would no doubt be under routine surveillance.

With only a carry-on bag, she passed through Customs quickly. She stopped at the currency exchange and traded in all her roubles for yen.

As she made her way to the cab, she spotted them. Two bulky women and one man. One woman and the man pretended they were a couple, the other woman operated independently. They were dressed in quality Western clothing, but their unsmiling Slavic faces gave away their roles.

She hailed a cab. They got into the next one in line.

The second team discovered Broken Nose and Hairy One, both conscious and struggling against their bonds. They called their boss at Nakhodka.

He was forced to call Vladivostock headquarters and confess what had happened.

The string of obscenities he heard from the general at the other end made him wince. The Vladivostock KGB man slammed down the phone and got on a secure line to the *rezidentura* in Tokyo.

"Dr. Sultana Mirnov is in Tokyo," the general growled. "I want her back immediately. On the next plane. She is guilty of assaulting an officer of the KGB, theft of state property, treason. This is top priority. Understand?"

"Understood."

The KGB *rezidentura* had never heard the general so agitated. He called down to his aide. "Get six of our *grazny rabota* men and meet me in the garage."

The aide scrambled the "dirty work" team, strong-arms who could muscle a reluctant defector into a car or intimidate local busybodies out of the picture.

Dr. Mirnov got out of the taxi and raced into the Mitsukoshi department store. It was not suspicious behavior. Russians in a consumer paradise were like bargain hunters at a once-a-year sale. She breezed by the petite, white-gloved Japanese girls who bowed to customers, endlessly repeating *"Irasshaimase,"* Welcome.

She stopped at the perfume counter, taking the time to

51

size up her shadows. She had lost one of the women. Maybe the female KGB agent had seen an irresistible blouse.

Mirnov played with an atomizer of Shiseido perfume, slowly turning around, scanning the faces. Without really thinking what she was doing, she bought the bottle of perfume. It cost as much as two months rent on her Vladivostock apartment.

She stopped at a nearby counter and bought a pale red scarf with a crane pattern on it. She hurried to the dress section, found one a size too big and entered the dressing room. She put the dress on over her own, and snipped off the labels.

The female KGB agent came in and saw what she was doing. The woman grinned. Shoplifting was unusual to the Japanese—to the Russians it was a fair assault on the materialistic, capitalist structure.

"Go get yourself a dress. I'll wait here," Mirnov said.

As the woman turned, Mirnov shoved her hard into a small dressing room. She slammed the door and wedged a chair against a knob.

The KGB agent pounded on the door and yelled.

With the scarf on her hair and the new dress, Sultana barreled out of the dressing room.

She spotted the male KGBer easily. Mirnov spun and made it to the exit. The surveillant caught her movement. He ran after her.

Outside, she hailed a cab and jumped in.

"The American embassy. Hurry."

"*Wakari masen.*"

"*Sprechen sie Deutsch?*"

"*Wakari masen. Gomen nasai.*"

The KGB agent was pushing his way across the crowded sidewalk.

She began humming the "Star-spangled Banner."

"Base-beiru. Yankees okay. *Dai ichiban,*" the cabbie said with a grin.

"Yankees. American. Please hurry."

"*Ah, America-jin. So desu.*"

He pulled away from the curb as the KGB agent got his hand inside the window. He clamped down on her arm. She bit his hand. The man yelped, shouted a Russian obscenity and fell back. The cab pulled out into traffic.

"Miami Vice," the cabbie said, clearly enjoying the excitement. He was watching her in the rearview mirror, and nearly struck a car. Horns honked. The KGB agent ran in between cars.

Then the light changed, and they were off. The KGB man got a face full of exhaust fumes.

CHAPTER
6

The private dining room in the MacMillan Building ha
panoramic view of Manhattan and beyond that rivaled
one offered by the World Trade Center or the nearby Em
State Building. Even the numerous heads of state who
been MacMillan's guests had been impressed by the vie

The chef had previously cooked for Giscard d'Estaing
waist-jacketed waiters were paragons of courtesy and s
ice. The place settings were antique silver and china,
seum pieces.

Benedict MacMillan sat at a table, nursing a Cha
Latour 1953 bordeaux. Opposite him was Marshal
Zabotin, under secretary general for political and sec
council affairs at the United Nations, the position once
by Arkady Shevchenko. He was a marshal in the KGB, 1
highest-ranked official in the United States.

Zabotin was a stocky, balding man, with thick gla
thick lips, and a perpetual scowl on his face. His v
however, was a mellifluous baritone, and his speeches o
floor of the U.N. were rousing moments of demagogu
He was in his late sixties, with thinning gray hair.

"Your father is a great man," Zabotin said, swirlin
Remy Martin around the glass.

"He speaks highly of you as well," MacMillan said.

"He will be remembered as a great philanthropist,"

botin said. "Of course, you wouldn't need philanthropists if your capitalistic system took care of its people. But still, he is a great man. We've known each other, thirty, forty years," Zabotin mused. "I remember you as a boy. You always dressed nicely, very serious."

"How is your son? Does he still play soccer?" Calvin MacMillan's files recorded that Zabotin's son had been a leading soccer player for the Leningrad Dynamos. Now his grandson was following in his footsteps.

Benedict let Zabotin tell him that and acted properly interested. The KGB marshal produced photos of his grandson in uniform. They made polite small talk for several minutes.

Then the senior Macmillan entered, using a cane. Benedict wondered why. He'd never seen his father need any support.

There were hugs between the two older men, and catching up on mutual acquaintances. The waiters brought appetizers, and then the meal. Roast quail with lamb's lettuce, radicchio, and fig vinaigrette. There was more chitchat and appropriate comments on the food.

"You remember my favorites," Zabotin said, pushing away from the table and patting his belly as the waiter brought out the dessert—chocolate mousse. "I daresay you have files that would do my comrades justice."

When the plates were cleared, waiters brought a selection of after-dinner liqueurs.

"Now that you've stuffed me like a Christmas goose, what do you want?" Zabotin asked, a grin taking the edge off his words.

"I'm getting old, Yuri Ivanovitch," MacMillan said, using Zabotin's patronymic as a term of friendship.

"We all are," Zabotin answered.

"The doctors say a few more months for me."

Benedict was stunned. Could it be true?

"Doctors know nothing," Zabotin said.

"I feel it. There is one thing I would like to see."

"And I can help?" Zabotin asked. "I owe you, you know that."

MacMillan nodded. "This constant saber rattling by the superpowers scares me. It's time for sensible men to take action." MacMillan took a slow sip of water. Zabotin and his son waited. "I want to show your government and mine

55

that they are playing dangerous games. I'm going to take one of their toys and scare the daylights out of them."

"How?" Benedict asked.

MacMillan gave him a sharp look. "There is research being done on biological warfare."

Zabotin made to interrupt; MacMillan raised his hand for silence. "Please, hear me out. Both sides are doing it. Don't deny it. You people have come further along with the actual germs. We have gone further in terms of delivery systems. I want the results of the Soviet research."

"*Tovarich,* this is more than I can deliver."

"I don't think so."

"What will you do with it?"

"I will begin to put together a plant to make whatever germ you people have developed. Along with the American technology. It is a weapon to end all weapons. I know, others have said the same thing. The inventor of the Gatling gun naively believed his weapon was so horrible it would stop war. Now, it is nothing but an antique.

"But I can shake up both sides. I am an outsider. Weapons have developed to the point where an individual, not just a sovereign nation, can destroy life on this planet. They must stop this arms race stupidity. In a few years, they'll have nuclear weapons that a child can detonate." Zabotin drained his glass. A waiter reappeared and filled it, then disappeared.

"If we wait for our leaders to recognize the road we're going down, we will all die," MacMillan said. "They need a rap on the knuckles."

"Incredible," Benedict said.

"What happens if what you develop falls into the wrong hands? A Kaddhafi, a Khomeni?" Zabotin asked. "Even your own government?"

"Don't worry about my government. They stockpile these things, assuming they will never be used. For all the tough talk, they're as sensible as the Politburo."

"Which might not be saying much," Zabotin said. He looked around the empty room after the indiscretion escaped his lips.

"As far as other governments, I will observe the tightest security." He leaned forward. "I won't actually put the plans into effect. Like a Potemkin village, it will be a front.

But enough to shake those fools in the White House and the Kremlin right down to their booties."

Zabotin leaned back in his chair. "You never cease to amaze me, Calvin. I must think this over."

"Please do. In the meantime, there's someone I'd like you to meet."

Benedict said good-bye, as prearranged with his father, citing vital business. Zabotin and Calvin looked out the window at the city.

"You capitalists have done quite a lot," Zabotin said, a sweeping gesture taking in the New York skyline.

"I want to preserve it. As well as Red Square. And the Eiffel Tower, and Big Ben."

"What about your Statue of Liberty and the Imperial Palace in Beijing?" Zabotin asked, smiling.

"Mankind has done so much," MacMillan said.

"True," Zabotin responded.

A waiter came over carrying a large padded manila envelope. MacMillan took it, and handed it to Zabotin. "Please accept this small token."

Zabotin protested, then reluctantly accepted. He opened the package. It was a jewel-encrusted Fabergé egg, created by Peter Carl Fabergé, the goldsmith to the czars.

While delicately rolling the egg in his hands, Zabotin renewed his protests. "I can't take this."

"You may keep it for yourself or return it to your countrymen if you wish. It recently came on the black market and I was able to get it at a reasonable price."

"It's priceless," Zabotin said, gingerly turning the egg around in his blunt fingers. "There is no way I can express my gratitude or that of my country."

"Oh yes there is," MacMillan said.

Benedict MacMillan crouched behind the parked car. He held a telephoto-equipped Polaroid, loaded with high speed film. He checked the light meter. Definitely bright enough.

The scope and grandeur of his father's vision amazed him. The idea sounded far-fetched, but so had so much of what his father had done. Playing off capitalists and communists, and collecting profits from both. Getting the CIA to do the dirty work when a South American leader threatened mining interests. Arranging a delay in an African tribal war so MacMillan industry property could be sold off.

Benedict wondered how far his father would go with the preparations. He'd have to do more than just set up a shop with a few beakers. Benedict felt a tingle of pride. What if the old man held onto the microbes and hinted that he'd swap all he'd made for a Nobel Prize? What could they do then?

The squeal of a car's tires broke his reverie. Peter Hornaday's BMW pulled to a stop right near the private elevator.

Deputy National Security Advisor Hornaday got out of the car and looked around. Benedict ducked lower.

The private elevator opened. Zabotin and MacMillan stepped out. Zabotin was carrying a bulky manila envelope.

MacMillan introduced the two adversaries.

Benedict clicked away with the camera. His father had craftily stepped back, out of the way.

"You gentlemen know each other," MacMillan said.

"We know of each other," Hornaday said tersely.

"I thought it important that you meet," MacMillan said. "We may all be working together soon."

"I doubt that," Hornaday said.

MacMillan just smiled.

Hornaday wondered what the hell was going on. He had provided the younger MacMillan with details about the U.S. biological warfare plans. But it was Cheez Whiz, nothing top secret. A few things were classified, but only at the lowest levels of security. Hornaday could tell what was important and what was just someone with a hush-hush rubber stamp flexing his muscles.

MacMillan said good-bye to Zabotin and invited Hornaday up to the penthouse.

"What's going on?" Hornaday demanded of MacMillan as they settled into the old man's office.

"I'm going to need more information from you in the future," MacMillan said. "I might need you to take some action at my behest."

"I was contemplating retiring in the near future," Hornaday said.

"In good time. When I say so."

"That's my decision, Mr. MacMillan," Hornaday said. He didn't like the old man's condescending tone.

MacMillan hit a buzzer on his desk and his son sauntered in. He dropped three of the Polaroid pictures on Hornaday's lap.

"What—what does this mean?" Hornaday demanded.

"I have the information you've given us. It's not much, but would be embarrassing. Your fingerprints are all over the paper. Plus, there're tidbits I've picked up on the Star Wars nonsense, which I would throw into the package. You see the envelope Marshal Zabotin holds?"

Hornaday nodded.

"Who's to say what's in there? I've got plenty of friends at the FBI who'd love a few of those prints. Along with details of the info you've been giving the Russians."

"You wouldn't."

"He would," Benedict piped up.

Hornaday sagged into his chair.

"What I'll be asking you to do is for the good of humanity, the good of our nation, Mr. Hornaday. You should be happy to be involved in the project."

"Is Zabotin involved?"

"This is bigger than your government or his. You're getting a chance to work for world peace."

Hornaday tugged at his face, nervously pulling at his cheeks.

"I don't need to point out what would happen if we went to the FBI," MacMillan said. "The arrest. Pictures of you in the newspaper with handcuffs on. The long trial. Tremendous legal expenses. Your children branded the progeny of a traitor. Maybe you'd be acquitted. But everyone would believe you guilty anyway. Your life would be over."

"What do you want me to do?" Hornaday asked weakly.

PART
II

CHAPTER
7

Brazil—1987

The man with bad teeth ground his gun into Robert Stark's ear. "Any tricks and I kill you," the man said in Portuguese.

"No tricks," Stark said slowly in Spanish-flavored Portuguese.

They were just outside a *favelas,* a suburban shantytown, on the northern edge of Rio de Janeiro. It was a universe away from the beautiful beaches that curved for fifteen miles along Guanabara Bay. Visitors saw Ipanema, Copacabana, the statue of Christ the Redeemer on Hunchback Mountain, Sugar Loaf silhouetted against a gorgeous sunset, and the maniacal fun of Carnival. They were unaware or indifferent to the *favelas,* where families of eight lived in what wouldn't pass as a shabby garden shed in the United States. There was no running water, no electricity, and no hope.

As Stark and Bad Teeth waited, a shoeless girl with large brown eyes and a tattered yellow dress watched. She had a runny nose that she kept wiping on the remants of a doll she held pressed against her chest. Flies buzzed around her— she didn't bother to shoo them away.

The nearby shantytown inhabitants ignored Stark and Bad Teeth. The last thing they wanted was additional troubles.

A decrepit red Chevy van with terminal suspension swerved around the corner and Bad Teeth shoved Stark into it.

A second kidnapper held an Uzi across his lap as if it was a beloved child. He glared balefully at Stark, eager for a chance to try his weapon.

A third man inside the van blindfolded Stark, moving too quickly for Stark to see much of his face. There was a butterfly tattooed between the thumb and index finger of his left hand. His hands smelled of cigarettes.

"We should hang on to him, too," one of his captors said. "Two pigs are better than one."

The van smelled of rotting fruit and sweat.

"Do you have the money?" Uzi demanded. His voice was quivery, but had the sound of authority.

"A good faith payment," Stark said. He slowly reached into the pocket of his bush jacket and took out an envelope. Bad Teeth, who had patted him down for weapons, had missed it. He sneered as the quivery-voiced leader took it. Uzi opened it and counted the money.

"Now you must show good faith, and take me to see him," Stark said.

"I spit on you and good faith," Uzi said, lobbing a mouthful of saliva on Stark's face.

Stark calmly took a handkerchief from his pocket and wiped his face. "You are asking for twenty million dollars for the return of the Associated Press bureau chief. He's not a wealthy man. He's a worker, with three children. He is sympathetic to—"

"Shut up!" Uzi said. "Take your money back. We will deliver the body tomorrow."

"There are insurance policies," Stark said. "Maybe his company can come up with more money. A hundred thousand perhaps."

The kidnappers argued rapidly in Portuguese. Stark knew enough of the language to get by. He could handle basic needs in eleven languages. He couldn't understand completely what they were saying, but by tone, he assumed Bad Teeth wanted to accept the deal. Uzi wanted to kill Stark and make off with the ten thousand dollars. The man with the tattoo voted to let Stark live. Tattoo and Uzi were vying to be top dog.

"Take off your clothes," Uzi said.

"Why do you want him to do that?" Tattoo challenged.

"I've heard about clothing with radio transmitters built in," Uzi said.

Stark removed his jacket and shirt. Uzi threw them out the window. Children scurried up, grabbed them, and raced off.

"Shoes and pants too," Uzi said.

Stark stripped down to his briefs. Bad Teeth tried on Stark's shoes, found that they fit, and tossed his own out the window. They, and the pants, were snatched up by the urchins.

Uzi ripped the watch from Stark's wrist and put it on.

Stark felt his adrenaline pumping. The van was stifling. He desperately wanted to pull the blindfold off, to lash out.

Uzi was waiting for a response. The wrong reaction, and Stark would lose face, making negotiations even more difficult.

If a man is rowing on the water, and another boatman bumps him, the man is angry. But if his boat is bumped by an empty boat that was bobbed about by the wind, he can laugh at it as mild misfortune.

"Don't forget to wind the watch," Stark said, relaxing his shoulders and keeping a calm half-smile on his face.

"Let's go," Uzi said, and the man who had blindfolded Stark started the engine.

The Lear Jet sat parked on the runway at Rio's Galçâo Airport. Pedro Quesada leaned against the fuselage. Hidden under his bush jacket was an Ingram M-11 Lightweight Individual Special Purpose (LISP) machine pistol, capable of spewing out 850 rounds of .380 subsonic ammo per minute.

One of Quesada's arms had been injured when he was a child growing up in Oaxaca. Quesada, a stocky fifty-year-old with a bushy mustache, had developed the other, giving him a lopsided appearance. His ethnic looks allowed him to pass for anything from a Sephardic Jew to a Colombian coke dealer. A one-time gang leader, he was adept at blending in on city streets. Quesada was a deadly shot, a ferocious street fighter, and Stark had trusted his life to him many times.

Inside the plane, Lester Halliwell sat at a console, watching the beep on the transponder screen. The flashing dot had blipped in one place for ten minutes. There was a long console of communications gear before him. On the seat next to him was an aluminum Haliburton suitcase with a half-million dollars in gold inside.

Halliwell watched the screen without moving. He had lots of practice being patient. For twenty years he had been a Secret Service man, rising to command the Executive Protection detail. He'd retired, tried a couple of businesses, had a few modest successes. Then he'd met Stark at an expatriate bar in Tokyo. They'd hit it off, and Halliwell-Stark Associates had been formed.

The firm had a total of six full-time personnel at offices in New York and Los Angeles. HSA didn't just offer bodyguards, they had a contract that mandated complying with their security recommendations. They were security consultants who believed that anticipating problems was much more effective than coping with them.

HSA was known for its expert crisis management and hostage negotiation. The company averaged two dozen calls a year and had not lost a single hostage.

The van bounced through the countryside, kicking up clouds of dust as it passed through small villages. Children and scruffy dogs ran out of the way as it sped onward. The only cheery colors came from the filled clotheslines. Obese women chattered in doorways of corrugated tin huts. Elderly men, or men who looked old, indifferently watched them pass. Potholes the size of craters jarred the four men inside.

The blindfolded Stark guessed they had circled and doubled back on their route a couple of times. Then Bad Teeth down-shifted and the road got even rougher.

The sun baked down on the top of the van and the air was fetid. The windows were open but the humid air did little to cool them. Uzi repeatedly hissed threats in Stark's ear. Though he was wearing only his briefs, Stark was sweating profusely.

The van stopped. Uzi jerked Stark's blindfold off. They were at a hut in a clearing. A creek ran nearby. The Brazilian Highlands loomed in the distance.

A scrawny man came out of the house, a double-barreled shotgun in his hand. A home-rolled cigarette drooped from thin lips.

"How's the prisoner?" Tattoo asked.

The man with the shotgun shrugged. They went inside the hut. Two hammocks were slung up in the twelve-by-twelve-foot space. There were a few pin-up pictures of Sonia Braga. The four windows had cracked panes.

The AP bureau chief lay on the dirt floor, clutching his stomach with bound hands. His feet were tied together with hemp and his face was bruised.

"He has the shits," the man with the shotgun said.

The bureau chief looked up.

"I'm Robert Stark. Your company sent me to see you are okay." Stark studied the man. It was indeed AP bureau chief Allen LaGrange, though the stubbled, pale figure hardly resembled the photo of the pudgy, middle-aged journalist Stark had been shown.

LaGrange was a two-time Pulitzer nominee who had exposed brutality and corruption in a half-dozen Latin American regimes. When he had first disappeared, it was assumed that some death squad had repaid an old debt. His family and employer were overjoyed when they got the ransom note. It gave them hope.

Stark had warned that it might be a ploy, that LaGrange might be dead already. He was glad his skepticism was misplaced. But it was a bad sign that the kidnappers were not wearing masks. They weren't afraid of being identified. That could mean they didn't expect survivors.

"We want five million dollars," Bad Teeth said.

"I told you, they can't raise that much."

"I will give you his eyeballs for insulting us," Uzi said.

"Let's talk man to man," Stark said to Tattoo. "We can work out an honorable solution."

"It's a trick," Uzi said. "Kill them both. We have ten thousand dollars more than before."

"I told you I can get a hundred thousand," Stark said, ignoring Uzi. "Is it worth ninety thousand for us to make a deal?"

Tattoo took a snub-nosed .38 out from under his loose-fitting guayabera shirt. "We'll talk. José, you walk behind us. Keep lookout." José was the one with the rotten teeth. "You others guard the prisoner."

"Why can't we all go?" Uzi demanded.

"Stay here," Tattoo barked.

Uzi took a few steps forward. Tattoo stood on his hands,

and his right leg swirled up and hit Uzi in the cheek. The entire movement was over in barely a second.

Uzi stumbled back.

"Stay here," Tattoo repeated. Uzi grimaced, but obeyed.

Tattoo and Stark walked down a narrow path. José trailed ten meters behind.

"Was that *capoeira?*" Stark asked.

"What do you know about *capoeira?*" Tattoo asked.

"Not much, just how difficult it is," Stark said.

Tattoo grunted.

Capoeira is a martial art popular among rural blacks in Brazil. Developed from Angolan tribal fighting dances, it is often practiced to music, and involves cartwheel kicks.

"You are a reasonable man," Stark said, as Tattoo kept the revolver pointed at his middle. "LaGrange needs medical attention."

"That is his problem."

"It's the problem of us all. Maybe I could get the company to come up with more money. Say, two hundred thousand."

"We'll take no less than a million of your imperialist dollars."

Stark saw a movement out of the corner of his eye, someone watching them from the thick brush. They continued their walk. Stark offered four hundred thousand. Tattoo held out for six hundred. He added a demand for the release of six prisoners being held in Brazilian jails. None were political prisoners—they were bank robbers and truck hijackers. It confirmed what Stark had believed. The kidnappers were not politically motivated. They were career criminals.

José stumbled and Tattoo was distracted from Stark. Stark grabbed his wrist, tugged forward and spun, executing a *shiho nage,* a wrist lock throw. He kept his hand on the barrel of the revolver. Although Tattoo squeezed the trigger, the cylinder couldn't turn, and the gun couldn't fire.

Stark jerked the gun from Tattoo's hand. Tattoo jumped up, whipping out a switchblade. He danced a little jig, and a kick caught Stark's shin.

Tattoo lunged.

Stark stepped aside like a bullfighter avoiding a determined charge. As Tattoo passed, Stark snapped a punch into his temple. Tattoo staggered, spun, and launched a deadly

68

roundhouse kick at Stark's head. Stark twisted and ducked simultaneously. Tattoo's legs were widespread, practically begging for the elbow Stark rammed into his groin.

A stunned Tattoo opened his mouth to shout and Stark hit him in the throat with a knife-edge hand. The kidnapper gagged, but slashed sideways. His knife just barely touched Stark's skin, drawing a thin bloody line. Stark grabbed the hand with the blade and twisted. At the same time, Tattoo lunged again. The movement bent his wrist double, and impaled him on his own weapon. The blade sliced his aorta, and he was quickly dead.

Stark picked up the .38 and trotted over to where José lay. Quesada was wiping the blade of the K-bar knife on José's leg. José's throat was slit.

"The others?" Stark asked.

"Watching the hut. How many are there?"

"Five. Minus two. Shotgun, Uzi, and a pistol. Uzi's the one to watch. Our client was lying on the floor along the west wall."

Quesada nodded and repeated what Stark had said into a dime-size collar mike. The two men, bent double and concealed by tall grass, hurried back toward the hut.

Halliwell was lying prone, a silenced, sniperscope-equipped rifle tracking the guard with the shotgun. He had an earplug in one ear.

"Ready when you are," Halliwell said. "Boy, it's great to get out from behind a desk."

"I'll bet LaGrange doesn't think so," Stark said.

"Want to do the honors?" Halliwell asked.

Stark nodded. Halliwell took a 9mm Walther PPK from a belly holster, gave it a cowboy twirl, and handed it over. He passed a silencer to Stark, who screwed it onto the end.

Stark bent low and moved toward the hut from the rear. The back was made of strips of wood, with two- and three-inch gaps. He crawled up close.

"They shouldn't be taking this long," Uzi said, and kicked LaGrange. "You want to go back to your soft *latifundio*, don't you? I say it's a trick. What do you say?" He moved to kick LaGrange again.

Stark aimed the Walther at Uzi's breastbone. "Drop the gun."

Uzi spun, lifting his weapon. Stark fired three times. Uzi

managed to squeeze off a burst, which tore up the thatched roof.

"What's going on?" the man with the shotgun shouted.

There were two muffled reports.

Stark bulldozed through the back of the hut and leaned over LaGrange, his gun trained on the doorway until he heard Halliwell shout, "All clear!"

Quesada went from body to body, double-checking that the kidnappers were dead.

"Thank God, thank God," LaGrange kept repeating.

Halliwell entered, produced a compact medical kit from the pocket of his camouflage safari jacket, and gave LaGrange a pill with a flask glass of purified water.

Stark bent over Uzi and retrieved his stolen Rolex.

"How—how did you find us?" LaGrange asked. He brushed his hand across his gray-flecked hair, knocking off caked-on mud.

As an answer, Halliwell took out a walkie-talkie-shaped gadget and turned it on. It made rapid beeping noises. He waved it slowly through the air. It got louder and louder, until he touched Stark's abdomen, and it whined continuously.

"He swallowed a transponder," Halliwell explained. "It emits a steady radio signal. We can pick it up from as much as fifty miles. State of the art."

"Fantastic," LaGrange said. He began to cry.

"Yeay, but who gets stuck cleaning it afterward?" Pedro kidded.

"I think there might be a pair of coveralls in the chopper," Halliwell said. He pointed to Stark's legs. "Betty Grable doesn't have to worry." Halliwell went off to get the helicopter, parked a half mile away. Quesada patrolled the area, alert for additional kidnappers. Stark was alone with the sobbing man.

"I was scared," LaGrange said. "Oh God. I'm not usually such a crybaby."

"You did great," Stark said, putting a reassuring arm over LaGrange's shaking shoulders. "This is a normal stress response. We've seen it dozens of times. Let it all out. By the time we get to Rio, you'll be ready to yell at reporters again."

LaGrange managed a smile.

70

CHAPTER
8

In 1942, the U.S. set up the Office of Malaria Control in Atlanta. Within three years dengue, yellow fever, and typhus were included in its responsibilities. It grew over the decades, changing names, adding diseases to its enemies list. In 1970, it was renamed the Centers for Disease Control.

More than two thousand people work at the CDC, a complex of squat, white buildings, the headquarters for some of the world's leading medical investigators. More than 250,000 samples of bacteria, viruses, rickettsia, and fungi are carefully stored in the CDC's library of disease.

Dr. Sultana Mirnov had been taken to a modest, two-story safe house a mile from the CDC, to be near the scientists and the lab. She had been inside the United States—counting U.S. embassy property as American ground—for four days.

The Soviets had raised the expected diplomatic uproar, pressuring Japan, doubling their surveillance at the airport, threatening to expel American diplomats. Which made Sultana all the more a prize.

When State Department brass confirmed she was indeed a prominent scientist, a task force was assigned to safely smooth the way. The operation was classified top secret, and half the people initially involved were no longer allowed to take part, since they didn't have a high enough clearance.

She was escorted to Camp Zama, seventy miles from

Tokyo, by a plainclothes Special Forces squad—who didn't know her identity but knew she was a hot commodity. A military jet took her from there to a Virginia safe house.

The house was equipped with electronic security and two-way mirrors. CIA staff and contract psychologists could study her as she was questioned.

In the lead debriefer's initial report, she was described as a questionable defection. He emphasized that she had papers identifying her as a KGB captain, although she denied working for them. She kept insisting that she had a major secret which she could only discuss with the President of the United States. The lead debriefer had been involved in the bogus defection of Vitaly Yurchenko, and he was wary of disinformation plants nowadays.

A certain amount of disorientation, resistance, and connivance is expected of defectors. The approach to breaking down the barriers varies. It can be as severe as physical abuse or threatening to return them to the Soviet Union. In Mirnov's case, it was decided a gentle approach was best. CIA officials hoped that by allowing her to speak to fellow scientists, she would reveal more.

She was moved to a two-story stucco house not far from the CDC. The light blue building was one of a dozen similar models built by a developer back in the 1960s. A few peach trees and a high hedge offered a little privacy. A chain-link fence was the only unusual feature visible.

CDC scientists dropped by and chatted with her. She opened up a bit, pleased with the vitality of her American colleagues. During the first few conversations, she was excited over exchanging information with the Americans. She told them of her concerns about germ warfare and insisted she would only go into detail with the President. What did U.S. officials know about Soviet BW? What was the U.S. doing? she wondered.

It was quickly obvious that the scientists had been told to draw out information and give her nothing. She grew frustrated at the one-sided exchange.

The time zone changes, the constant questioning, sometimes going over the same ground again and again, made her short-tempered. She kept demanding to speak to the President. Her keepers had heard such demands from defectors before and sloughed it off. She refused to talk.

She tried to walk out. The guards gently, but firmly, dragged her back.

She stood at the window in the safe house's dining room and looked out. The glass was polycarbonate—bullet and bomb resistant. She had orders to keep the curtain drawn, but disobeyed them.

There were at least two guards in the house at all times. They were young men, clean-cut, muscular, with alert eyes. They reminded her of movies she had seen of American cowboys. They were polite, noncommittal, always in sight, except for when she was locked into a room.

A large, dark government car pulled up in front of the house. A lean, well-groomed official got out and moved briskly up the front walk. His salt-and-pepper hair was blow-dried, a wave atop his head. He wore a lab coat over a gray pin-stripe suit.

She faced the wall, and turned around disinterestedly when he entered.

"Sultana, I've been informed we're not communicating," he said. His eyes, behind black glasses, were sharp, feral. He spoke and carried himself with confidence. Power clung to him like a hint of aftershave. He had a bland, contented smile. "Would you prefer I question you in Russian?"

"Who are you?" she asked.

"That's not really important, Sultana. Call me Dr. Hobbs."

"Then call me Dr. Mirnov."

"Okay. Sit down and let's talk."

"I'm not talking until I meet President." When she got excited, her precise command of English slipped.

"Are you having second thoughts? Maybe you'd like to return to the Soviet embassy? Would you feel more talkative then?"

"You threaten me?"

"Let's not commence negatively," he said. "Please, sit down."

They sat at the dining room table, a bowl of fruit between them. She leaned her elbows on the table and rested her head in her hands.

"I'm an epidemiologist," he said. "I'd like to talk with you about some of the ways diseases are spread in Russia."

73

They had spoken for a couple of minutes when she decided he was not what he said he was.

"Who are you truly?" she demanded suddenly.

"I told you. Dr. Hobbs. An epidemiologist with the CDC."

"Then why do you not know proper words? Why do you talk about the way diseases are spread, instead of saying vectors? How come you do not know what monoclonal antibodies are?"

"I'm a little rusty. I've been involved in administrative work."

"You are liar."

Hobbs narrowed his eyes and pursed his lips.

"Sultana, we want to assist you in acclimating yourself to a new environment. But you have to help us first. Prove your value. You've been implying you have a major secret. This is not a game of twenty questions we're playing."

"What is your position?"

"That's not important."

"It is important to me."

"I work for the White House. In an intelligence gathering capacity. Now, you were employed at the Lenin Institute. Tell me about it. Exactly what did you do there? What is the organization, mission, and functions of the Institute?"

"You work for CIA," she persisted.

"If I did, I wouldn't say so anyway."

They smiled at each other without warmth.

"Can we start again?" Hobbs asked.

Growing up in the Soviet Union, Sultana had been raised to believe that the CIA was all-powerful, even more important to the U.S. government than the KGB was to the Kremlin. She began to believe the conniving man in front of her was her best way to get word to the proper authorities.

"My main interest is the relationship between viruses and cancer. A virus is a fragment of DNA, sometimes RNA, in a protein shell. It commandeers a cell's genetic mechanism, gives it new orders, and the cell generates viruses. With cancer, the cell reproduction mechanism goes away itself, reproducing irregularly, in disorganized manner.

"A key to solution involves how do viruses target certain cells. For example, mumps and parainfluenza viruses look exactly the same under electron microscope. But mumps

74

attacks salivary glands, pancreas, or meninges, and parainfluenza virus attacks respiratory tract."

"How is that important?" Hobbs asked.

"If we can understand mechanism of attack and selection,
we can thwart it," she said. "And we can use information
to make treatment better focused. Medicine in chemother-
apy would be directed right at affected organ, without systemic side effects."

They talked for a half hour. He didn't take notes, but
could repeat accurately details of what they had discussed
earlier. There was a quiet authority about him that she found
both reassuring and threatening.

"What about the germ warfare experiments?" she demanded. "How come you don't care about that? I must talk
to President. He has to stop them."

"Don't be concerned, it's on my agenda," he said calmly.
"Frankly, the previous visitors thought your evidence was
weak."

She repeated her account of the strange diseases appearing in clusters of six, the vanishing bodies, and her belief
that the Soviets were conducting germ warfare research.

Hobbs nodded. "Are you asserting that you didn't defect
solely because Colonel Arkov, your GRU boyfriend, de-
ceived you?"

"I told you it was relationship of convenience. He bullied
me into it." She seethed. She had expected a shocked
reaction, or a triumphant "what do you expect from the
Russians" expression. But Hobbs was unfazed.

She rapped the table. "They were doing research on live
subjects."

"That's terrible," he said, putting on an upset face. His
reaction didn't ring true. "Do you have any hard evidence?"

"You do not believe me?"

"Oh yes, I do."

"Results of test were sent to a Marshal Zabotin in New
York."

He reacted as if he'd been given an electric shock, then
quickly brought a controlled look back to his face. He took
the bowl of fruit and put it on the far side of the room, then
dropped his suit jacket over it. She watched, puzzled, as he
returned.

"You didn't mention that before," he said.

"I just remembered."

"What else do you know? There's no reason for you to be coy, Sultana. We're on the same side."

"President knows about Soviet research on human beings?"

He wiped a bead of sweat from his forehead. "What else do you know?"

"I know top officials at Lenin Institute were involved. So I came here. What will you do?"

"It will be taken care of."

"How? They might be doing experiments on people right now. You must get the President to act immediately."

"It's under control."

"It is not under control," she said, slamming her hand down on the table. "I want to talk to President. To newspapers. To TV. Russian people will not tolerate this if they know."

"Listen, your words won't get back to Russia. They'll censor it. They'll say it's a CIA fabrication. You've been naive, Sultana. You'll have to trust our judgment. What else do you know?"

"I will not tell you. I will only tell President."

He stood up. "Suit yourself. Don't discuss this matter with anyone else. Don't discuss our encounter with anyone. Do you understand?" The bland grin was gone.

"No."

He leaned over her. "What you have mentioned is classified information. If you breach security, I will personally see that you are sent back to the Soviet Union as a bogus defector. You know what that means?"

He glared until she nodded. He retrieved his jacket, returned the bowl to the place on the table, and marched out. She hurried to the door and pressed her ear against it.

"You keep a tight watch on her," Hobbs was saying.

"My pleasure," the guard named Benson responded.

"What's your clearance level?" Hobbs barked.

"Q-clearance," both guards answered.

"As I suspected. She's brought up matters above your authorized level of access. I neutralized the electronic surveillance."

"Do you have the authority for that?" one of the guards asked.

76

"I'll be speaking to Brent Crofton later," Hobbs said, naming the CIA's director of security. "You'll get the proper paperwork."

"I guess it's okay then," the other guard said.

Hobbs fought down his sigh of relief. Crofton was an old buddy and a notorious cocksman. Hobbs could tell him that he wanted to loosen Sultana up by flirting with her and not have it on the record. Crofton would leer and send the necessary memo through the pipeline. All that was missing was a few minutes anyway.

"I don't want her leaving the house," Hobbs said, full of confidence as he mentally resolved the problem.

"She's got an appointment over at the CDC later today," the other guard piped up. "She's going to give them a hands-on demonstration of Russkie lab techniques."

"Cancel it."

"No can do," Benson said. "We need Cabinet level authority to change her schedule. It was arranged by the head of the Public Health Service herself."

The men spoke in lower voices and Dr. Mirnov moved away from the door. She was convinced Hobbs was not surprised by her revelations. The only information that had drawn a response was Zabotin's name. What did it mean?

Was the U.S. allowing the Soviets to get away with BW research on live subjects? Why? If they pressed them on human rights, freedom for Soviet Jewry, ending brutality in mental hospitals—all information she had picked up from reading international medical journals—how could they allow this heinous abuse of science to go unmentioned?

She checked the waxed fruit in the bowl. She found the transmitter, concealed in an apple, and stared at it numbly. She felt as trapped as she had been in the Soviet Union.

"Is this phone secure?" the man who'd introduced himself as Hobbs asked.

"Yes, Hornaday, it's secure," Benedict said. "What's the matter?"

"A woman's defected from the Soviet Union," Hornaday said in a near panic. "Her debriefing report came across my desk. She's babbling Zabotin's name around. And germ warfare. Do you know what this can mean?"

"Let me think," Benedict said. "Let me think."

77

"No, I'll tell you. It could blow the whole project out of the water. I'd be the first to get caught."

"Just shut up a minute," Benedict hissed. "Can you discredit her report?"

"That's why I contrived to visit. But someone will get interested in it eventually. I've already activated a program to isolate her. We've got a safe house in the back country. But that's just delaying things. Our plausible denial has been compromised."

"What if she was shot trying to escape?" Benedict heard Hornaday's sudden intake of air.

"It's feasible, but dangerous. There would be an investigation."

"Do it," Benedict urged. "We can cover it up later."

Peter Hornaday hung up the phone, leaving behind a sweaty sheen on the black handle. The phone was one of five on his desk, still another sign of his clout. It was Hornaday who had three locks on his door, while others only rated two. It was Hornaday whose office had the same view of the Ellipse, the Mall, and the Washington Monument as the President did from his living quarters.

He toyed with his Rolodex, the largest model they made. He had dozens of contacts at high levels in the legislative and executive branches. His talent for leaking carefully orchestrated information made him a darling of the Washington press corps. Though his name never appeared in print, his policies received excellent play.

More than once, the President had consulted with him privately and chosen his recommendation over that of the CIA director or the National Security Advisor.

There are thirty-two major U.S. intelligence organizations, from the narcotics cops at the Drug Enforcement Administration, to the State Department's Bureau of Intelligence and Research. Hornaday had sources at all of them. He had always been under the national security umbrella, and he knew how to use it. He had a knack for getting his few failures classified as top secret, and having the files buried, or destroyed. All in the interest of national security, of course.

Hornaday had survived five changes in administration, building up contacts, doing favors, collecting favors. He knew who owed who what, the secretaries on the payroll

78

strictly for extracurricular activities, which lobbyists owned which congressmen, and which senators were so senile they'd sign whatever was put in front of them. He didn't depend solely on his files, which were nearly as detailed and damning as J. Edgar Hoover's. He could be as charming as the most successful lobbyist while twisting an arm to get what he wanted.

He'd need all his savvy to get himself out of this jam. The Russian woman would have to die. If she went public, it would ruin his career. And that would be bad for the country. He was one of the few people who could get things done. Without him, who knows what sort of advice the President would get.

He decided to work through the CIA deputy director for operations. The man owed him, and they were both members of several top secret Restricted Interagency Groups. The sweat had evaporated from the headset as he picked up the phone.

Hornaday was confident he was acting in America's best interests. And God was on his side.

Dr. Sultana Mirnov spent two hours in the lab, watched constantly by a half-dozen scientists. She showed them the latest Soviet techniques for harvesting cells.

Midway through her demonstration, one of her guards, who had been watching her from the back of the room, was paged. When he returned, he whispered in the other guard's ear.

There was a change in the guard's expression. A coldness. He had always looked at her flirtatiously. Now, his expression was blank, as if she was a slab of meat.

"What were you saying?" one of the scientists asked, breaking into her thoughts.

"Oh, yes, with epithelial cells, the techniques are different," she continued her patter. It was a speech she had given at an Academy of Sciences, and she could repeat it without thinking. "I can demonstrate some of our newer techniques," she volunteered. She requested a half-dozen different chemicals, including ether, acetone, peroxide, as well as several chlorides and catalysts.

She used several of the chemicals to remove the cell culture from the glass intact. The mixture was put in a stainless steel centrifuge. By the time it was done whirling, the pure cell culture had separated from the rest of the fluid.

She added a mitotic inhibitor to stop the cell division. She titrated in a hypotonic solution—which puffs up and separates the cells—and finally a special agent to burst the cells and make them spill their chromosomes.

"Then mixture is treated with fixatives, and we have a karotype," she said.

"That's well and good, and interesting, but there was an article on it two months ago in *Cytology Today*," said a woman whose spectacles kept sliding off her nose.

"But we'd never seen it done before," a male scientist piped up. "And so proficiently."

"It's the sort of work a lab technician could perform," said another female researcher.

"I personally found her commentary on chromosomal damage quite interesting," a male researcher responded.

"I am very, very tired," Dr. Mirnov said. "Maybe tomorrow I show you more."

"You're booked up already," another man said. "I understand you'll be with the gas chromotagraph people."

"Derek!" the woman with the sliding glasses reprimanded.

"Don't Derek me. I know why those people get priority over everyone else. I tell you, it's because the whole project is being funded by MacMillan Industries. I saw the truck making a delivery."

"Derek! This is classified information," the woman scientist said. "You shouldn't be talking in front of her." The woman nodded at Dr. Mirnov.

"She's on our side now, right? Besides, what's she going to learn, that private industry has invaded our hallowed halls? That they get first crack at new equipment, better funding for supplies. That public health is being subverted for private enterprise. That—"

"No more complaining," one of the men said. "You're going to get yourself in hot water one of these days."

"Big deal. What will they do, fire me?" Derek challenged. "I can go to the private sector the next day and make three times what I'm getting here. It could be the best thing that ever happened."

As the scientists bickered, Dr. Mirnov maneuvered until

she was in the right position. Her elbow banged a beaker. Fluid smashed to the floor. The scientists jumped back. Her body concealed her smooth movements from the group, as she pocketed five of the vials of chemicals.

After proper apologies and maintenance coming in to clean up the mess, her escorts came forward to take her back to the safe house.

"I have to use bathroom," she said.

One guard stood at the door, another went outside to stand by the window. There was no way she could escape.

Inside a stall in the ladies' room, she dumped the expensive Japanese perfume into the toilet. Holding the ether and two catalysts at arms length, she mixed the chlorides and the catalyst and then chlorinated the acetone. She held her breath as she poured the mixture into the atomizer. It was a trichloromethane derivative, but even more volatile and effective. She had used it as a student, when she was forced to anesthetize mice.

She flushed the toilet, dropped the tubes in a wastepaper basket, and breezed out. She gave the guard a big smile. No response.

They got back into the unmarked van that had brought them over. She rode in the back, with Benson. They were separated from the driver by a steel wall, with a small window in it.

They had driven a short distance when she said, "This is not the way back."

"We're taking you to a place in the country," Benson said.

"Why the change?"

"It's just routine."

"I have things at other house I need."

"We'll pick them up for you."

"I don't want to go," she said, reaching for the door handle. She tugged at it. There was a lock on the inside. "Let me out."

He unbuttoned his jacket, baring a 9mm Beretta in a shoulder holster. "Afraid not. Just take it easy."

The road got bumpy. She peered through the round window in the side of the van. They were on a narrow country lane. On one side was a sparse forest. On the other, a twenty-foot drop, and a fast-moving creek. There were no cars or houses in sight.

She took out a pocket mirror and put on lipstick. Benson looked on, bemused. She adjusted her dress, lowering her neckline. She took out her perfume.

"Is makeup okay?" she asked.

He nodded without really looking at her face.

"You're sure?" she asked. "I want to look my best."

She leaned forward, lips partly opened. Benson looked away. He didn't want to meet her eyes. She had the atomizer barely a foot from his face when she squeezed it.

He reached for his gun. She threw herself against him. He struggled for a second, and then was unconscious.

The road got narrower and bumpier. Holding her breath, Sultana unscrewed the top of the atomizer and poured the remaining mixture through the small window into the driver's compartment.

She bent over Benson and rooted through his pockets. She took money from his wallet and his set of keys.

The van was swerving. She peeked through the window. The driver was rubbing his eyes and yawning. He glanced in the rearview mirror and saw her face.

"Hey, what the hell—"

The drowsiness and the distraction were too much. He lost control of the van. They came dangerously near the twenty-foot drop, but the driver slammed on his brakes. They skidded. The van swerved to the opposite side of the road and rammed into a tree. Sultana was knocked back, tumbling against the van wall.

Dazed, she got up, and tried Benson's keys until she found one that opened the rear door. She climbed out on wobbly legs. She tugged the driver and Benson out, and dragged their unconscious bodies off the road. She used the two ropes from the van to tie the men together. She checked their pulses and respiration. Both were fine. She took out their wallets and pocketed the cash. There were plastic cards she knew were for credit, but she wasn't sure how to use them and had to leave them behind.

She walked down the road for about a mile when a pickup came by. The driver was a leathery-faced man of unguessable age.

"That your van cracked up back there?"

She tensed, ready to run into the woods.

"Hop in, I'll give you a lift," he said.

She eyed him warily, then looked at the long road, and then climbed in. They rode without talking, an easy-listening radio station the only sound. Periodically, the driver spit green. At first she thought he had some respiratory ailment. Then she realized it was tobacco, and laughed. He looked at her like she was not all there.

As the news came on, he reached over to change the station.

"No!" she said, pushing his hand from the knob.

He moved away from her on the seat, convinced now that she was crazy.

"I—I am sorry," she said. "I want to hear news very bad."

"I reckon you do," he said.

The newscast came on. She listened intently, wondering if they'd mention her. They didn't.

A great deal of time was devoted to the repercussions of the armed rescue of an AP bureau chief in Brazil. A Brazilian Radical Party spokesman accused the U.S. of assassinating four peasants during the mission.

Allan LaGrange, the kidnap victim, said, "I don't give a damn what anyone says, when I saw Bob Stark and the others from Halliwell-Stark, it was like seeing a band of angels."

Robert Stark declined comment.

The reporter said Stark was a former CIA agent, who had resigned as a protest against an unspecified incident in 1974.

She knew that name. From where? Think. Think.

During her first trip to Japan. She had escaped the KGB watchdogs. It had been a foolish thing to do, she recalled. She'd gone shopping at a department store. Later she'd found out that several of the scientists on that trip had done the same.

But on the way back, she'd stopped at a newsstand and bought the *Japan Times*. She'd devoured the foreign newspaper. There was a front page story about a Robert Stark, a CIA agent, and a man named Kenji Matsumoto who'd been killed.

It had to be the same man.

The tobacco chewer dropped her at a gas station on the

outskirts of Atlanta. He sped away as soon as she stepped out. She phoned for a cab. She would go to New York. Yuri Zabotin was in New York.

She could no longer trust any government. She was convinced the guards were taking her to be killed. There was something about the man she knew as Hobbs, and the way the guards had changed.

She counted the money she had taken from the guards. Close to five hundred dollars.

When the cab came, she asked the driver to take her to the airport. Then she recalled all the stories she'd read in *Pravda* and *Izvestia* about American planes being hijacked. There must be many police officers at the airports. And that would be the first place they would look for her.

"To the bus station, please," she told the cabdriver. It would take much longer, but she gambled that they wouldn't check there. She'd have a better chance of slipping off a bus than a train, she had decided.

"You're running up quite a bill, lady," the cabbie said, altering his course.

In the bus station bathroom, she took out the three remaining vials of chemicals, put the hydroxide bleaching agent in with the catalyst, mixed that with the peroxide, and poured it over her brown hair. She went inside a stall and locked the door.

The bathroom smelled foul. Time passed slowly. She could hear the voice of an announcer calling out arriving and departing buses. Finally Sultana stepped out and gazed at herself in the mirror. She was a cheap-looking blonde.

Her first step was to get to New York. She had read a great deal about the city. It was an enclave of corrupt politicians, murderers, drug addicts, Mafioso, and rioting black people. She hid her money in her shoe and boarded the bus.

CHAPTER
9

Benedict MacMillan sliced through the water in the Olympic-size pool at his father's home in Connecticut. His perfect musculature, coupled with the bathing cap over his hair, goggles on his eyes, and deliberate movements, made him look like an android.

His regimen included a fifty-lap swim, five-mile jog, and at least ten-mile bicycle ride. He varied his routine to keep in shape for triathalons. MacMillan was a fierce competitor, who treasured the prize-winning extra large T-shirts he'd received more than the silk dress shirts that filled his closets.

He had been banned from several triathalons before becoming a secret sponsor. Although his participation in the sport went back to its beginnings—the first was held in San Diego in 1974 after a number of athletes and military people began debating who was in the best shape—MacMillan was not a popular entrant.

Twice he had "accidentally" knocked over his closest competitor during the bicycling part of a triathalon. Both times the other bicyclist had been seriously injured. During a final spurt toward the finish line, he had once elbowed another runner so hard that he'd broken the other man's nose. That match had been televised, and the intent behind the blow was clear.

As he put on a burst of speed for the final few laps,

Benedict thought about all those weak Willies who couldn't take the pressure. He had been like that once. Until his father had taken over rearing him. Calvin had made him into a man, Benedict thought, recalling the Vince Lombardi-isms that had been beaten into him.

Twice divorced, Benedict spent weekends and spare time at his father's place. Since he was often on the road it made more sense for him to maintain a *pied-à-terre* in Midtown Manhattan and enjoy the grounds of his father's estate.

He climbed out of the pool, and the pool boy, who policed the area and attended MacMillan and his guests, handed him a towel. He was a scrawny Hispanic teenager, dressed in neat whites.

"The water's too warm," MacMillan complained as he briskly rubbed the towel across his shoulders. He used it to dry his hair, then threw it at the boy. "This smells terrible. Don't you wash the soap out of it?"

"I'm sorry, sir."

"That's not good enough. You're fired," Benedict said.

"But the laundry isn't my responsibility," the young man protested.

Benedict MacMillan towered over the youth. "I said you're fired."

MacMillan shoved the young man and headed toward the house. He wasn't looking forward to what he had to do.

He found his father in the study, reviewing a report from their chemical division. The old man didn't look up as he came in.

Benedict hadn't had the nerve to ask him if the story about his health was true or just a way of manipulating Zabotin. He looked healthy.

"Uh, sir," Benedict began.

"What is it?" Calvin MacMillan asked, still not looking up.

"It's about the BW project."

MacMillan turned his eyes on Benedict like a tank locking on target. "Yes?"

"There's been a little problem."

"What is it?"

"A woman doctor defected from the Soviet Union," Benedict said. "Hornaday found out she was throwing Zabotin's name around. I told him to have her killed."

"You did what?" MacMillan shouted.

"To keep her quiet," Benedict said. "But it looks like she got away."

MacMillan's hand drifted up and pressed the side of his head. His glare was replaced by a pained expression.

"Are you okay?" Benedict asked.

"Who gave you permission to order a murder?" MacMillan asked. "Who told you you could do that?"

"But you always said to act swiftly and decisively," Benedict said. "I was trying to save you aggravation."

"Aggravation? Aggravation!" MacMillan took a step around his desk, as if he was going to spank his son. But he moved jerkily and banged into a corner of the antique piece.

"Damn son of a bitch," MacMillan said.

"Maybe you better sit down," Benedict said.

"Get out of here. Leave me alone."

"I was only trying to help."

"Get out, get out, get out," MacMillan shouted, his face reddening.

Benedict backed out. He strode across the lawn, on the verge of tears. He was heading toward the guest house where he had his private gym when he saw the pool boy. Benedict ran at him, overcome by a blinding rage.

"I told you you were fired," Benedict yelled. He smashed the boy in the face, grabbed him, and held his head underwater. The young man struggled for air but Benedict was too strong.

The houseman and a couple of the gardening staff saw what was happening. They raced to the pool and pulled Benedict off. The pool boy was unconscious. Benedict stormed off without saying a word.

When the pool boy came around, the houseman cradled his head. The boy moaned. His jaw was shattered, would need reconstructive surgery.

"We'll call an ambulance," the houseman said. "Don't worry. You'll get the best medical attention." He leaned forward, whispering conspiratorially. "It's happened before. There'll be a big settlement. Whatever you want. A big car, a college education. Their lawyer will handle it."

The houseman tried to sound like he was giving the pool boy good news. But his face as he looked at Benedict's private gym showed pure hatred.

87

Benedict MacMillan bashed the heavy sandbag, each powerful blow rocking the one-hundred-pound bag on its chains.

Why could he never do right? He tried, he was trying, and still he failed. No matter what he did, he was no good.

When he heard the ambulance pull up, he wondered what it was for. He had forgotten his assault on the pool boy.

A few steps out the door, he saw the maid running toward him.

"Mr. MacMillan, Mr. MacMillan, come quickly. Something's the matter with your father."

"The only reason he's alive is because the ambulance had been dispatched to pick up your pool boy," the doctor said. "The one who fell and broke his jaw."

MacMillan nodded, not really hearing the doctor's words.

The doctor, in his late sixties, had been the family physician for as long as Benedict could remember.

"I won't beat around the bush, you probably already have guessed it," the doctor said. "A cerebrovascular accident. A stroke. I've just gotten the results of the cerebral angiogram and the CAT scan."

"Can you make any predictions?"

The doctor put his hand on Benedict's shoulder. He didn't like MacMillan's son, but he hated to see anyone going through grief. "It struck in a particularly quirky spot. By the reticular activating system of the brain stem. Do you understand?"

"That's the narrow spot where the brain connects with the spinal cord," Benedict said.

"Right. A millimeter in one direction, coma. In another, death. The third possibility is locked-in syndrome."

"What's that?"

"The patient can see, hear, and smell. The autonomic system works fine. But the rest of the muscles are nonfunctional."

"Oh, God. That sounds like being buried alive."

"Well, at least he's alive. And sometimes patients do recover."

"How often?"

"About one in six. Usually with younger patients. I'm not

going to build false hopes," the doctor said. "But you know he'll have the best medical attention there is."

"Anything he needs, anything, just get it," Benedict said.

"Of course, I've contacted specialists. They should be here later today," the doctor said. "You can go in and see your father if you like."

It took several minutes for Benedict to muster the courage to step into the private ICU room. Since the hospital wing he was in had been paid for by MacMillan, he received the best care, with two nurses on full-time duty.

The room was dark, easier on Calvin MacMillan's eyes. A nurse was putting drops in, keeping them moist. His father sat, propped up in bed, staring straight ahead. Two IV tubes fed into his body. A catheter drained fluids out.

Benedict sobbed, and hugged his father's body.

The nurse left the father and son alone.

"Oh," Benedict hesitated, "Dad. Oh, Dad."

He sat by the bedside, staring at his father.

Nurses came in periodically and aided him in his bodily functions. Filling an IV tube, checking the catheter. Benedict heard the doctor come by, confer with the nurses, and leave.

It grew dark outside.

MacMillan moved a chair close to his father.

"Dad, it's okay to call you that, isn't it?"

No answer.

"I've been thinking about your project for world peace. I'm gonna do it. You'll be proud. But I've got an idea.

"We'd never be able to pull off a bluff. We're going to have to go ahead with it. On a small scale, of course."

No answer.

"In time for your birthday. I know, that's just a few months away. I'm going to do nothing else. I've got a bunch of ideas. Want to hear them?"

No answer.

"This bacteriophage they've been working on is self-limiting, noncontagious. That means we don't have to worry about the disease spreading where we don't want it. Only those directly exposed to it will die.

"What I figure on doing is skywriting 'Peace' above a bunch of major cities. Only the letters will be seeded with the bacteria, and the phage that destroys it. That'll be for the United States, Britain, Japan, India. In the Soviet Union, we'll send a couple of people through the subways with the aerosol dispersion attaché cases. I haven't figured out Red China yet.

"Atlanta and Vladivostock are on my list. That way, the major disease control investigators will be taken out. Isn't that clever? I haven't decided on the other cities yet, but they'll be big ones, I promise. You see, Dad, this way, they'll have to take us seriously. When I make the speech at the United Nations, they'll all be listening. I'll make sure you're there too.

"I know what you're thinking. People will die. It's true. But you always said you can't make an omelet without breaking a few eggs.

"There're too many in the world anyway. That's the beauty of the plan. With no wars, the population explosion will get worse. But this approach solves that problem as well. Isn't that great?"

A tear trickled down Calvin MacMillan's cheek.

Benedict reached over and wiped it away with his finger.

"You're so happy, you're crying," Benedict said. "I'm happy too, Dad. This will be great. Just wait and see."

CHAPTER
10

KGB Marshal Yuri Zabotin sat on a bench in Central Park, tossing bread crumbs to the pigeons. A radio next to him played a baseball game. He was dressed casually, in American clothes, and looked like a grandfather waiting for his child.

Benedict MacMillan walked up casually and sat down. He unfolded a newspaper and pretended to read. The paper covered his lips while he spoke.

"Is this really necessary?" he asked.

Zabotin, who kept a hand near his mouth and had mastered the art of mumbling to frustrate lip-readers, nodded.

"I took two hours to ensure I was free of your FBI watchers who harass me day and night," Zabotin said. "As well as the bodyguards from my own organs of state security."

"Do you have the BW information?" Benedict asked.

"Most of it. You'll find it inside the newspaper I'm sitting on."

MacMillan glanced down and saw the edge of the *New York Post* sticking out from under Zabotin's posterior.

"I must warn you. The disease they were working on is exceedingly dangerous," Zabotin said. "Some fool decided we should develop a bug that was easily manufactured and handled. There was talk about offering it to one of the

91

Middle East madmen. Your government is so frightened of terrorists."

"I understand."

"I'm glad they are shutting down the lab at the Lenin Institute," Zabotin said. "There was a defection. A woman doctor. Have you spoken with your Mr. Hornaday about it?"

"No," MacMillan lied.

"I recommend that you do. She knows my name. I am being temporarily recalled to Moscow. There are questions about why I was getting the reports."

"Are you in trouble?"

"*Nyet*. At the United Nations, there were discussions on the Convention of the Prohibition of the Development, Production, and Stockpiling of Bacteriological and Toxic Weapons. I have plausible excuse. Also, my cousin serves on the Politburo. There will be no problems."

"When do you leave?"

"By the end of the week."

"Are you sure this woman didn't confide in anyone in Russia?"

"If she did, it's being taken care of."

It was nighttime in Vladivostock, and a KGB wet work specialist waited outside Dr. Dorokhov's *dacha*. When the lights went out, the wet work man crept in, holding a device similar to a tear-gas pen. Sultana's mentor had taken a couple of painkillers to help him sleep. He didn't hear anything as the intruder leaned over.

The assassin pressed a button and the steel plunger slammed into a glass ampule holding hydrocyanic acid. The cloud of acid jolted Dorokhov's circulatory system, sparking massive contractions of blood vessels and causing what appeared to be a natural heart attack.

The obituary on Dorokhov's role as a brilliant scientist and the paperwork to award him the Order of the Red Banner posthumously had already been prepared.

Simultaneously, a heart attack claimed Sultana's lover, the GRU colonel. The KGB had been aware of his relationship with her from the start. He had been compromised, and in looking for someone to blame for her defection, he was an easy target. The KGB relished a chance to punish the rival intelligence agency.

"I don't want you to think about what effect those pictures would have on your career," Benedict MacMillan said soothingly. "I need to know I can count on your enthusiastic response."

MacMillan was playing games with him, Peter Hornaday realized. Hornaday had no choice. After more than thirty years in the Washington corridors of power, Hornaday was used to manipulating, and being manipulated.

"Your father's idea of developing BW materials outside the government was quite innovative," Hornaday said. A slap and a stroke. "I heard he's not feeling well."

"He slipped and fell. Nothing serious," Benedict said. "Now, what about that woman? Mirnov."

They were in the study in MacMillan's Connecticut estate. The study held as many books as a medium-sized public library. It was furnished with burnished teak shelves, well-tanned leather chairs, and lamps strong enough to read by without destroying the mood. The teak desk had no frills. The top was freshly polished, free from clutter, dominated by a sophisticated phone setup.

"No wonder the United States is losing allies left and right," Benedict MacMillan fumed. "You can't even keep a woman locked up in a house. I could've had a couple of security guards from one of our department stores do a better job. Then she overpowers two guards and disappears. Poof!"

Hornaday had seen to it that the two guards from the safe house were assigned to duties more commensurate with their skills. Every day, the CIA shredded a ton and a half of paper. The guards were now working the feeder on the shredding machine.

"You're sure she hasn't gone to the FBI?" MacMillan asked.

"You know about my network of contacts. I'd have heard by now."

"We're going to have to accelerate our plans," Benedict said. "I'm going to need a few things from you." He pulled a sheet of paper from the pocket of his custom-tailored suit. "Here's a list of cities. I want to know their traffic condi-

93

tions, weather patterns, wind currents, rain, et cetera, for the next couple of months.

"Also, I want all the specs on the aerosol dispersion attaché cases the army used in their germ warfare tests in the subways."

"Why do you need that?" Hornaday asked.

MacMillan slammed his fist down on the desk. "Don't question me." He paused, breathing heavily. "My scientists say they need to know the density of the spray, and such. I'm planning on setting up the plant in Mexico. I'm going to need a couple of dozen men. Rough-and-tumble security types, who'll follow orders. Like the kind that helped on Watergate."

"I'll see what I can do."

"Good. One other thing. Zabotin. He's become a weak link. He's going back to Russia. He has to be taken out right away. The woman doctor has to go, too. ASAP."

Hornaday rushed back to the airport. He had a reception at the French ambassador's residence that he couldn't miss.

Waiting at the airport for the Eastern Airlines shuttle, he made one phone call.

Hornaday had no great love for the Russian who'd been such a pain in the butt at the U.N. He blamed Zabotin for indirectly getting him into this mess.

Hornaday was not as comfortable with the thought of having the woman doctor killed. But he knew it was necessary. There could be no screw-ups this time. He thought of several capable individuals he knew in the CIA.

He decided Charon was the best man for both jobs.

CHAPTER
11

The fifty-seat auditorium atop the corporate headquarters of the third largest soda manufacturer in the world was packed with upper-echelon executives. The audience had been carefully screened and identities checked.

At the podium, Robert Stark was finishing his remarks. Stark, in his custom-tailored, dark gray three-piece suit, was every inch the proper corporate man. He was deliberately stiff, assuming the old-boy manner cultivated in the Central Intelligence Agency.

He had finished the slide presentation showing dead executives and explaining what they had done wrong.

"In conclusion, I urge you to remember a few facts," Stark said. "Eighty percent of terrorist attacks occur when the target is in his car. Vehicular safety is a primary concern. Varying your schedule is the cheapest, most effective form of insurance. Other than that, avoid a high personality profile and be on good terms with local governments and the indigenous population wherever possible. I recommend donations to appropriate charities. Any questions?"

A young man in a blue blazer began asking a long question. He was a vice-president in sales, the sort who liked to hear himself speak.

"We have to have bodyguard chauffeurs, armored limousines, security guards and alarms all over our homes and

95

businesses, change our route to work every day, and you tell us we should donate to charity in these countries?" the salesman demanded. "These people should be grateful. We're paying them more than they make in their own industries, we have higher safety standards in our factory, we're providing jobs. They're lucky we're there."

There was mumbled assent from half of the executives in the room.

"There's a Zen parable about a prominent professor who went to see a Zen *roshi*," Stark said. "The professor was impressed with himself. The monk hardly had a chance to talk. Finally, they sat down to tea. The *roshi* poured, and poured, and poured. Tea overflowed the cup, ran down the table, and onto the floor.

"The professor yelled for him to stop. 'It's overfull. Nothing more can go in.'

" 'Like this cup, you are full of your own opinions and speculations,' the *roshi* said. 'How can I show you Zen unless you first empty your cup.' "

Several executives bobbed their heads. The intense sales exec who had asked the question said, "I don't get it. Why'd the monk make a mess like that?"

Stark just smiled. "I'll address your question in more direct terms. First off, I recommend against limousines of any sort. It is an expensive perk and can cost you your life.

"And I do recommend charitable donations. You can talk to your comptroller about the tax advantages, but I can't emphasize enough the security benefits. Terrorists depend on the people in the country. If you are perceived as a benevolent intruder, you're far more likely to get assistance from the local regime, as well as the people in the countryside. Get known to the general populace for day-care centers, medical clinics, schools, all with your company name prominently displayed. I urge you to consider it a form of preventative security. It's far better than having to pay my operational fee or the ransom money. Or even worse, funeral expenses."

Stark collected his notes. There was enthusiastic applause. Les Halliwell, who had been standing in the back of the room, gave Stark a thumbs-up sign of approval.

The soda company's CEO chatted with Halliwell and

Stark, and they made an appointment to work out a retainer.

Bunny Washington had been Halliwell-Stark Associates secretary for three years. Before that, she had run a middling-size marijuana dealing operation in Spanish Harlem.

Bunny weighed 250 pounds when Stark first met her. She was a tough piece of work who handled her own collecting on bad debts and never went anywhere without a .357 magnum. Now she weighed 110 pounds, and few men who came into the office didn't take the time to flirt with her.

"Marry me, Bunny, and I'll have your babies," Halliwell said, repeating his usual joke as he and Stark entered the office.

"It's a good thing you know business better than biology," she said. "Anyways, I'm holding out for Mr. S."

She handed Halliwell his stack of messages, and the ex-secret serviceman, with mock sulk, retired to his office. Stark picked up his stack of mail and began going through it, tossing junk mail into the wastepaper basket.

He opened a letter from the rescued AP man from Brazil. LaGrange's gushing first-person account of the rescue had run in three hundred papers around the world. In the newspaperman's account, he had helped Stark and his team overpower the two dozen armed terrorists who were holding him captive.

Stark had mixed feelings about the publicity. As complimentary as it had been, and despite the thirty-five business inquiries it had generated, it violated his dictum of keeping a low profile.

"I know you're probably pissed about the article," LaGrange had written in his letter. "The story was self-serving bullshit, but if I hadn't written it, everyone would've wondered why.

"You may be curious why I'm in Chicago. I decided I was too old for that foreign correspondent crap. Leave the cattle prods and death squads to a younger buck.

"If there's ever anything I can do, just ring. When you're in Chicago, give me a holler, and I'll take you to the best Brazilian restaurant in town. A nice thing about selling out is the pay is good."

Bunny broke in on Stark's thoughts.

"A woman has been calling for you," she said. "Claims she's a Russian defector in trouble with her own government and the Americans, too. She wants you to protect her."

Stark sighed. HSA suffered from the usual crank and psychotic phone calls—people who had exclusive information on the Kennedy assassination; paranoids with bombs implanted in their heads; defectors from the Venus armed invasion of earth. Publicity brought them out of the woodwork.

"Give it to Les," Stark said, winking at Bunny. "He's handling all our potential accounts."

"She insists on you. Says the CIA is involved. She was pretty upset."

"Wouldn't you be if the United States and Soviets were both hot on your heels?" Stark said skeptically. "What's the name of that psychiatrist we refer paranoids to?"

"I tried that already. She was very persistent."

"They usually are. She give a name and phone number?"

"She refused. She did say she knew about Kenji Matsumoto." Bunny pronounced the Japanese name slowly, phonetically.

Stark, who had been reviewing the mail, abruptly turned to Bunny. "What did she say about Matsumoto?"

"Just that she knew what had happened. That's why she wanted to talk to you."

Stark walked into his private office and shut the door. Matsumoto. He inhaled and let out the air slowly.

Unlike Halliwell's office, which was loaded with hardware and souvenirs of the partners' globe-trotting, Stark's office lived up to his surname. His desk, which held a Wang computer terminal, was a thick smoked-glass plate across two chrome file cabinets. The walls were white—the only hanging a reproduction of a calligraphy by Miyamoto Musashi, the most famous swordsman in Japanese history:

> *Under the sword lifted high,*
> *There is hell making you tremble.*
> *But go ahead,*
> *And you reach the land of bliss.*

Stark undid his jacket and tie and did a hundred push-ups, a hundred sit-ups and a hundred jumping jacks, then repeated the sequence. He pulled the blinds shut, sat on a small pillow, and closed his eyes. He didn't have time to meditate.

Stark kept thinking back to Matsumoto, unable to focus on business. Monkey mind. He'd have to take a week off, head to his retreat near the Mohave Desert. No phone, few comforts. He'd have his own private *sesshin*, the intense week of meditation performed several times annually at Zen monasteries. His retreat was the only place he'd be guaranteed absolute privacy. Not even Les knew where it was.

Stark reviewed architect's plans for a new auto company headquarters in Mexico. He had already decided there were too many entrances and exists, too much glass, and too few secured parking facilities. He would have to tour the site to get more detailed ideas. It was important to see what was really there, not what other people thought was there.

Les Halliwell sauntered in, waving a color brochure. "Look at this car. This baby's got armor plate, tear gas and oil vents, gun ports, an infrared viewer, and oxygen tanks built in. The glass is bullet-proof, the ramming bumper's titanium, and it comes with a built-in scrambler phone."

Halliwell inevitably pushed to expand, hire more full-time staff, get high-tech gadgetry. Stark preferred the small, simple operation, with low overhead and emphasis on their skills.

"When will we need it? Can we afford it? How many miles does it get to the gallon? We're better off with a used Chevy." Stark realized his tone was too harsh and tried to soften his words with a smile. The woman caller had hit a nerve as surely as a dentist probing for a root canal.

"Cranky, aren't we?" Halliwell said. He sighed. "I knew what your answer would be. I guess I just wanted someone to rain on my parade. What about that Caribbean security contract? Sun, sand, sweet young things in itsy-bitsy teeny-weeny bathing suits."

"It's one of the most repressive regimes in the world," Stark said. "Some of Papa Doc's top torturers got work there."

"We won't be torturing people, just making sure our boy doesn't get blown up."

" 'Our boy' is psychotic, sadistic, and has chronic halitosis. Maybe his getting blown up wouldn't be bad for human- ity."

"He's talking about a million-dollar retainer," Halliwell said. "I don't see anything wrong in keeping him safe."

"That's probably what Wilson and Terpil said when they got into bed with Idi Amin. I'm just being pragmatic. Think about our world image."

"The guy's a U.S. ally. If he's good enough for Uncle Sam . . ."

"He's also number one on the Amnesty International parade of human rights violators. Do you remember what his secret police do to dissidents?"

"I read the report," Halliwell said. "A million bucks is a million bucks."

"And a sadistic dictator is a sadistic dictator," Stark said.

"Sometimes, you can be a bleeding heart pain in the ass," Halliwell said.

"I'm willing to compromise," Stark said. "You forget the dictator, and I'll re-examine the super car. Deal?"

Before he could answer, a buzzer went off and a red light on the wall began blinking. An intruder. Stark calmly reached into his desk drawer and took out a gun. Les pulled a .38 from a shoulder holster.

Both men stepped out into the hall.

Steel bars had slid from concealed niches in the wall, compartmentalizing the office. Inside the hallway was a blonde with a stunned expression. On the other side of the bars from her, Bunny Washington held a .357 magnum.

"She barged in, ran past me," Bunny said.

"Who the heck are you?" Halliwell demanded.

"Dr. Sultana Mirnov. Are you Mr. Robert Stark?"

Stark and Halliwell kept her covered while Washington opened the bars on her side. She stepped in and gave Mirnov a thorough, none too gentle frisk.

"Clean," Bunny pronounced.

Stark signaled for her to lift the bars. She hit a button near her desk and they rose.

Mirnov patted her hair, composing herself.

Stark admired the way she stayed cool, even after being caged and having three guns pointed at her. "I'm Stark."

"I must talk to you."

"Some guys have all the luck," Halliwell said, before walking away.

In Stark's office, he switched on his computer and tapped in his password—Satori. She sat on the edge of a leather chair, facing his desk.

"I don't have money, but I need to hire you," she said.

"The consultation is free. What's your problem?"

She hesitated. After what had happened with her mentor, and at the safe house, she suddenly didn't know if she could trust him.

He was good looking, smug. Reminded her of her GRU lover. Which was a mixed blessing. There was a reassuring calm about him.

"What are you doing?" she asked, as he continued to tap at the computer.

"Cleaning up some paperwork," he said.

He punched her name in. The data base held brief entries on over 100,000 people around the world, drawing info from the *New York Times* index, *Who's Who, Reader's Guide to Periodical Literature*, thirty-seven different trade publications, as well as a private intelligence data base.

"I need your full attention," she said.

"You haven't told me anything," he said, reading the four-line entry on her. It described her as an expert in several biological disciplines assigned to the Lenin Polyclinic Institute near Vladivostock. It cited her speech in Vienna and gave places to look for more detailed information.

"You work at the Botkin Polyclinic?"

"No," she said. "The Lenin Institute."

"I must have you confused with someone else. Did you give a speech in Prague?"

"No, Vienna."

"Okay," Stark said, returning to the opening menu. "You're a defector in trouble. What went wrong?"

"The CIA tried to kill me."

"Uh-huh."

"You don't think I am telling you truth?"

"Let's say I'm a naturally suspicious person."

She sat tall in the chair, arms folded across her chest. A pretty woman—with a crummy dye job—used to getting her way, Stark decided. He tapped "virology" into the computer and memorized a few items that appeared on the screen.

"Have you eaten?" he asked.

She cocked her head, and realized how hungry she was. "No."

"C'mon, I know a good place." Providing a primal gratification like food, and keeping her off balance, would aid in his questioning.

Besides, he was hungry.

CHAPTER
12

Chuckie Lee bowed to Robert Stark, then shook his hand warmly.

"Long time no see," Lee said, with sing-song intonation and a New York accent.

"It's only been a couple of weeks, Chuckie."

"I thought you'd found another place that makes pan-fried noodles the way you like," Lee said.

"Actually, I've switched to McDonald's."

"That *kwai lo* crap will kill you."

Lee, whose actual first name was Chang, had nearly been the lightweight champion for two years back in the early fifties. He was nicknamed "The Great Yellow Hope." Lee was smart enough to have gotten out of the business with his brains intact. The only signs of his former career were the peculiar shape of his ears and his athletic grace. That grace, coupled with his Oriental sense of aging dignity, gave him a distinct and commanding presence. He had once so spooked an armed robber, with only his calm gaze, that the thief had run from the restaurant empty-handed.

Stark and Lee were in the foyer to Lee's bar and restaurant on Lexington Avenue in Murray Hill. Sultana stood behind Stark, nervously eyeing the restaurant.

The restaurant had the mandatory framed fading photos of prizefighters, dark red vinyl booths, and the long redwood bar off to one side. The bartender, an old pug named Barney, waved his soiled dishcloth at Stark, who bobbed his head back as a greeting.

"How's things?" Stark asked.

"Same old, same old. That young man I sent over last week, is he behaving himself?"

"Seems to be," Stark said. "He still hates the world, but I think we're at the point where he only dislikes me a lot."

"If he disrespects you, kick his ass back over here. I'll straighten him out."

"Bunny already did."

Lee gave a high-pitched laugh. "Speaking of pretty young ladies, who's the one hiding behind you?"

"Alice Brown, meet Chuckie Lee."

They shook hands. Lee led them to the table. He gave Stark an approving thumbs-up as he walked away.

Stark slid into the booth, close enough to her that they could whisper.

"Are you sure is safe here?" she asked.

"The health department has never closed it down. Chuckie pays them off."

"You make joke?"

"Yes."

"Is not funny."

"Maybe. I'm friends with the owner," he said reassuringly. "If there was anything amiss, he'd let me know. I've been here enough that I could find my way around it with my eyes blindfolded. There are two entrances, both of which we can see. There's a fire exit in the kitchen that has an alarm on it. Barney has a short, double-barreled twelve-gauge under the bar. There are no microphones by the table. The food is as good as you're going to get. Any other questions?"

"No."

"Dr. Mirnov, I know you know your business. If there was a germ I couldn't identify, I wouldn't hestitate to give you a call. You must have confidence that I do my job as well as you do yours."

The waitress brought warm sake for Stark and wine for Mirnov.

"Before we get to your problems, I'm curious as to what you know about the Matsumoto case," Stark said.

"I was in Japan," she answered, after taking a long sip of wine. "I read about it in the newspaper."

"You've got a good memory."

She nodded. "It is unusual for a CIA man to have a conscience."

"Not as unusual as you might think. Most just don't have the courage to defy orders. Like people in any job."

"That is true."

He noticed the intensity of her response and filed a mental note.

Mirnov did not like the man sitting across from her. He was too cocky, too American. He did not seem to take her seriously. He didn't look at her the way most men did. She had adjusted to that kind of look. He was more bemused than attracted. She did not know how to play him.

The waitress came. She let him order for both of them—hot-and-sour soup, pan-fried noodles, Mu Shu pork, and shrimps in black bean sauce.

"Tell me about your defection. Why did you do it? Surely a respected scientist like you can't have it too rough over there. Were you asked to do something that violated your principles?"

"Yes."

"What?"

"I can't tell you."

"Okay."

They ate in silence. Sultana devoured her portion, pausing only to ask about different ingredients before she gobbled them down.

"You don't ask me any questions?" she finally asked.

"Sitting quietly, doing nothing, spring comes, and the grass grows by itself."

"What?"

"You came to me. You want something. You'll either tell me or decide not to. Either way, the food is good here, isn't it?"

He was wary because it was too convenient. A beautiful defector pleading for help. A dangle operation. An agent would pretend to defect. She would get the rival intelligence service to gear up, reveal its own secrets, and then return to her real masters with the names of counterintelligence officers and details about procedures.

The plates were nearly empty. She set down her fork, he lowered his chopsticks. He refilled their teacups.

He might be of more value to the KGB now than when he was with the Company. He knew corporate security plans from dozens of the Fortune 500.

Who's to say it was the KGB? He had stepped on the toes of U.S. officials enough times to earn more enemies in high places than friends.

The career spook's mind was a Byzantine one, with ghosts of Machiavelli and Sun Tzu haunting the crevasses. Stark forced himself to put his predilection toward conspiracies aside and open up to his own perceptions.

"You were allowed to travel abroad, so you had a fair amount of clout over there," Stark said. "I presume you were well treated. Leaving one's country is never easy. It must have been quite a motivation."

She answered by sipping her tea.

"Then you defect. I presume you were thoroughly debriefed. Something went wrong, and you go on the run. Now you say that the United States government is out to get you. What did you do?"

She shook her head and sipped again.

It was a positive sign that she did not rattle something off. It meant either she felt reluctant to lie to him, or she didn't have the textbook paranoid's imagination of exotic persecution.

"I'm sorry to have troubled you," she said.

"It's no trouble. It's not often one gets to spend lunch with an internationally renowned biologist. One thing I am intrigued by. Why did you choose to study in many disciplines, rather than concentrating on one?"

"In every branch of science there is a grand old man and his cronies. And their rivals. To get to the top you have to join one clique or other. I never did. Anyway, when I get bored with one, I can switch to other."

"You like a new challenge?"

"Yes. I also think scientists become too specialized. Virologist can learn much from molecular biologist, oncologist can be helped by immunologist."

"I understand. Like Werner Henle."

"You know about Doctor Henle?" she asked, clearly surprised, and pleased.

"Oh, just a little." Stark had memorized his entry when it had appeared on the computer screen, figuring that it could keep the conversation moving.

"What do you know?" she asked suspiciously.

"Let's see, Henle and his wife, who was also his research partner, developed tests for the effectiveness of mumps vaccine and influenza. They also did pioneering work with gamma globulin and hepatitis."

"Yes, yes," Mirnov said.

"But you're probably most familiar with him from his work in the late sixties, when he first showed the link between infectious mononucleosis and a cancer that's common in Africa."

"Burkitt's lymphoma," she said. "His work with that cancer and Epstein-Barr was brilliant. I wished I could have met him." She launched into a detailed technical account that Stark had trouble following, but he nodded along.

He could see her relaxing as she began to cite case histories. At one point, she slowed and seemed to stiffen, but he got her going again by prompting her, asking a question about viruses that showed he understood, as well as a layman could, what she was talking about.

"Viruses are microscopic parasites, as small as thirty microns, a thin protein coat around central core of DNA or RNA," she explained. "There's debate whether they are even alive, for they cannot reproduce by themselves. They float in an organic sea, until the encounter a suitable cell. Like pirates, they commandeer nucleus and use its mechanism to reproduce. Then they blow the cell up and move on to infect neighboring cells."

She drew diagrams on paper napkins as she explained "taming a hot virus" to produce a vaccine. She segued into a lecture on viruses and the immune system, the link between stress on the body and the reemergence of dormant viruses.

"I talk too much," she said.

"Not at all," he said. "It's fascinating. Have you really found a substantial link between viruses and cancer?"

"A cancer is a cell with the wrong genetic information,"

she said. "Can be caused by radiation, chemical irritation, spontaneous mutation, Or virus." And she was off again.

The more absorbed she became in her subject, the more beautiful she became. Her green eyes flashed as she made a point she felt significant. Her finely tapered hands gestured, her body shifted with excitement.

"But I am going on too long," she said.

"Believe me, I'm enjoying. Did you ever wonder what the Kremlin intended to do with your information?"

"The peace-loving government of the Union of Soviet Socialist Republics?" she said sarcastically. "I thought my project was going to save lives. Biological research is not like a gun. It is not necessarily a weapon of aggression."

She had told him a lot with her cynicism.

"Yes, it's more like a knife. You can use it to peel an orange or slice someone's heart out."

She nodded. "That's a good analog."

"Analogy."

"Yes, analogy." She set her coffee cup down in her saucer. "I cannot afford your fees. I beg you for help."

"I'm not so world weary that I won't help a damsel in distress."

"Bolshoye spasibo," she gushed.

"You're welcome."

"You understand Russian?" she asked.

"Just enough to get myself in trouble."

Helping her would be a minimal commitment. A few hundred dollars and a little time. If she was bait, he wanted to see whose hand was on the fishing rod. It was such a clumsy attempt at trapping him, it was almost plausible.

Back in the office, Les, after ogling Mirnov and giving Stark a broad wink, produced paperwork from a new account—a food franchise corporation in California that was going to open a plant in Latin America.

"They want us to give them the once-over. Pronto," Les said. The two men talked in the hallway while Mirnov waited in Stark's office. "Can you fly out there tonight?"

"I've been wanting to take time off anyway."

"What about the lovely Russkie? What's her problem?"

"Not sure yet."

"She a wacko?"

"Possibly. But I doubt it."

"Is that your intuition again? Or just your gonads?"

"Maybe both. But I'd like to believe it's more intuition."

"Ah, I wish I was single again." Les leered.

"Can you put out feelers? Find out about Dr. Sultana Mirnov, what the story is on her defection. Why'd she do it, what's she got that's valuable, how serious the spooks are in getting her back?"

"Might take a bit. My best contacts are retiring left and right. I've got a half-dozen résumés from them on my desk right now."

"Whatever," Stark said, and entered his office. She was sitting primly in the chair facing his desk, making it clear she was not used to being kept waiting.

"I need to find out about Yuri Zabotin," she said abruptly.

Stark turned on his computer and punched in the name.

"Yuri Zabotin, born 1924, in Soviet Georgia. Graduated Institute for International Relations." Stark paused. "You know what that probably means?"

"KGB."

"Right. It's got a listing of his postings, a gradual rise in the bureaucracy. Deputy Minister of Heavy Industry in 1960s. Switched to Foreign Ministry. As of late 1986, he was posted at the United Nations. The FBI believes he's the KGB *rezidentura* in New York."

"Anything about germ warfare?"

"No."

"How about a man in your government named Hobbs. With the CIA."

Stark tapped out the buttons. "We've got several Hobbs. I need more information."

"Mid-fifties. Gray hair. Weak chin. Expensive clothes."

"The mid-fifties helps."

Stark played with the keys. "The only one who seems possible is with AID. But he's currently in Zaire. And he's only forty years old."

"Are you sure?"

He looked up from the terminal. "It's probable he gave you a bogus name. That's pretty standard."

"Can you identify him somehow else?"

"Not with such sketchy data. Do you want to tell me about Zabotin?"

"Not yet."

"I'm patient. But if your life is in jeopardy, you're only hurting yourself."

"Can you find out more about Zabotin? Where he lives, what he does exactly?"

"Let's see." A brief riff on the computer. "He's a big cheese, so the wire services should have a file photo on him. I can access UPI. You want to go see him? It's good to get a feel for the opposition. If he is the opposition."

"What if I am recognized?"

"We're going to the United Nations. There's inevitably crowds there. To be on the safe side, we'll alter your appearance. Change your hair color with a quick, temporary dye. How'd you like to be a brunette?"

"I am brunette. I did this myself as a disguise."

"Forget about a career as a hairstylist. Sorry. How would you like to be a redhead? Puff out your cheeks with cotton balls, give you rings under your eyes. Get some baggy clothes. You just have to agree to keep quiet while we're out in public. Your accent might draw hostiles."

"You believe me then?" she said hopefully.

"It never hurts to take precautions," he said. "Expect nothing, be prepared for anything."

No one paid any attention to the couple walking on the grounds of United Nations Plaza. Overhead, flags snapped in the wind. The man was wearing a gaudy Hawaiian print shirt, and a camera dangled around his neck. He wore dark sunglasses. He talked in a loud voice, with a Southern drawl. His red-haired wife nodded docilely at his words.

"Look at all them flags. See that one? That's the British flag. Over there, that's France. Damned if I know them other ones. Says here in this guidebook there's 159 of them. One for each of the member nations. That makes sense, don't it, honeybunch?"

The woman nodded.

"Says that they got more 'n a thousand prize-winning rose bushes, and cherry trees, and dwarf fruit trees, and daffodils. Reckon they'd mind if we took a couple back home? Just kidding. You having fun, cupcake?"

The woman nodded.

Stark was hamming it up, enjoying himself and hoping to put her at ease. But behind his dark sunglasses, he scanned the faces of the people around him. A black in a dashiki. A pair of Turks in caftans. Several tourist couples and families. Cabdrivers leaning against their vehicles. Three-piece-suited diplomats with regal posture and fancy attaché cases.

He had checked the schedule. They had just missed a speech by Zabotin.

They entered the sloping, domed General Assembly building and loitered by the gallery elevator at the north end. The sun was setting and the light filtering through the translucent panels set in marble pillars gave the airy lobby a gloomy gray feeling.

Stark reluctantly removed his dark glasses. They meandered about, pretending to eye the Marc Chagall stained glass and bronze plaques dedicated to slain soldiers from the peace-keeping forces. Stark prattled continuously, pretending to be absorbed in a guidebook but watching for the face he had committed to memory.

After fifteen minutes he spotted Zabotin striding across the lobby. Stark gave Sultana a covert squeeze.

"Recognize him?" he whispered.

She shook her head.

"Back up a smidge, sweetheart. Lemme get your picture."

She did as he directed. Stark snapped away. He got two shots of the Russian.

Zabotin exited through the revolving doors. They followed at a safe distance. He seemed to have something on his mind.

Suddenly Stark squeezed her arm.

"What is it?" she asked.

"The two guys over there."

Two men had begun tailing Zabotin. KGB heavies, by their look. They only had eyes for Zabotin and hadn't noticed Stark and Sultana.

"Hang back," Stark whispered. "Probably just his bodyguards."

A cold wind was blowing off the East River. The sun was beginning to set. Shadows fell across the plaza. Tourists were squeezing off their final shots before hurrying to their hotels.

Zabotin reached the curb. It looked like he was going to take a cab, then he changed his mind. His last chance to walk in New York for a while. The Fabergé egg was in a safe deposit box. He could decide whether he would give it to his government when he got back to America. It might even be a bargaining chip if they punished him by keeping him in the Soviet Union.

As he stepped out into the street, a car jumped the red light. It picked up speed and hit him with a lethal impact.

The two KGB men drew their guns and began firing.

Before she could be sure what was happening, Stark had hustled Sultana in the opposite direction.

"What is going on?" she demanded.

"No talk. Move."

At first, people thought it was a backfire. Then they saw Zabotin's body. The shouting started. Cops on duty at the U.N. ran out, saw the KGBers firing, and drew their own weapons. Pandemonium.

Stark and Mirnov were already several dozen yards away.

He hailed a cab on Forty-second Street and they headed west. Sirens were shrieking past them.

"Wonder what's going on?" the cabbie mused.

"New York is a heckuva exciting place," Stark said in his Southern accent. "You can drop us at Grand Central Station."

Stark breathed slowly, in and out, in and out.

He had only gotten the barest glimpse at the face of the hit-and-run driver.

But deep down, he knew who it was. A face from out of the past.

Charon.

CHAPTER
13

Pedro Quesada sat in the aisle seat next to Dr. Mirnov. He held a Red Diamond private eye novel with his good hand, deftly turning pages with his thumb. Stark, one seat behind him, pretended to doze, keeping his eyes barely open. The "soft eyes" made him particularly sensitive to movement. Mirnov had no sooner settled into the seat then she fell asleep.

The trio was alert when they deplaned in Los Angeles. Stark led, Mirnov a few paces behind him, Quesada bringing up the rear. They scanned the crowd, paying particular attention to people's hands. Neither Stark nor his aide had a gun, though Pedro carried a special fiberglass knife that he was deadly with up to about twenty feet.

A driver under contract to Halliwell-Stark Associates was waiting at the curb. He was a former bank robber and expert wheelman. He was not suitable for chauffeur security work since he insisted on wearing a bush-size Afro and clothes that looked like Salvation Army rejects.

The car he picked them up in was a beat-up Dodge Dart. It had 195,000 miles on the odometer and several coats of paint. It also had a new turbo-charged engine under the hood, a racing car suspension, and Kevlar bullet-resistant lining around the passenger compartment.

113

He dropped them at a hotel Stark named. Then the trio walked five blocks to a motel.

"You don't trust your own workers?" Mirnov asked.

"I don't even trust myself most of the time," he said.

The Welcome Motel was the kind of respectable place salesmen, middle management, and families might go. Stark knew the owner and had placed clients who needed security there before.

"You settle in," Stark had told Mirnov after he went over the second floor room and assured himself there were no bugs or anyone waiting in the closet. The metal bar was in place in the sliding glass door to the terrace. The locks worked and appeared untampered with.

"Don't go outside."

"I can take care of myself."

"You're my client now, my responsibility. Either you follow my instructions or we part company."

She stifled a defiant response. "What will happen now?"

"I've got to go to work. I don't want to do anything unusual. If I think it's safe, we can do a little sightseeing later. Okay?"

"Is all right."

She threw herself down on the bed and stretched out. "America," she said, and sighed. She saw the TV at the foot of the bed and turned it on. A soap opera was playing.

"Keep the curtains closed and a chair against the door," Stark said. "I'll give four short knocks and say my name. Don't open it for anyone else."

She nodded.

He thought about leaving her a gun, then decided against it. He didn't know yet what her real story was. And a dead chambermaid would dampen his relations with the hotel manager.

As soon as he left she put the chair against the door. She ignored his order to stay away from the window, and peered out cautiously. He got into his car and drove off.

She gazed out at the street. The two- and three-story buildings looked well kept, glossy. A billboard showed a handsome man and woman standing in the water, splashing each other, and puffing on cigarettes. Many cars, few pedestrians. The people wore brightly colored clothing, exposing as much of their flesh as sunbathers at Yalta.

She hopped into the bed and stared raptly at the drama on television. The commercials were as captivating as the soap opera. She couldn't believe her escape was real. She had actually made it to America. But what happens now? she wondered.

Could she stop the BW experiments? Would she be forever a fugitive, or would she be able to do research again? Could she trust Stark? Could she stay alive?

The man Stark knew as Charon had also been known by a dozen other names. But his knack for taking on an identity was not what made him valuable. It was his ability to see through others' false identities that made him the head of his own small section in the Central Intelligence Agency's Clandestine Services.

Charon was a hunter who specialized in tracking down those who could embarrass the CIA. After the revelations about the activities of ex-CIA agents Frank Wilson and Edwin Terpil, who sold classified equipment and their services to Libya, and former agents like Philip Agee, who published books naming active agents, the Director of Central Intelligence had ordered, in National Security Memo 357, the formation of the Office of Career Evaluation and Guidance.

Charon's section, which included six men and two women, anticipated problems and neutralized them. Sometimes that meant talking to an agent about to go bad, threatening him with biographic leverage or physical force. Sometimes, a rogue agent had to be terminated with extreme prejudice.

OCEG had handled sixty-one cases since its inception. In more than half the cases, they found fears about an agent embarrassing the Company were unwarranted. In twenty cases, they were able to convince the agent to keep his secrets to himself. Several times, they arranged for the departing agent to write a biography that would never be seen outside of Langley. One of the books had actually been turned into a CIA training manual.

In nine cases, the subjects had to be TWEEPed. Charon felt it was a responsibility that shouldn't be delegated. Besides, there were few people as skilled at it.

Peter Hornaday had been around for ages, always at the

upper levels of government. He had given Charon a number of special assignments over the years. Confidential matters. For the highest levels of government. Hornaday had once introduced Charon to the President. It was an honor Charon would cherish.

Charon had returned to Langley immediately after fulfilling half of Hornaday's latest assignment. The car he'd used had been stolen, and was ditched minutes after Zabotin's death. Charon had worn gloves at all times and no one had seen him leave the vehicle. CIA records showed that he was in Washington while the incident was occurring.

Emil, one of Charon's assistants, dropped Dr. Sultana Mirnov's file on his desk. He thumbed through it, memorizing her particulars. Before Emil left, Charon told him to put a confidential flag on the file, as well as similar files at Defense, State, the National Security Agency and the FBI.

While the agencies did not share files, they had worked out an informal agreement to share information about access. The deal had been worked out after the Freedom of Information Act, where outsiders were able to piece together the whole story by getting dribs and drabs from the individual agencies.

He dispatched an investigator to Atlanta to interview personnel at the Centers for Disease Control who had been in contact with her. The investigator would also do follow-up interviews with neighbors of the safe house and the Atlanta police. The investigator flashed IRS identification and said Mirnov was a material witness.

Charon went to the shredding room on the other side of the seven-story CIA complex at Langley. Although every office could get a burn bag pickup, and many had their own shredders, the disposal center housed four twenty-five-thousand-dollar units that could reduce a full loose leaf to rice size confetti in seconds.

The two screw-ups who had been guarding Mirnov when she escaped had been reassigned there. Charon questioned them individually, while the mammoth shredders growled in the background. He garnered no new information.

Three hours after the investigation began, Charon got his first break. Mirnov's file at the FBI had been pulled. Grilling the agent who had pulled the file, an OCEG investigator found out the man had done it for an old buddy, an ex-Secret Serviceman named Lester Halliwell.

Emil accessed the retired federal personnel listing in the computer and came up with Halliwell's career history, including his present role as president of Halliwell-Stark Associates. He brought up Halliwell and Stark's biographies.

Charon remembered Stark from their days at the Farm, and the incident in the Tokyo subway. At the training school Stark was a maverick, questioning teachers, wanting to know the why. For Charon the who, what, when, where, and how was sufficient.

His doubts about Stark had been proved right in Tokyo. The man had failed and dropped out of the Company. He'd challenged a direct order. In the military, he could've been shot. But because America was a country of freedom—and the Agency didn't want to embarrass itself with messy disciplinary proceedings—Stark was allowed to drop out.

Then, Charon had been a mere field troubleshooter. Now he had OCEG to eliminate problems.

He had the secured telecopier fax his New York–based investigator a photo of Mirnov, Halliwell, and Stark. He didn't tell her the reason for the inquiry. She was a competent agent—she would follow orders without asking.

The building at Langley emptied around six P.M. Documents were locked in file cabinets and safes. Authorized cleaning personnel collected the burn bags and material to be shredded.

Charon continued to work, tidying up papers, reviewing the fallout from a State Department defector who'd gone over to the Reds. Charon wished there was some way he could get to the man, neutralize him in the Soviet Union itself. That would put the Commies on notice.

At one point, he had come up with a plan to get Kim Philby. Terminating the renowned British traitor would've been a blow for freedom. Revenge for the Russian murder of the Bulgarian. But the weak-kneed bureaucrats had decided Philby was already milked dry, and a symbolic murder was too risky to international peace to be worthwhile.

Charon sent Emil to get them supper from the twenty-four-hour commissary. Charon paid for their meals. It was the least he could do. Emil didn't get overtime. Not that the young man minded. He had not much of a life outside the

Agency. His deepest relationship was with the Octopus, the nickname for the CIA computer.

It was eight o'clock in Washington when the phone on Charon's desk rang.

"Bingo!" the New York OCEG investigator said. "The subject was seen by a building maintenance worker entering the premises. Subject was not seen to leave. Deuce left at the usual time, but Ace left early in the day. With a staff member identified as Pedro last name unknown. With them was a white female, fortyish."

"The doctor?"

"Roughly similar. My source didn't really notice her."

"What time did they leave?"

"Yesterday at 1400 hours. I can return tomorrow and confirm it with additional personnel. Or make a surreptitious entry tonight."

"No. They've probaby got precautions. Come up with a cover story and get in there during business hours tomorrow. Get informational brochures, the layout of the place. See if there's any sign of the subject."

He hung up and signaled Emil. "I've got a hunch Stark's taking her out of the city. Check the airline computers for me. Starting from yesterday at about 1400 hours. I want two men and a woman traveling together. Maybe not sitting together."

"Domestic or international?"

"Domestic first."

At 11:30 that night, Charon called Hornaday at home. "We have reason to believe the individual you asked me about is currently in Los Angeles, with an ex-CIA agent named Robert Stark. He runs an executive security agency named Halliwell-Stark Associates, with offices in New York, Los Angeles, London, and Tokyo."

"I'm familiar with the firm," Hornaday said. "Do you know where the woman is?"

"A name search at the major hotels came up negative. He had her fly out there under the name Gretchen White. He used to use White as his own cover name. Old habits die hard."

"True enough."

"I can dispatch a few operatives, canvass the hotels,

check out his office and residence. According to records, he has a small house in the Hollywood Hills."

"Do you think he'd set her up there?" Hornaday asked.

"I doubt if he's that sloppy. Of course, it could happen. Especially if he doesn't think we're on to him."

"Send someone by his place. Maybe we'll be lucky. I'll put the screws on through overt channels," Hornaday said. "I want you to establish a command post out there."

"Can I tell them what this is about?"

"Negative. Strict need-to-know. This comes from the highest level of government. Do you understand?"

"Yes, sir."

"You do excellent work. Keep it up."

"That's what Uncle Sam pays me for," Charon said.

CHAPTER

14

Stark's office was on the top floor of a steel and glass skyscraper in Century City. It offered an excellent view of the former Twentieth Century Fox backlot that had been turned into an enclave of expensive offices for doctors, lawyers, and producers.

It was late afternoon as Stark got out of the elevator. Chief assistant to the United States Attorney Lawrence T. Peters, who had been waiting impatiently in the reception area, breezed up to him. Peters has a boyishly handsome face, the kind that jurors would love. But there was a go-for-the-jugular determination in his eyes.

Gina, Stark's secretary in the L.A. office, introduced Peters. Stark could tell by her tone that the prosecutor had been giving her a hard time. Gina was a striking blonde who had a knack for affecting different accents. Before Stark hired her, she was a renowned scam artist. She could be a British princess or a southern belle with equal facility. When she spoke with a pronounced New York accent, she was annoyed.

"Dis guy got here a half hour ago," she said. "He's been threatenin' all kinds a things if I didn't let him into your office."

Peters stood with arms folded across his chest. "I merely

informed her of the consequences of obstructing a federal officer."

"I oughta give you an obstruction," Gina said. "But I didn't let him in."

"My office is always open to our friends in the federal government," Stark said, giving Gina a covert wink. "Of course, this spirit of amicable cooperation is quickly withdrawn if I think anyone abuses my staff."

"I was not abusive," Peters said.

"Well, why not just apologize to her, and we can get on with it."

The boyish-faced prosecutor reddened. "I expect to be taken seriously."

"I take you very seriously."

Peters snorted. "I have here a subpoena deuces tecum for all of your records, as well as an order commanding your immediate appearance before a grand jury. We can go into your office and talk right now, or I can call several federal agents and have you escorted downtown forthwith. Of course you'll be held overnight in the lockup. Which do you prefer?"

Stark turned to Gina. "I'd like a stiff cup of coffee." He turned to Peters. "Won't you please step in to my office?"

The only major difference from his spare New York suite was the view out the window. Stark had a corner office, and could see much of the Los Angeles basin on days when the smog didn't blanket it with a yellowish-brown pall.

"Harvard or Yale?" Stark asked as Peters lowered himself into one of the off-white upholstered chairs.

"What?"

"Did you go to Harvard or Yale?"

"Dartmouth."

"Oh, I see." Stark said it like he had just heard a major confession from the prosecutor.

"Are you belligerent because of a guilty conscience?" the prosecutor counterattacked.

"Only when I get visited by federal prosecutors. I presume you're not here to sell U.S. bonds. If you are, then we can have a friendly talk. If not, my hackles are going to be up. Are you selling bonds?"

Peters took out the subpoena and tapped it against his hand like an old-fashioned copper playing with a blackjack.

"I have a grand jury currently investigating certain acts of international terrorism. Violations of the Neutrality Act. Illegal transportation of weapons. Commission to serve against friendly nations. Acts of violence and murder in defiance of existing treaties. Your mercenary activities have not gone unnoticed."

"I am not now and never have been a mercenary. At least no more mercenary than any other businessman."

"I doubt that a jury would see it that way if they had all the evidence," Peters said.

"I'm sure you didn't come here just to threaten me."

"I'm not threatening."

"I'm sure you didn't come here to tip me off to the investigation so I can flee the jurisdiction."

"We have reason to believe you know the whereabouts of a Dr. Sultana Mirnov."

Stark steepled his fingers in front of his face. "If I do, why is that of interest to you?"

"She is a material witness to a crime and an escapee from federal custody."

"What crime is that?"

"I'm not authorized to divulge the details. Do you know where she is?"

"Not at the moment," Stark said. Which was true. She could be anywhere in the motel room. It was the kind of weaseling around the truth an attorney would appreciate.

"Can you find out where she is?"

"I might be able to."

Peters stood and returned the subpoena to his pocket. "You have twenty-four hours to find her. If you do, call me." He handed Stark a card.

"If I don't?"

"The grand jury room is on the tenth floor at the courthouse. In addition to your terrorist activities, we will ask about Dr. Mirnov. If you do not answer, we will grant you immunity and order you to comply. If you still do not, we will have you held in contempt, and jailed."

"Have a nice day," Stark said.

Peters strode out. Stark walked around his desk to the window and looked out at the city. The filth in the air made a solid line across the sky.

Stark's secretary rapped on his door and entered.

"More bad news?" he asked.

"Les called a couple of times from New York. He asks you to call him back right away. He's staying in the office until he hears from you."

"Les working late? This must be an emergency."

Gina smiled. "He sounds uptight."

"Okay. Give me a few minutes to clean up my desk, and then ring him for me."

Stark returned his attention to the file on Dr. Sultana Mirnov, telecopied from the New York office. One of the data analysts had put together a half-dozen pages, with information from Les's government sources and the public record.

Stark read through it. The information jibed with the little she'd told him.

The most intriguing thing was what was not in the file. There was no mention that she had defected five days earlier. Mirnov was not being groomed as an agent-in-place. There was no need for secrecy. The Russians would know immediately that she was gone. Why not update her file to indicate she had come over to the side of the angels?

Putting out the word in the espionage establishment would bring together all the experts, let everyone get a crack at her while her information was fresh and she was still safe. It was possible some functionary wanted to keep her under wraps. Maybe it was just a bureaucratic slip-up.

But the federal government was obviously quite aware of Dr. Sultana Mirnov.

The intercom on his desk beeped. "Les on line two," the secretary said. Stark picked up the line. The phone had a scrambler attached, which decreased volume and made it harder to hear the party on the other end.

"Hey, Les, what's going on?" he said loudly.

"What's going on? That Russian cutie of yours is what's going on. Have you had any visitors yet?"

"Only a lovable prosecutor who threatened to jail me if I didn't give her up."

"I had one of those here, too. Also the bank called and said they were reevaluating our loan. They hinted there was some kind of outside pressure. Listen, how much is this Russian gal paying us? Is she worth the grief?"

"We've never backed out on a client yet."

"We've never had the feds come down on us like this before. I called my old buddy to see how serious it was. He wouldn't take my call! I've know this guy for fifteen some odd years. What's she paying us anyway?"

"Maybe you could shop around at other banks. It'll blow over."

"Bob, we operate in a gray area. They can nail us on weapons violations. They can revoke our passports. And that's for openers until they can sic an IRS SWAT team on us. You still haven't answered my question about her account with us. I didn't see anything in the computer."

"She's pro bono."

"A freebie? A goddamn freebie and we're risking our business? I hope she's a great lay at least."

"I wouldn't know," Stark said. "We can't let them push us around on this. If they get the idea they can, they'll keep doing it."

"What do you mean, get the idea they can push us around? This is the federal government of the United States of America. You know the kind of resources they have?"

"Les, they gave me twenty-four hours to think about it."

"What's to think? Give her up. We don't owe her anything."

"I'll talk to you later."

"You bet you will," Les said. "By the way, where is she anyway?"

"Right now, I'm not sure," he said.

Halliwell had asked the question too casually, after his heated tone throughout the conversation. Stark didn't think his partner would betray him, but he knew how much the business meant to Halliwell. Halliwell had a wife, two kids, a mistress, three cars, a house in Westchester, a summer home in Southhampton, and a taste for lobster.

It was hard to tell when someone had reached the breaking point, when they would compromise their principles to maintain the status quo.

CHAPTER
15

For a half hour, Stark dry-cleaned himself, making sure no one followed him to the motel. He stopped off to buy a curly blond wig and a knee-length, floral-patterned dress. It was attractive but not elegant and hopefully wouldn't call attention to its wearer.

Mirnov responded quickly to his knock.

"I'll take you out for dinner," he said. "But I'm afraid it will be costume party time again."

He gave her the items he'd bought, and she hurried into the bathroom to try them on. He noticed that she chastely closed the door. She had made no effort to seduce him. A positive sign.

He still didn't know how much to trust her, whether she was legit, emotionally disturbed, or a KGB agent. The contact was clumsy and flagrant, even by KGB standards. But he recognized that he found her attractive. She was bright and beautiful; tough and vulnerable.

She came out and spun around in front of him. She was pleased with her new outfit. He slapped on a bushy mustache and put a "Beverly Hills Polo Club" cap on. Hats were a great disguise: They called attention away from the face and altered the hairline.

He told her what had happened with the prosecutor as he drove down Wilshire Boulevard in his Toyota Celica. The car boasted stiffened suspension, tougher brakes, and four-point seat belts.

"Will you tell them where I am?" she asked.

"Not yet. You can keep your secret a while longer."

She frowned. If she couldn't trust her government, her mentor, or the U.S. government, why should she trust him, she wondered. But she would stay with him. At least for now. She had considered slipping away during the day. Maybe he had changed since the Matsumoto incident. What would happen when he knew her story? Yet every moment she delayed could mean another person being experimented on, another BW weapon being developed.

"What did you do today?" he asked.

"Watch television. America is strange place. People get paid money to act like fools on game shows. The drama programs, they have sad stories like Russian drama, but everything's so superficial. Everyone's beautiful. Do people really live like that?"

"Like what?"

"In such fancy houses. And always everyone is sleeping with everyone else. How do they have time to make money to get such fancy houses?"

"Do you believe what you see on Soviet TV?"

"*Nyet.*"

"There's probably about as much truth on American TV."

He paused, watching the rearview mirror. He had made a few extra twists and turns to ensure no one was following them. It would take a while for the hounds to pick up Mirnov's trail. If indeed there were any hounds after her.

They turned up Rodeo Drive and parked north of Santa Monica Boulevard, just north of the chichi commercial strip. They walked from shop to shop, with Mirnov gazing in the windows hungrily while Stark stood back, bemused.

They had dinner in Santangelo's, a quiet restaurant with white table cloths, waist-jacketed waiters, and outstanding Italian food. There were candles on the table, soft lights reflected off crystal and gleaming silverware.

"Why are you helping me?" she asked. "You could get in trouble."

"I like a challenge. The only time a sword gets sharpened is when it rubs against stone."

They talked about Zen and its emphasis on the intuitive

and the nonverbal. She got frustrated at his inability, or unwillingness, to put it exactly into words.

"Everything can be quantified," she said.

He held up a fist. "What's this?"

"Fist."

He opened his hand. "Where is it now?"

She pursed her lips. It made her even more attractive. "Just the name has changed. It's still there."

"How important is the name? What was your face before you were born?"

She pondered for a minute. "It's nonsense question."

"No more than any other."

It took the two men fifteen minutes to get into Stark's Hollywood Hills apartment—five times longer than it usually took them to gain entry. They were black bag specialists, but Stark's apartment was equipped with a hard perimeter alarm, pressure sensitive pads by the doors and windows, and an interior motion detector.

They cut the power and bypassed the alarms with short jumper cables. The only sign of their intrusion was a dime-size jimmy mark by the rear doorjamb.

Neither man was a CIA employee per se. They were contract workers who'd do the odd dirty jobs. Mitch, an ex-FBI agent, had a private detective firm that was frequently used by the Agency. Steve was a semireformed cat burglar. Mitch favored pungent aftershave and picking up cocktail waitresses. Steve lived alone, disliked doing burglaries, and kept vowing each job would be his last.

They went over the house cautiously, looking for any signs of a woman's presence. The house was neat, relatively bare. There was only a man's clothes in the closet.

"What do you want to do?" Steve asked.

"Let's wait around."

"Guy's probably armed. A tough piece of work."

Mitch had had a slow few months. He was eager for some excitement. "We'll wait outside in the car. Make a dupe of his key. If he goes into the place alone, we go home. If the woman is with him, we'll see just how tough he is."

Steve forced a soft plastic compound into the keyhole. It hardened in one minute and he withdrew it. They returned to the van where Steve took out his toaster-size key-making machine. He used the plastic prototype to make a perfect copy of Stark's key.

"How long do we have to wait?" Steve asked.

"As long as it takes," Mitch said. The ex-FBI man adjusted his seat so he could keep an eye on the house. Steve sat in the back of the van and fretted. Mitch loosened his jacket, for easy access to his .357 magnum. He was a big-fisted man who had used his gun four times during his years of law enforcement. He had killed two bank robbery suspects, earning an FBI commendation. He wished he was still with the Bureau.

The wine and rich food had served their purpose. She relaxed more and more with each course.

"Sultana, why did you decide to come to America?" He avoided the word "defect." No matter how it was pronounced, it sounded ugly.

She was silent.

"I can guess it involved biological warfare. Were you assigned to a project?"

She nodded.

"I don't understand why the feds weren't interested in debriefing you. What happened at the safe house?"

"Do all Americans live like this?" she asked, changing the subject as the waiter wheeled over a silver dessert cart.

"No."

"On TV in Russia, they show poor black people rioting all the time. Where are they?"

"Most of the time the poor don't riot, they just get ground down by the poverty. What happened at the safe house?"

"Please, I will tell you. But give me time."

"How much time do you think we have?"

"I—I have to think things through some more. Can I ask you to trust me?"

"You can ask. I will, for now. But I will need to know the whole story if I'm going to protect you properly."

The mood had been broken. They finished their meal, he paid, and they headed out into the night. She asked to see Hollywood, and they rode down the boulevard. Traffic moved sluggishly, jammed up by gang members cruising in low riders. She laughed long and loud as a car in front of her went up and down on hydraulic lifts. She could laugh like a little girl when she saw a new sight.

There was an electricity when they brushed against each other. Getting involved with clients, even non-paying ones, was bad business, he knew.

She had decided that she would slip away from him that evening. He was nice, but she was better off alone.

They got out at Mann's Chinese theater, and she compared footprints with the stars. They watched punk rockers and break dancers strut their stuff, while boom boxes blasted rap music. Hookers in hot pants fled before sweeps of cops in black-and-white patrol cars. A psycho in bikini briefs and a sombrero, his pale body covered with tattoos so it almost looked like he was clothed, got into an argument with a bag lady.

"Your country is strange," she said. "There is much freedom, much craziness. It's scary." She watched the street scene with fascination.

"To us, a lack of freedom is scarier."

"In Russia though, you can walk almost any street at night. Not so here, right?"

"Right. But in Russia, you can't talk in the privacy of your own home."

"Where is your home?" she asked.

He pointed at the Hollywood Hills, a dark mass covered with dots of lights.

"I would like to see it," she said.

"It's late."

"I'm not sleepy. I want to see how a typical American lives."

"I don't know how typical I am." She had awakened feelings in him he usually suppressed. How long had it been since he was with a woman?

What if it was a honey trap? But what pressure could they hope to exert? There was no betrayed wife to threaten with. He was not the kind to spill his soul in pillow talk. Nothing they'd do was illegal between consenting adults.

"Okay," he said. "I've got a nice view of the city lights from my window."

He drove over to Beachwood Canyon, and north into the hills. His apartment was located on a narrow street that dead ended two blocks past his building.

But he didn't go up his street. He went a block over. One of the reasons he chose the house was because of the second way in. By walking up a short, steep flight of stairs cut into the hillside and pushing through overgrown bushes, he could enter his apartment virtually undetected.

As they shoved their way through the bushes, Mirnov commented, "You don't have a gardener?"

"It's deliberate. The same reason I grow roses around here. They're beautiful, but a prowler would have a helluva time. It's a particularly thorny hybrid."

She pulled her hand back from the brush.

"Don't worry," he said. "I keep it trimmed away from this walkway."

They stepped into the house, and he froze.

To help see better, she flicked the light on.

He turned to face her, a momentary rage sweeping across his face. For most of the night, he had had a peculiar half-smile. She couldn't read what he was thinking. Now he had gotten angry. For what? She felt out of place, awkward. And suddenly scared. Maybe he was a sex maniac. She had read in *Pravda* that California was full of them.

"The light just went on," Mitch hissed and Steve clambered forward to the front of the van.

"Musta had it on a timer."

"I didn't see any fucking timer. He must've snuck in through a back way."

"But how?"

"Maybe he dropped down the chimney like Santa Claus," Mitch snapped. "The point is, he's in there. People don't sneak into their own house unless they're sneaking something. I bet he's got the dolly with him."

"We can't be sure."

But Mitch was already checking his gun. "Give me the key. Go knock at the front door. I'll let myself in the back." As they walked up the front steps, Mitch pulled on a ski mask. He crouched low and worked his way through the shrubbery toward the back of the house.

CHAPTER
16

As soon as he'd stepped into the house, Stark had smelled the aftershave. And something else—fear sweat. Someone had been inside his apartment.

Then Mirnov had turned on the light. He'd nearly yelled at her to shut it off, but there was no point. It was too late. Perhaps she was setting him up and that was the signal. No one attacked them in that first second. He reached into a desk drawer and grasped his Browning Hi Power.

"What's going on?" Mirnov asked.

"Someone's been here." He moved to the walk-in closet and threw the door open. No one. "Get in," he told her.

She hesitated. He gave her a gentle shove.

"Get in the closet," he said, softly. "That way I shoot anything that moves."

He shut the door and prowled his apartment, gun at the ready, checking any space where a man, no matter how small, could hide. He was finishing his search when the front doorbell rang. It was nearly midnight. It could be the neighbor who repeatedly invited him to come skinny-dipping in her giant jacuzzi. He just as repeatedly had declined.

He looked through the peephole. A scrawny, nervous-looking man stood on the doorstep. Stark opened the door, holding his gun down low, out of view.

"Yes?" Stark asked.

131

"Uh, I'm looking for my friend, uh, Scott."

"Sure, he's right inside."

"Huh?"

Stark put out a friendly arm and tugged the man in. As he did, he swung up the gun and cracked the butt across his temple. The visitor crashed to the floor, knocking over an end table.

Stark heard the hallway floor creak. It was a nightingale floor, modeled on similar ones in Japanese castles, an ancient burglar alarm system.

He crouched out of view behind the sofa. He waited. His breathing was level, maximum intake, minimum noise. Belly breathing, his tongue pressed to the roof of his mouth, his diaphragm moving out with each inhalation. He was in a state of *munen muso,* no mind. Completely focused on the problem at hand. Yet completely unfocused, acting instinctively.

"Steve?" the intruder hissed from the doorway to the hall.

Stark took the change from his pocket. He tossed it to the far side of the room. As the intruder spun toward the sound, Stark vaulted over the couch. He planted a fist, with raised knuckle, in the man's beefy abdomen. The man grunted, but didn't fold. There was muscle under the flab.

The intruder tried to raise his gun. Stark chopped down hard on his wrist, and the .357 magnum dropped to the floor.

The man swung a wild roundhouse right. Stark dropped under it, and drove another punch into his abdomen. This time the man folded. Stark hit him with a chop on the side of the neck. It shocked the carotid artery, and the intruder fell to the floor unconscious.

Stark rummaged through the intruder's pockets and found his FBI identification. He went through the other man's pockets, found a driver's license, and jotted down the information from both sets of ID. He dragged the two men next to each other in the middle of the living room, and using a pair of handcuffs from Mitch's pocket, attached their right wrists together. Mitch's hands were covered with blood from his pushing through the rosebushes.

The closet door opened a crack, and Stark gestured for Mirnov to stay inside. She saw Stark over the two men lying on the floor and shut the door.

He returned his attention to the intruders, who had both regained consciousness.

"What's the story, boys?" Stark asked. He held Mitch's gun and aimed at the two men.

"We thought no one was home, and we heard you had a lot of money," Mitch said. "If you let us go, you'll never see us again. I promise."

"That doesn't cut it, Mitch. What's a nice FBI agent like you doing on a job like this?"

"I'm on a national security assignment," Mitch said. "I demand that you let us go immediately."

"That's two lies. We could stay here all night coming up with stories. How about we go for the truth?"

Steve looked pleadingly at Mitch, but the FBI man said nothing.

Stark got a length of rope from his camping gear. He pointed the gun at Mitch and tossed him the handcuff key.

"Undo your bracelet and slap it on your partner," Stark said. "His hands behind his back."

Mitch did as he was told. Stark tied Mitch's arms to his side, used another section of rope to tie Steve's feet together, and turned on the stereo. A sixties oldies station blasted the Rolling Stones' "Sympathy for the Devil."

"Enjoy the music," Stark said, then marched Mitch into the bathroom and shut the door.

"What do you think you're gonna get outta me?" Mitch asked.

Stark took a dirty sock out of the hamper and shoved it in Mitch's mouth.

Then Stark gave a pained gasp. A few seconds later, he yelped. He slapped his hands together, then turned on his electric razor. After a few more seconds, he yowled painfully.

The ex-FBI man glared at him like he was crazy. Stark turned on the electric razor and yowled again.

Mitch struggled, trying to butt Stark. Stark used a few more feet of rope, and hog-tied him.

"Any more out of you, and I'll use my old gym shorts as a gag," Stark said. "That's cruel and unusual punishment."

Mitch thrashed and growled.

Stark turned on the razor one last time, and let out a truly horrible scream. He rubbed his hands on Mitch's hands, getting the ex–FBI man's blood all over him. They were just superficial cuts from the thorns, but there was enough leakage to give Stark's hands a grisly look.

"Damn bloodstains," Stark said as he walked up to Steve. The burglar's eyes bulged.

"Your partner's tough," Stark said. "Didn't get all I needed out of him. Your turn."

The radio was playing "Honky Tonk Women." Stark turned it up.

"We were just supposed to get the girl," Steve blurted. "We weren't supposed to hurt no one."

"What girl?"

"They didn't tell us her name. Just gave us a picture. A pretty brunette in her thirties."

Stark asked questions. Steve answered. Eagerly.

They were to take the woman to an abandoned warehouse in Torrance and drop her off. Mitch had a syringe full of sedative to give her. They were not supposed to talk to her. They were not to harm her. Steve did not know who hired them. Mitch was frequently hired by mysterious people from the government. Steve didn't know what agency they were with and didn't want to risk losing his job by asking. Mitch was no longer with the FBI. Before retiring he had reported his credentials missing and had never been forced to hand them in.

Stark took the syringe from Mitch's pocket and rolled up Steve's sleeve.

"What are you doing?"

Stark gave him a shot full of the sedative. Steve lolled off to sleep.

Stark went to the bathroom and took the gag out of Mitch's mouth. Mitch cursed long and loud. Stark shoved the sock back in.

"Listen up, cupcake," Stark said. "I'm letting you go. I'm going to untie you, and you'll carry your friend out to the van. With all the excitement, he went to sleep."

Stark untied Mitch, who rubbed his arms and legs, and eyed Stark.

"Don't even think about it," Stark said. "Get going."

As they walked out, Stark reached over to his liquor cabinet and removed a pint bottle of Puerto Rican 151-proof rum.

Mitch put his accomplice in the back of the van and climbed into the driver's seat. He balled his hands into fists. He was about to make his move when Stark chopped his carotid artery again. The FBI man passed out.

Stark shoved him away from the driver's seat, got in the car and drove them a few blocks. He parked so it looked like they had banged into a hydrant. He took the Puerto Rican rum, opened Mitch's mouth, and poured a little in. Mitch coughed, but swallowed. Stark poured a half a bottle over Mitch's lips and lap, wiped his prints from the bottle, and dropped it on the floor.

He wiped his fingerprints from the syringe and laid it in plain view next to Steve's unconscious body. He took the .357 magnum and put it back in Mitch's holster. He returned their identification.

He walked to a coin phone five blocks away and dialed 911. Los Angeles had the enhanced system which displayed the caller's address on the operator's terminal. In a high-pitched voice, with a slight British accent, he said, "There's two gentlemen seated in a van. One of them has a firearm, I believe." He gave the street address and hung up.

Mitch might beat the drunk driving rap, but they'd certainly get him for having an open bottle of liquor in the car. The gun and the syringe would go over real big, too.

He was grinning as he walked back to his apartment. Mirnov was in the living room, sweeping up an ashtray that had been broken when Steve fell over in the living room.

"You shouldn't have come out of the closet until I told you to," he said.

"I saw everything was okay."

"Our lives may depend on your trusting me completely."

"But there was no one here."

"If we were in a lab with dangerous microbes, and you told me to stand in a corner and not touch anything, I would do it," Stark said. "If you're being hunted by professionals—and I now believe you are—you have to listen to what I say. To keep us both alive. Understand?"

She nodded. "Did you torture that man?" she asked.

He told her about his bluff, then said, "Before we go any further, you have to tell me what this is all about."

She had been watching from the closet. She knew now that she needed him. That he was willing to risk his life to

protect her. She told him everything, from her late
discovery to her suspicions about the trip to the safe h
"What can we do?" she asked when she was done.

"First thing get you someplace safe. Then we'll wo
a plan." He filled his picnic cooler with food fror
refrigerator.

"Where are we going?" she asked.

"I have a little house about two hours north of her
not much, but no one knows I have it. Not even my pa
It's my Fortress of Solitude."

"What is that?"

"Forget it. Let's go."

CHAPTER
17

The command post was set up in El Segundo, a 5.5 square mile working class community just south of Los Angeles International Airport. Although it enjoyed ocean breezes, the air usually stank of petroleum by-products from the numerous oil pumps and refineries that dotted the landscape.

The Premiere Manufacturing Corporation had shut down in early 1984, unable to compete with overseas competition. Their huge warehouse had remained shuttered, a victim of occasional vandals.

Charon had arranged for use of the site for a month. The cover story was that they were a marketing research firm doing advance work for a new product which was going to be test marketed in the Los Angeles area. No doubt the owner thought they would be storing dope there, but Charon paid top dollar, and the owner promised to keep his mouth shut.

"I'm sure you will," Charon said, as he rattled off where the owner lived, his wife's habits, and the schools his children went to.

A security team repaired cuts in fences and added an alarm system. Two guards with Dobermans were always on patrol.

A central cable tray power distribution system was set up and Emil got his computers humming. A phone bank, files, and modular work stations had been provided. The ease with which the money was appropriated was just more proof to Charon that this was a priority matter that reached the highest levels of government.

Charon's investigative staff worked with telephone modems to access various data bases at the speed of an electronic blink of the eye. Besides gathering data, they planted traps for Stark in the federal system.

If he was stopped for a traffic violation, a cop checking NCIC would see an outstanding warrant. Border guards and customs officials would find his name in their listings as a suspected drug trafficker. There was a hot line number for any law enforcement official to call who stopped him. The phone line ran straight to Charon's desk.

None of the listings would hold up under scrutiny—they were easily dismissible as a bureaucratic foul-up, someone with a name just like Stark—but they would serve to detain him long enough for Charon to locate him.

None of the OCEG staffers knew exactly why they were looking for Robert Stark and/or Dr. Sultana Mirnov. None of them really cared. For some, it was just a job. Others enjoyed the challenge. Whatever the motive, they had demonstrated aptitudes in logic, languages, data processing, forensic sciences, or investigation.

Charon didn't like to have so many involved in the operation, but he had to run Stark down fast. He was glad he'd picked up three hours going east to west.

It was the middle of the night, but banks of fluorescent lights made it seem as bright as day. A half-dozen workers were hunched over terminals.

At least none of the staffers had to know what was going on. Hell, Charon didn't even really know what was going on. But it had to be hot for a special assistant to the President to have met him at Dulles Airport with a suitcase full of cash. No question, it went right to the top. And Charon was their field man.

For Charon the best jobs were where he could operate on his own outside U.S. borders. There were fewer problems with queasy local cops who couldn't hold a prisoner's head in a bucket of water. It was easy to buy guns, drugs, or people.

In the United States, he had to be more careful. After all,

the Agency's charter forbade them from even operating in the country. The liberals made a big deal out of that, like it was written in the Constitution. It was just a presidential concession to J. Edgar Hoover, who had feared the CIA would intrude on his turf.

Charon had to waste lots of his energy being clandestine. Energy better spent on tracking. The big advantage was the millions of files kept on people by credit agencies, government agencies, employers, insurors, utilities, social groups, market researchers.

They had gotten access to Stark's personal and business phone records for the past five years. The computer, with dialer attached, was printing out the address and available information on every number. There were thousands of numbers.

As the computer spat out sheets, an analyst passed them to various staff members. The staffers reviewed the list, using criss-cross directories and various data banks to determine who they belonged to.

During work hours—misrepresenting themselves as anything from police detectives to marketing people needing information about soap products—Charon's staff would call selected numbers. Conclusions would be typed on terminals hooked up to Emil's machine.

Any they couldn't figure out and connect logically with Stark, or anywhere the party answering refused to divulge relevant information, were referred to a supervisor for follow-up. Field investigators were dispatched to local sites. CIA staffers in cities around the world were asked to make discrete inquiries.

The tapping of the computer printing and the air conditioner running to keep the machine cool were the only noises in the large, well-lit room. Food or beverages were not allowed. There was no smoking permitted inside the building. The atmosphere was as serious as in a classroom the day of finals.

Although work was continuing, it had slowed during the nighttime hours. Charon called over to the federal prison on Terminal Island. He used the galvanizing password of "national security." The warden was wakened at home.

Terminal Island is one of the ugliest places in the civilized world. Signs warning against trespassing, hazardous materials, restricted entry, dangerous cargos, hang from barbed wire topped walls. Shipyards, weather-beaten marine salvage businesses, container terminals, and grimy canneries fill the acres. Cranes and derricks jut skyward. Like El Segundo, oil pumps work in the open areas, and the air has the same pungency. Mixed with it is the smell of fish from the canneries.

The medium security prison· itself is one of the nicer looking buildings, despite the guard towers, high Cyclone fence, and massive coils of ribbon wire. At least there are a few palm trees, patches of grass, and yellow picnic tables surrounding the squat brown building. The facility is relatively new, and clean, and even the spotlights gleaming off the concertina wire have a perverse charm.

A respectful guard buzzed Charon through the gate and led him through two sets of heavy metal doors and a sally-port. Their footfalls echoed off the cinder-block walls as they marched down the long corridor to a small room with a formica table and two plastic chairs. The guard left. Charon sat motionless, patient. A few minutes later, Samuel "Cheech" Castellano was led in.

"You must got a lot of juice to get me outta bed in the middle of the night," Cheech said. Castellano had a jockey's build and carriage, and managed to look well groomed even in his prison clothes. He wore a dark green jumpsuit with his number stenciled on it. Castellano was cruelly handsome, though his face bore the pits of bad adolescent acne. He studied Charon's face. "Hey, don't I know you?"

"We met in Colombia."

"That's right. You was the guy with the friends in government. The one that got my people out of that sewer jail those stinking spics threw 'em in. Fucking bunch of extortionist bastards."

"What are you in for?"

"You got the pull to haul me over here, you must know."

"I'd like to hear your version."

"The feds say I was shaking down the garbage truck companies," Castellano said. "It's bullshit. And the wire they used to record it was illegal anyway."

"How long?"

"Eleven fucking years. That means I got to eat this shit

government food for at least another four years. I'll be sixty when I get out."

"I'm in the position to do you another favor."

Castellano cocked his head and squinted. "What's in it for you?" Castellano asked.

"I want you to put the word out. I'm looking for a woman named Sultana Mirnov. She's probably with a man named Robert Stark. There's five thousand in it for whoever finds her."

Castellano snorted. "Five gees. For five gees, I ain't got time to make a phone call."

"That's for whoever finds them. If I get word of it through you, I'll pull whatever strings I can."

"You get me out?"

"Maybe not out, but at least cut time off your sentence."

"How much time?"

"I can't guarantee anything. But I'd say two years at least. Maybe more. And I can arrange for you to go to the prison of your choice. Minimum security."

Castellano picked at a tooth with his fingernail. He nodded. "The names ain't enough to go on."

Charon took out an envelope and held it up. The guard overseeing the room glanced at it and nodded. He was supposed to check that no weapons or tools that could aid in an escape were passed.

Castellano took the envelope and opened it. Inside were the pictures of Stark and Mirnov, with height, weight, and eye color written on the back.

"Cute piece of ass," he said, looking at the shot of Sultana. "I can sell it to the guys here to jerk off over. Some of 'em would fuck a cow if you put a skirt on it. What do you want her for?"

"She's just an assignment to me." Charon got up. "How long before you start getting word back?"

"My *gumbah* comes out to see me in the morning," Castellano said. "He'll beat the bushes. I figure no more than a coupla days. You got any clue where this bimbo's hiding?"

"Could be anywhere."

"In Southern California?"

"In the world."

CHAPTER
18

Stark had dropped Sultana off and left the Daggett house a little before sunrise. He couldn't learn what was going on while hiding out. He had to go into the city to patch in to the information nexus.

His first order of business was a stop in Orange County, at the offices of a conglomerate that was branching out into Latin America. It was the appointment that ostensibly had brought him to Southern California. To skip it would have been an admission that something was up and confirmed the opposition's suspicions. Also, it would make Les happy if Stark successfully handled the account.

Associated Food Industries owned a fast-food chain called Taco King, which had more than 125 outlets in the southwestern United States. They were moving into the country that had invented the taco, and, hopefully, pushing southward from there, despite threats from Guatemalan terrorists.

AFI's corporate headquarters was a three-story, blue glass building, just off the freeway, in a belt of similar corporate bastions. Stark drove up to the gatehouse.

"My name's Robert Stark. I have an appointment with Mr. Kline."

The guard, obviously an ex-cop gone to seed, checked his clipboard.

"Nope."

"Better doublecheck. I'm due at his office in ten minutes."

"You ain't." The guard set his clipboard down and came out, his hand on his gun like a kid clutching a security blanket. "Meeting's been canceled."

"Can I use your phone to call up to him? I'm sure there's some mistake."

"Only mistake is you showing up."

Stark got out of the car. "Let me call up, please."

"Get your ass in gear and get out of here." The guard sounded like an actor doing an impression of a tough Southern sheriff.

"Where's the nearest pay phone?"

"Ain't my problem," the guard said, withdrawing his nightstick from a metal ring on his belt. He poked Stark in the stomach.

"Git!"

"Don't do that," Stark said, brushing the nightstick aside.

As the man went to jab Stark again, Stark caught his hand in an *ikkyo* grip and twisted slightly. The guard yelped and released the baton. Stark took it and twirled it. The guard reached to pull out his gun. Stark rapped the top of his hand with the baton. The man yelped again, and clutched his numb hand. Stark took the gun away from him.

At gunpoint, Stark relieved the guard of his handcuffs and walkie-talkie. He handcuffed the man to a knee-high radiator in the guardhouse. The guard cursed proficiently and profusely.

Stark got back in his car and drove up to the parking lot. He sat in his car where he had a view, through the front door, of the security guard watching video cameras behind the desk just inside the door.

Muffling his voice, he put the walkie-talkie mike by his lips and said, "Front desk. Got a prowler in the first floor ladies room. West wing. Need help, forthwith."

"Who's this?"

Stark played with the "speak" button and said, "Mahstegale."

"Who?"

"Get your butt over here forthwith," Stark said, trying to mimic the guard he had handcuffed. "We got an emergency."

Stark watched the guard hesitate, look both ways, and then leave his post. Stark walked inside and headed up to the executive suite.

The only one between him and Steven Kline was a ferocious looking middle-aged woman with her hair teased up into a bush atop her head.

"I'm here for Mr. Kline. The name's Robert Stark."

"Didn't the guard tell you? That appointment's been canceled."

"I just need a word with him."

"He's not in."

The intercom on her desk buzzed. "Bring me the Smithson file," a man's voice barked.

"My gosh it sounds like there's an intruder in your boss's office. I better go see."

"Wait, don't you . . ."

But he was already past her. He opened the door. Sitting behind the desk was Steven Kline, a crusty gent who reminded Stark of a Gold Rush prospector. He had a bushy white beard, but a youthful entrepreneurial spirit. His company had been among the first to take advantage of trade opportunities in the People's Republic of China.

"I tried to stop him," the secretary said.

"She did. So did your guards. That's what I'm here to talk about. Your security needs revamping."

Kline made a gesture of dismissal at his secretary and she retreated back to her den. Stark dropped the guard's gun and walkie-talkie on Kline's black lacquer desk.

"You got balls coming here," Kline said with a grin. "I like that."

"Then why did you cancel our appointment?"

"Sorry we didn't get a chance to call your office. It came up real sudden-like." Kline hesitated, gazing at Stark. His eyes twinkled mischievously, like a kid about to do something that he knows he shouldn't.

"Early this morning, some snot-nose from the IRS called, threatened me. I don't take that stuff well. Like when some loudmouth from the John Birch Society called to tell me I better not do business with the Reds. I gave him a lesson in laissez faire. Anyway, this federal snot-nose threatens me with an audit if I do business with you.

"Then they threaten to audit me personally. I laughed at

the son-of-a-bitch. I'm probably the only person in America who doesn't cheat on his taxes. This country's been good to me, and I always played square with those that've been good to me."

There was no point in trying to rush Kline. The septagenarian talked like he was telling stories around a campfire.

"Anyways, I start getting calls from other federal snotnoses. FTC, ICC. A whole damn alphabet soup worth of 'em. I been here since seven A.M., and the phone hasn't stopped ringing. I didn't think them damn pencil-necked pencil pushers were up so early.

"They won't tell me why, but they're all warning me that I'm going to be investigated. I tell 'em to go pound salt. None of them would tell me why you'd become such a bad person overnight. Then I get a call from Benedict MacMillan. You know who he is?"

"As in International Sales and Services?"

"Right. Son of Calvin. Calvin and I go way back. He's sharp as a whip. I'm on the boards of a couple of charities with him. We old coots get together and talk about what we did during the Depression. Anyway, his son gives me a call. Pleasant chitchat. Then your name comes up. He starts telling me not to deal with you. I ask why. He says the feds are building a big case against you. They claim you been handing over security secrets from the companies you work for to the Reds. I tell him I don't believe it. He said he had proof, he's seen the documents. He said you were a fugitive. I said you weren't the type to run from nothing or nobody. I've checked you out, my boy. Now you turn up, which shows me I was right. You going to tell me what's this about?"

"They think I've got someone that they want."

"Who's they?"

"The federal government."

"You're harboring a fugitive?"

"It's not that simple."

"You've got to trust the system."

"I can't. Not this time."

Stark got to his office in the early afternoon. Two supercilious IRS agents were waiting.

"We want to see your records from the past five years,"

one of them demanded. "We have orders to instigate a jeopardy assessment against your firm."

Stark called his tax lawyer.

The lawyer said, "Robert, I have to withdraw as your attorney. A conflict of interest."

"You've been my counsel for seven years. What happened?"

"It's a long story. I can't go into it right now. I've got another client here. Good luck."

The attorney hung up.

Stark's secretary walked in. "They picked up Pedro Quesada on an outstanding traffic warrant. They also picked up six of our contract workers. Jenny, Mike, and Pete tendered their resignations, effective immediately. And I got Les on the phone. He sounds bent outta shape."

"I can't imagine why," Stark said. "Thanks for sticking with me, Gina."

She nodded. "Can you tell me what's going on?"

"The feds think I have something they want."

"Can you give it to them?"

"It's not an it. It's a she," Stark said. "I'd understand if you went on a leave of absence. It's not going to be fun around here."

She shrugged. "I don't believe in deserting a sinking ship."

He smiled, got up, and gave her a peck on the cheek. "I just doubled your salary. Assuming there is a salary. Set those IRS men up in the conference room. Give them the old files to start with." He reached into the desk where he kept various medicines. Traveling all over the world, his stomach was subject to a variety of assaults. He took out a package of Ex-Lax. He handed it to her. "Why don't you make a fresh pot of coffee for our federal friends?"

"You're really gonna shake the hornets' nest, ain't you?"

"If you prefer not, I'll do it."

She took the Ex-Lax. "You ain't gonna have all the fun. You better take Les."

"After they've had a solid dose, make sure there's regular brew in the pot. We don't want them to suspect."

She grinned and walked out. He picked up the phone.

"Les, how are things?"

Les answered with a string of obscenities. "I always knew

146

you were an obstinate son-of-a-bitch. But this is too much. You know what's been happening here?"

"I can guess."

"Are you going to give them what they want?"

"No."

"I just spoke to my attorney, Bob. I'm dissolving the company. I've got to protect as much of my investment as I can. I have a family to think of."

"I know."

"Our business is dependent on our good name. It's being dragged through the mud."

"No one ever said integrity came cheap."

"That's a low blow, Bob."

"I'm a low kind of guy. You have to do what you have to do, Les."

Stark hung up and called the headquarters of International Sales and Service. After getting through a half-dozen layers of corporate buffers, he found himself speaking to an assistant to Benedict MacMillan.

"Mr. MacMillan is out of the city right now. If you tell me what you want, I will relay the message."

"Just tell him Robert Stark called. And thank him for the referral. I'll be getting back to him soon."

"Do you care to elaborate?"

"He'll understand," Stark said.

Stark called a few contacts looking for a safe place to send Sultana. Many who he had considered friends refused to even take his phone calls. Those he did get through to were clearly uncomfortable.

The Ex-Lax hit the IRS men. They hurried out after a short time of reviewing files.

The phone rang all afternoon with bad news. Stark's credit cards were canceled. Clients withdrew. Crews came in to repossess the photocopying machine, computer system, and telecopier.

Stark took fifteen hundred dollars from the petty cash drawer and gave it to Gina and told her to take a few weeks off.

"If I'm still in business when you come back, you've got your job back."

"I'll hold you to the raise."

He grinned. "It was made under duress. I'll have to consult my attorney. If I can find one who'll talk to me."

She smiled back, dropped a stack of unpleasant messages on his desk, and walked out.

He was alone in the office. He thumbed through the messages. One of them was from the company that managed the building. He guessed he'd have to find new quarters soon.

He walked to where the IRS men had been working. They had left without putting the files away or sealing them with a court order. He took stacks of documents to the shredder and reduced them to confetti. He had been doing it for a half hour when he heard the electric eye alarm at the front door trill.

His gun was in his desk drawer, out of reach. He stepped to the side of the door and grabbed the heavy glass ashtray. They wouldn't kill him. They still needed to know what was up. That gave him an edge in any fight.

He heard a man's tread in the foyer on the parquet floors. No effort to walk softly.

He waited.

"Stark?"

The voice was familiar.

Stark stepped out, casually holding the ashtray, ready to fling it like a discus.

Charon stood in the middle of the room.

"It's been a while," Charon said.

CHAPTER
19

"Let me guess. You're here to tell me about our class reunion from the Farm," Stark said. "Spooks, class of 1965."

"You're still a wise guy," Charon said. "From what I've seen of your file, you've got nothing to be wise about."

"Lesson five: Let the subject know you have," Stark paused and made his voice melodramatic, "seen his file. This puts him at an immediate disadvantage and makes him wonder what you know."

"You've been quite busy these past few years," Charon said, ignoring the sarcasm. "Brazil, Israel, Venezuela, Mexico, Australia, Singapore, Lebanon, England, Italy, France, Canada. All over the United States."

"Sounds like a great tour. Book me passage."

"Wherever you go, things happen. You visit Montreal, and an FLQ terrorist is dropped off unconscious at a police station. In Italy, two Red Army leaders are found dead. In Singapore, a kidnapped American businessman is set free by his kidnappers with no explanation."

"I'm just a lucky guy at picking hotspots."

"We know what goes on. We're not fools."

"You feed me lines like that, and I'll get you a job as a straight man."

A muscle at the corner of Charon's eye twitched. He

opened his mouth as if to say something, then swallowed his words. "Can we sit?" he asked, indicating Stark's office.

"Well, I've got a very busy schedule today. But for you, old chum, there's always time."

They sat in Stark's office. Charon put his feet up on Stark's desk.

"Your body language is saying you think you're in charge," Stark commented. "But your shoes need to be resoled."

An embarrassed Charon took his feet down. He looked at the soles. They were fine.

"You played your hand and found out we hold all the aces," Charon said. "Now it's time to pay up."

"I never figured you for a gambler. You've been listening too much to Kenny Rogers."

"We want Dr. Sultana Mirnov."

"But she doesn't want you."

"You admit you've been in contact with her?"

"You could say that. I get calls from lots of people."

"Where is she?"

"Damned if I know."

"We know she was in your former apartment last night."

"Former apartment?"

"You've been evicted," Charon said. "A forensic team went over the place, found her hairs in the closet. Also, the sniffers detected her perfume in there."

"Sniffers? You brought bloodhounds in? I'm amazed the landlord allowed any dogs on the premises."

"Olfactory sensors. Better than animals."

"C'mon, nothing's better than a cuddly dog."

Charon slammed his hand down on Stark's desk. "Cut it out. I want to talk seriously."

"You just violated lesson seven: Never lose control of your emotions, except by design."

"I could have you arrested right now."

Stark reached into his desk drawer and took out two Browning Hi Powers. He worked the action on both of them. "These hold fourteen shots each," he said in an exaggerated tough-guy tone. "Get your twenty-seven best men, and we'll meet at the O.K. Corral."

"Don't be such an asshole."

"I'm not amused by what you and your bosses have done."

"We wouldn't want to kill you, but accidents do happen."

"That would be too bad all around, wouldn't it?"

Charon shifted to a conciliatory tone. "I'd like to straighten things up. There's no reason for this bad blood between us."

"Have you forgotten Matsumoto? He had a wife and a kid. He was innocent. But you probably forget those details."

"I had my orders."

"That doesn't cut it. What about Zabotin?"

Charon couldn't hide his surprise. "What do you know about that?"

"A lot more than I did a few seconds ago."

"I'll make you a simple deal. Give us the girl, and we give it back," Charon said, waving his hand to encompass the office.

"Who wants her?"

"The U.S. government."

"But who?"

"My orders come from the highest levels of government."

"Why do they want her so badly?"

Charon shrugged. "Give her back. All will be forgiven. In fact, maybe we can throw contracts your way."

"You don't understand, do you?"

"Understand what?"

"This whole business, the car, the apartment, those are trappings. The very fact that you can take them away from me indicates their impermanence. If I took it back, it would mean even less to me. If I accepted it back from you, it would mean less than nothing. It would be dirtied, a constant reminder of how I gave in to you."

"All this for a Communist bitch? You're going to throw your life away for her?"

"You're not hearing me. Tell them I'll contact Mirnov and ask if she wants to return to you. If she wants to, fine. If not, that's fine too."

"You prefer to give aid and comfort to the enemy rather than assist your own government. In my book, that's treason."

"It's time for you to go," Stark said levelly. "Because

I'm going to lose my temper. If I do, I will throw you out the window, and I don't like to litter."

"You don't like being called a traitor?"

"I know more about American ideals than you could learn in a lifetime. To you liberty is something you hear in a speech and name a bell, and then step on at work. Think about it on your way down in the elevator to kiss your boss's ass."

Charon got up slowly. "We'll be meeting again."

"I'll let you have the last word. Just get out."

He sat absolutely still while Charon swaggered out. After a few minutes, Stark walked to the window. He looked out at the city. It was a clear day, a breeze keeping the smog from building up. Stark could see all the way to downtown Los Angeles.

He locked the front door and continued his shredding. It would only slow them a little. Duplicates of most of the paperwork were on file, either at the New York office, or somewhere in the bowels of regulatory agency files.

When he had purged the most sensitive reports—mostly matters of personal embarrassment to corporate leaders who were kidnapped from the beds of their mistresses—he cleaned out his office.

He put the two Brownings in his aluminum Halliburton case, along with the thousand dollars left in petty cash. He took the change of clothing he kept in his closet and packed his suit carrier.

He rode the elevator down to the garage. He had no doubt he would be tailed. They wanted him to move. Why else had they left him his Toyota? They couldn't repossess it—he owned it outright—but it would have been easy enough to arrange for it to be stolen or totaled in an "accident."

He started the engine and pulled out slowly. He stopped. Two cars were pulling out from opposite rows. A blue Chevy and a brown Ford.

They were "lockstepping" him, an obvious tail, the Chevy about two car lengths behind him, the other hanging further back. He drove over to the main branch of the Beverly Hills library.

Why had MacMillan called Kline? Was MacMillan himself being pushed by the government? How much leverage did the government have over a muckety-muck with a multinational corporation?

He culled through *Forbes, Fortune,* Securities and Exchange Commission reports, the *New York Times,* the *Wall Street Journal,* and the *Los Angeles Times.* Stark found a couple of books on biological warfare, including Seymour Hersh's investigative book, and General Rothschild's pro BW book. He photocopied the sections of the Church Committee report focused on "Unauthorized Storage of Toxic Agents" as well as several magazine articles.

He kept hoping some clue, some answer, would jump out at him. His hopes went unanswered. MacMillan's companies had no apparent involvement with biotechnology, or even pharmaceuticals. The name "Hobbs" did not come up in any articles, and the Lenin Institute was only mentioned once, in an aside, as a place for the best and the brightest in Soviet medicine. But he knew it would take time to digest the materials. Time, and perhaps Sultana Mirnov's analytical mind.

He got back into his car and pulled out into traffic, feigned turning left on Santa Monica Boulevard, and made a right turn across two lanes of traffic. He had gotten rid of the Chevy, but the Ford remained. He drove into Beverly Hills, then up Coldwater Canyon onto Mulholland Drive.

He accelerated on the snakey road. It was a treacherous place, with several dead man's curves, and cars periodically went over the edge, landing in the swimming pools of multimillion dollar homes.

Two cars stuck with him. The Ford had been joined by a dark green Chevy. A three-vehicle tail, a by-the-book operation. After rounding a blind curve, he swerved into a driveway with a snap-spin U-turn. The Ford raced past him. He pulled out of the driveway as the second Chevy came around the bend. The driver hit the brakes, skidded, and smashed into the iron gate at the foot of a film star's driveway.

Stark hit the gas and got back on Coldwater Canyon. He headed south into Beverly Hills. He drove to a bank, and went to one of the safe deposit boxes he kept under a nom de guerre.

He retrieved a passport with a false name and a blank passport he kept for emergencies. As well as ten thousand dollars in gold Canadian coins, a Slim Jim lock opener and related tools.

His Halliburton was much heavier when he went back to his car.

It had been easy. Too easy. Underestimating the enemy was a fatal flaw. He stowed the money in his car, then locked the door and began going over the underside.

He found what he was looking for—a box the size of a cigarette pack, attached by a magnet. He yanked it off and strolled to a nearby Entenmann's bakery delivery truck. He feigned dropping something, then slapped the transmitter under the truck.

He drove to the Beverly Center mall and parked his car. With state-of-the-art electronics, Charon could've planted another transponder anywhere in the Toyota. It was time to say good-bye to his car.

He took his case and found a common, late-model Nissan in good condition. Using the Slim Jim, he opened the door and was inside within thirty seconds. It took a minute for him to pop the ignition lock and be off.

Charon was fuming, but happy. He was glad that the ex-CIA agent had not decided to cooperate. Renegades like Stark shouldn't be allowed to run loose, defying their own government.

Back at the command post, Emil handed Charon a report summarizing their findings. Unexplained contacts had been narrowed down to fourteen listings. Six of them were in the Los Angeles area, and investigators had already been dispatched.

"One of our field people came up with an interesting tidbit when she ran down his purchases at the Mindfulness Bookstore. They specialize in oriental religion and philosophy books. Stark is a Zen Buddhism adherent. The clerk suggested he try the Zen monastery at Tassajara, up near Monterey."

"Yes?"

"The subject told her he had his own retreat a couple hours out of Los Angeles."

"Did Stark say where it was?"

"No. But the clerk was pretty sure he specifically said a couple hours drive."

Charon went out into the main room. The walls were covered with maps, ranging from detailed Thomas Bros. maps of Los Angeles, to a giant world map, with blue pushpins stuck in every post Stark had ever been assigned to for an extended period of time. It was human nature for him to return to a locale he felt familiar with.

There were red pushpins for cities Sultana had lived in. Moscow, Odessa, and Vladivostock. Charon doubted she would flee back there, but he wanted to cover every eventuality.

On the map of California, Charon took a ruler and measured out a 150-mile circle, with Los Angeles at the center point.

"Now what do we have within that circle?" Charon asked.

Emil shuffled the computer printouts he was holding. "A half-dozen possibilities. One of them, we believe, is an ex-girlfriend in Palm Springs. She owns several pieces of property, including a golf course. Another is an apparent contact with a Perris insurance broker who has several arrests for flying marijuana cargo planes. Then there was a real estate man/survivalist leader in Rancho Mirage. Another in Barstow. He's dead, and the number's been reassigned. These others . . ." He looked at the map. "Actually, they're outside the circle you've drawn."

"Save them. We might have to expand the search."

"Should we prioritize any of the others?"

"Try the ex-girlfriend. A golf course is the kind of place Stark would go to. It's quirky enough. And Barstow."

"Why Barstow?"

"Because it sounds the most difficult. That's what I expect from Stark."

The private line in Charon's office rang, and he muttered an obscenity. Emil looked at him curiously.

"It's the President's man running this op," Charon said. "He's been calling every three hours, wanting an update."

"He should have confidence in you," Emil said. "You want me to take care of him?"

Charon, bleary eyed and operating on only a couple of hours sleep, smiled. "I do my own dirty work. You get the team going. Prioritize Palm Springs and Barstow."

CHAPTER
20

Dr. Sultana Mirnov paced around the house. It didn't take her very long. There was a living room, a bedroom, a kitchen area, and a bathroom. A total of thirty square meters, she calculated. Her hotel room had been more lavishly furnished. In Stark's living room, there was only a large wooden cabinet and a table with legs cut short. To use the table, you had to sit on your heels, Japanese style. The walls were bare white. A hanging samurai sword was the lone decoration. The floor was pale pine, brightly polished.

There was no door to the tiny kitchen, but a shoji screen depicting a misty oriental landscape hid it from view. The refrigerator had a dozen things to eat in it, necessities they had brought up from Los Angeles: eggs, bread, milk, vegetables, cheese.

In the bedroom, Stark had a futon bed, a giant sleeping bag that could be rolled up and hidden in the floor-to-ceiling wall cabinet. Also inside the cabinet were changes of clothing for Stark, miscellaneous household goods, a twelve-gauge Remington shotgun with a short barrel, and five boxes of 00 shotgun shells.

There was no telephone or television. The sole luxury—if it could be called that in an area where the temperature sometimes soared to 120 degrees—was the large air conditioner.

Hidden from sight was several thousand dollars worth of electronic security gear. Motion detectors were implanted in the ground along the dirt road coming up to the house. The road was hardly ever used, except by telephone linemen, plinkers going off to shoot targets, or teenagers in four-wheel-drive vehicles looking for a place to get drunk. He had shown her how to activate and deactivate it, and how to use the Remington riot gun. He emphasized that she shouldn't touch the weapon unless she was confident she could use it properly.

"In Komsomol, they teach us how to shoot," she said.

"Target shooting at Communist Youth rallies isn't like shooting a person," he said.

"Obviously. But I was best shot in my unit."

"Fine. Just don't be overconfident. Killing a man is different than you expect. You don't want to make a mistake and shoot some lost kid. You have to wait and see who you're shooting. If you're going up against a pro, you won't have seconds to decide. You have to be cautious and quick. A difficult combination."

"I take care of myself," she said.

Now she was alone. The shotgun leaned against the wall in the corner, a constant reminder of what could happen. She hated being confined. The view out of the window was of a bleak, dried up lake. Lifeless. On two sides was a bleached landscape, with a few Joshua trees—twisted, pre-historic-looking things—and arroyos that ran through the cracked earth. The other two sides had low hills, that ran into bigger hills, that ran into a mountain. The mountains were rocky and lifeless.

She thought of her childhood and the rich Russian land. Evergreen forest mountains damp with dew. White birch trunks glowing with the first light of dawn. Children shouting joyfully, wandering the hills with their families.

She was attracted to Stark, but still annoyed with him. She felt that he didn't give a damn about anyone, including himself. His Zen sayings got on her nerves. He had stuck her in this godforsaken place.

Her eyes were sore from reading. She had finished Raymond Chandler's *The Big Sleep* and Fritjof Capra's *Tao of Physics*. She tried to read D. T. Suziki's *Introduction to Zen Buddhism* but couldn't concentrate.

She had thought she was heading to freedom. Now she was dependent on a stranger. She'd be a fugitive the rest of her life. She hadn't done anything about biological warfare. Maybe Dr. Dorokhov was right. She was naive.

Who could tell what Stark was really up to? Why should she trust him? He had left her feeling stranded and helpless. She had thirty-two dollars left. She went over the house, looking for any money. Nothing.

She had seen a small grocery-gas station about two miles up the road. She would walk to the store and see if she could get a ride somewhere. Could she really trust Stark? Was he following the right course of action?

The sun was beginning to set, a ball of orange gradually lowering itself behind the mountains on the horizon. The few trees cast long shadows. The brutal heat of the day was spent. The first cool breezes of night were blowing as the desert sands cooled.

She had almost reached the store. Her shoes, not made for hiking, had abused her feet. She gazed around at the wide open spaces and felt very small.

Stark had risked his life for her. The adept way he had bested the intruders at his apartment confirmed that he was good at what he did. Could she really handle life on the run herself? He had not done anything to betray her trust. Much as she hated to admit it, she needed him.

She decided to pick up supplies. She would make a nice meal for when he returned and they would plan what to do next. How could he argue with her making a nice meal? She would soften him up, get control of the situation.

She had drunk a few glasses of water before she left, but by the time she could read the "Coke" sign on the store, her throat was parched from the dust.

The beefy man behind the counter must've weighed three hundred pounds. He had a bushy black beard, small brown eyes set in folds of flesh, and a T-shirt that said "Coors." His piggy eyes feasted on her.

"You a mirage, honey?" he asked in a squeaky voice.

"No. Just thirsty."

He reached into a cooler and cracked her open a cold beer. He had tattoos covering most of his meaty arms.

She gulped the cold beer.

"Want another?"

She shook her head and looked around the store. There was lots of beer, soda, boxes of crackers, beef jerky, canned beans, coffee, bread. Sitting on shelves and hanging from nails in the wall were spatulas, ladles, can openers, corkscrews, stationary supplies, hand tools, rat traps, room deodorizers, egg timers, and plastic toys. It was better stocked than most Soviet markets. But there was nothing she could make a meal out of.

"Do you have anything to eat?"

He waved at the shelves behind him.

"I mean real food," she said. "Meat. Vegetables. To make meal."

"Gotta go to Barstow you want that."

A pickup honked outside.

"I'm closing up shop. Where's your car?"

"I walked."

"You walked. From where?"

"My friend's house. It's not far."

"You staying with that screenwriter?"

"Who?"

"The fella lives up the road in the little house. Don't socialize much."

The driver of the pickup honked twice.

"That's my wife, Emmy. She's gonna get real jealous, I keep her waiting to talk to a good-looking lady."

A freckle-faced woman with thin red hair tied up in a bun walked in. "Jesse, what's keeping you?" The woman looked hard at Sultana.

"She's a friend of that writer fella," Jesse volunteered. "She's looking to buy groceries."

"You want to ride into town with us?" Emmy asked. "We got to stop by the Foodway anyhow."

"Would you mind?"

Jesse began closing up shop. "Heck, no. Not often we get to talk to strangers. Tell us about the writer. He famous?"

On the way into town, Mirnov fabricated a story about Stark. He was a screenwriter working on an adaptation of *Crime and Punishment*.

"I always wanted to be a writer," Emmy said. "Mrs. Johnson back in grade school said I had a gift with words. I just never get the time to set pencil to paper, what with the kids and Jesse here."

159

Emmy took over the conversation adroitly questioning Sultana. Mirnov tried to stick to a plausible story, that she was Stark's girlfriend from Los Angeles.

"You got an accent," Emmy said.

"I was born in France," Mirnov said.

"I was over there when I was in the service," Jesse said. *"Parlez-voo francis?"*

"Oui, je parle français. Comment allez-vous?"

"Tray bien. Mercy. Et vous?"

"You have a very nice accent," she said.

Jesse grinned. "That's about all I can say that's fitting to repeat in the company of ladies. Most of what I learned I picked up in cathouses. 'Course that was before I knew Emmy."

They got on the freeway. Jesse rolled up the window as he pushed the truck up to seventy.

"What do you think of America?" Emmy asked.

"It's very nice."

"Best damn place on earth," Jesse said. "Land of the free and the home of the brave."

They made small talk until they got to the supermarket. It took Sultana a while to get oriented in the brightly lit store. There was so much to choose from. She wandered the wide aisles in a daze.

She stopped at the fruits and vegetables counter, staring in amazement at the selection. She reached out and touched an artichoke. Even the *beryzoka* for the elite were never as well stocked.

The meat section was a miracle. The cuts were so fresh. Not a fungus-covered sausage in sight. There were no smirky clerks, hiding the best cuts under the counter, and "finding" them for a bribe. She squeezed the chop meat, stroked the chicken.

The store seemed to stretch for miles, with enough food to feed an entire collective. So many different brands, so many choices. Could Jesse and Emmy have taken her to a showcase store?

"You look out of sorts," Emmy said, coming up to her with a full cart. "I guess it's hard getting used to a new store. You want some help?"

"I want to cook him a nice meal."

Emmy helped her pick out steaks, fresh vegetables, wine.

160

Jesse carried her groceries out to the car. They dropped her back at Stark's house and promised that they would all get together and go bowling real soon.

"You tell your boyfriend to get a phone put in out here," Emmy ordered. "He shouldn't be leaving a gal alone out here. No car, no phone, no way to get help."

"I take care of myself," Sultana said.

Emmy gave her a wink. "You don't want to let him know that."

Then the couple rode off, waving as their pickup kicked up dust.

Sultana put the perishables in the refrigerator and set up the barbecue behind the house.

The headlights of cars on the road were shielded from view by the hills. But the stars twinkled and a full moon lit the landscape. It was beautiful in an eerie way.

There was no clock in the house, no way for her to tell time. Her belly grumbled, and she gobbled down a slice of bread. It had no life to it, unlike Russian bread. She checked the time of sunset in the newspaper, and guesstimated two hours had passed.

She cut the steak into cubes, basted it with sauce, and put tomatoes, peppers, and onions on the skewer.

When not tending the food, she tidied up and set the table. She arranged plastic silverware and paper plates, and set out two candles. She stepped back when she was done and admired her handiwork.

But where was Stark?

There was something cozy about the little house out in the middle of nowhere, Stark thought as he drove up. He felt like entering and shouting "Honey, I'm home" as if he were a happy husband returning to his comfy house in suburbia. But that was a lifestyle that would never be his.

He walked to the door and the lights went out. He grabbed his gun as the door opened.

"Hello," Mirnov said.

"What's going on?" He stepped inside and saw the candles burning on the table.

"I made us meal."

He took off his jacket and undid his tie. "What did you make?" he asked, sniffing the air.

161

"*Shashlik*. Russian shish kebab."

"Where did you get it from?"

"I went into town. The man at the store gave me ride."

"You went out of the house?"

"There was nothing to eat."

"Didn't I tell you not to go out?"

"I preserved cover story. You said to man in store you were movie writer."

"I never told him anything. I told that to the real estate agent when I bought the place. That gives you an idea how quickly gossip travels here."

"What do you think, he will tell the KGB?"

"No. Maybe the FBI. Or the local cops. Or some busybody who will."

"You leave me out here in middle of nowhere and expect me to rot. I have feelings. This is like prison."

She started to cry. The emotion she had bottled up was let loose, and she couldn't stop it. He went into the bathroom and brought back tissues. She seized them and dabbed at her face.

He took her in his arms to comfort her. "I'm sorry," he whispered.

They continued to embrace. He lifted her face to his, and they kissed.

She was light in his arms as he carried her into the bedroom. At first she was responsive to his touch. Then she stiffened.

"What's the matter?" he asked.

She began crying again. "I was thinking of the KGB agent, what he tried to do. And Dr. Dorokhov. It was as if, as if he was trying to . . ." She couldn't complete the statement.

"Roll over," Stark said. "Have you ever tried shiatsu?"

She looked at him like he was proposing sodomy. He laughed.

"It's acupressure. Think of it as a first-rate massage, with medicinal benefits."

She rolled over. He kneaded her shoulders, her arms, her back.

"Just relax," he said as he massaged her.

She felt strange tingles, almost shooting pains, but not quite.

"I read your book *Tao of Physics*", she said. "Very interesting."

"No talking. Just enjoy."

She started to speak, then stopped. The sensations were overwhelming, like a drug. He seemed to know where her muscles were most knotted.

"Let's try again," she suggested.

"There's plenty of time for that later."

He wore shorts, she wore only his shirt, unbuttoned, as they sat at the table and ate the cold, but delicious, *shashlik*. They sipped the wine.

"I have never been in desert before," she said. "Tundra yes, but this is stranger."

"The area was shaped at the end of the last glacial period when several nearby volcanos were active," Stark said. "Between vulcanism, earthquakes, and glaciers we got quite a mix. Bake the whole thing in the sun, throw in some erosion, and *voilà*."

"Does it ever rain here?" she asked.

"Sometimes. We get gully washers. Flash floods. They cut their way through the hills, making all those little rivulets that look like wrinkles on an old man's face. They call them *wadis*, like the ones in the Sahara."

"You know so much."

"Not really. One of my previous covers was as a geologist. Another time I was a naturalist. I've forgotten most of what I'd learned."

"Where did you work?"

He hesitated. He trusted her, and yet, she was Russian. There was something about telling her details from his past that stuck in his craw.

"All over the place," he said. "Don't get the idea rain is common. There's a place called Baghdad not far from here where it didn't rain for a couple of years. Usually we get no more than five inches. Temperatures can hit 120 degrees. Yet things live. Pack rats, bats, coyotes, jackrabbits. Creosote bushes, shadscale scrub, smoke tree, desert willow, jumping cholla."

She giggled at the unusual words. The bottle of wine had relaxed her.

"Then you've got sand lizards, spiny lizards, whiptail geckos," he continued.

"They have funny names. Nicer than scientific ones. Will you show me them?" She reached out and held his hand.

"I wish I had the time. We have to move you out soon. They gave me twenty-four hours to think it over, but there's nothing to say they're not continuing the search for you. Under Moscow rules, I'm assuming you'll be safe here for another forty-eight hours."

"Moscow rules?"

"The rules you follow when operating among hostiles. If the safe house is in friendly territory, it's assumed viable for five years. In neutral territory, it's usable for a year. In enemy territory, a week. Of course those are just rough figures. I'll get you out of here within forty-eight hours. Please don't go out yourself. There are scorpions and rattlers around."

"Rattlers?"

"Rattlesnakes. Especially in areas like the abandoned mines. They like the shade during the heat of the day. There's a joke that the way to catch a rattler during a summer day in the Mojave is to build a fire and grab him when he crawls into it to cool off."

"What kind of mines do they have? Gold?"

"That's further north. Here it's borax, tungsten, lead, barium. Lots of clay and gravel quarries."

He took a topographic map from his camping gear and showed her points he had explored in the surrounding areas. She listened raptly as he told her about fault lines, lava flows, and dry lakes. There were lots of long silences when they locked eyes and laughed for no reason at all.

"This would be your civil defense place to go if nuclear war breaks out?" she asked. "You need to stock it better with food."

"What makes you ask that?"

"In Russia, civil defense is high priority," she said. "Most of the people with any power have *dachas,* and many are outfitted in case you attacked us."

"There's only one Russian I'm thinking about attacking," he said.

She looked down, and then up, and her eyes were large and moist.

He switched to a serious tone, putting her off balance. "This would be the worst place in the world to be. We're surrounded by military bases. Edwards Air Force Base is east of us. There's the Naval Weapons Center, Fort Irwin National Training Center, and Goldstone Deep Space Tracking station north of us. The Marines have facilities southeast, as well as due east. This place is probably close to ground zero." He pointed out the restricted areas on the map.

"You know, in the Soviet Union, a map like this would be classified top secret." She studied the road map, fascinated, nibbling her lip. "So which way would you head?"

"If I was trapped here, I guess I'd go southwest. Towards Victorville. Besides the military bases, you've got pretty tough mountains in all directions. The worst thing between here and Victorville is Sidewinder Mountain," he said, tapping a spot on the map. "It's close to a mile high. But it's climbable, if you have the right gear."

"Do you bring many girls here?" she asked.

He chuckled. "Why?"

"Just curious."

"You're the first. Actually, you're the only other person who knows about my retreat here."

"I am sorry I went into town," she said softly.

"It's okay. Just don't do it again."

She took his hand. "Would you like to . . ." and she nodded toward the bedroom.

"Later. I want to review what's happened from the first moment."

She pouted, but followed him out to the couch. She recounted the events from her first suspicions at the Lenin Institute. He listened carefully, interrupting her narrative a couple of times to ask questions.

"There's no way you could have signed those reports at the Lenin Institute? You know, you're busy, and sign whatever is put in front of you?"

"Never."

"Why your name then?"

"Because I work in different departments, different disciplines. It would be harder for an administrator to check out."

"That sounds plausible. Now, you're convinced that this

165

man Hobbs who questioned you knew about the Soviet program?" Stark asked.

"Yes, but it is just my feeling."

"You've got to trust your feelings. Has anyone from your program defected?"

"No."

"Somehow U.S. officials know about this ultra-secret program. It could be a mole, I suppose."

"Maybe." She reached over and began kneading the flesh of his inner thigh. His response was clearly visible in his shorts.

"Assuming they do know about it, why are they going out of the way to scoop you up? They don't come on heavy unless they feel really threatened. Let's go over it again."

She pulled back, annoyed that he didn't seem to be getting the message.

"Deadly diseases in lots of six. Your name forged on the papers. Transferring you to another division. 'Hobbs' apparently knowing about it. Your being taken from the safe house. You find Zabotin's name on papers, then he's run over by Charon. Charon turns up at my office and pressures me. You say you heard MacMillan's name at the CDC?"

"*Da*. Yes."

"Kline mentioned him to me. And he's known for his dealings with the Soviet Union."

She folded her arms across her chest. "I think we don't have the facts to come to a logical conclusion. All this is speculation. Deductive versus inductive reasoning. We need more data." She seemed on the verge of tears again. "Maybe I made a mistake, maybe it is all a mistake," she said. "I could still be working in the lab. What if I never get a chance to do research again? What if we can't stop them? What if I'm wrong about everything?"

He took her in his arms. "You did the right thing," he said.

It was all she wanted to hear, what she was trying to convince herself was true.

They tried making love again, but once again she wasn't able to respond. She slept with his arms around her. She woke him once when she had a nightmare, yelling in her sleep in Russian. He didn't understand what she was saying, and she wouldn't tell him when he tried to reassure her.

CHAPTER
21

Benedict MacMillan would've preferred meeting the greaser on his own turf, someplace like the country club or in the company dining room. But he knew the country club management's attitude toward minorities, and having the man in the company dining room would be too conspicuous.

With all his reservations, he was still excited by the thought of meeting his first professional killer. Hornaday had arranged the appointment, and MacMillan had followed his instructions exactly.

He had flown into Fort Lauderdale, rented a car, and driven to this godforsaken spot. He was parked on the edge of a mangrove swamp, in a turnoff that was invisible from the road. He had tied a red bandanna around the antenna of his car. MacMillan leaned against the rear fender.

Hornaday had warned him if he deviated from the procedure, the man wouldn't stop. Or he might stop and kill MacMillan. The danger gave MacMillan an almost sexual charge.

Under his one-size-too-large suit, there was a sawed-off shotgun. The possibility that Hornaday might be setting him up hadn't escaped him.

A Ford LTD pulled into the dirt lot. The car slowed.

MacMillan was ready to move, watching for a glint of metal in the car window. There was a driver and one passen-

167

ger. The car stopped at the far side of the lot. The passenger got out.

He was tall, lean, with a bushy black mustache. He could've passed for a prosperous businessman in his late forties. He had a regal air about him as he casually approached.

Hornaday had told him that the man he'd be meeting had been one of the insider operators at the Bay of Pigs, actually inside Cuba before the operation, laying the groundwork with acts of sabotage. A vehement anti-Communist, he'd been caught, tortured, and imprisoned.

Released three years later, when President Johnson worked out a secret trade, the man had gone to Vietnam and become a specialist in helicopter antiguerrilla attacks, "lightning ops." Later he'd helped perform the same work for the El Salvador government, then helped train Contras. He was in between jobs, getting older, but still one of the best.

"Do you know anything about crocodiles?" the man asked.

"Only that they're more dangerous than alligators," Mac-Millan answered, feeling both sophisticated and silly from the cloak-and-dagger parole.

The man nodded. "Call me Jefe."

"That means chief, doesn't it?"

The man didn't answer. He wore lightly tinted aviator glasses. Beneath them were dark brown eyes that pinned MacMillan against the car. Benedict knew he had to take charge initially or he'd never be able to.

"All right, Jefe. My contact spoke highly of you. But I'm still concerned about your being able to handle the job."

"Mr. Hobbs knows my record," Jefe said. "If you do not trust him, then we are both wasting our time."

It took MacMillan a fraction of a second to recall that "Hobbs" was Hornaday's field name.

"Still, I don't know," MacMillan said.

"What do you want me to do to prove myself? Bite the head off a chicken? Tell you stories of operations I have run? Take away that big gun you have under your suit?"

Benedict grinned. "Okay. Can you get a dozen men? A few have to be pilots."

"Fixed wing or helicopter?

168

"Let's say two of each. All combat veterans. Willing to follow instructions to the letter."

"Yes. For what purpose?"

"Do they have to know?"

"They don't. I do."

"Anti-Communism."

"What will they be doing?"

"The U.S. has developed special bacteriological weapons. They want us to run tests. Covertly. They felt I'd be able, through private enterprise, to do a better job."

MacMillan held his breath, waiting for Jefe to swallow the bait. The Cuban said nothing.

"I'll pay two hundred dollars a day per man. You get five hundred a day. Plus there will be a one hundred thousand dollar account for expenses."

Jefe nodded.

MacMillan reached under his jacket. Jefe shifted slightly, and a .38 appeared in his right hand. Benedict took out a wad of bills.

"There's ten thousand there," MacMillan said. He showed no fear under the gun and gained respect in Jefe's eyes.

Jefe holstered his gun and took the money.

"When do we begin?"

"Immediately. Assemble your crew. A plane will fly you to our plant in Mexico. For now, just get your team in order and guard the facility. Very soon your men will be needed to fly to several locations. A couple might need to go behind the Iron Curtain on a mission. Can you handle that?"

Jefe nodded, pocketed the money, and walked back to his car without another word.

Dr. Crenshaw couldn't believe his luck. One minute, he was directing just another corporate program. The next, his salary had been doubled, he'd been given carte blanche to set up a new lab, and promised the opportunity to work on world-class research.

A messenger had been waiting at the airport with a stack of briefing papers from Benedict MacMillan. As Crenshaw read the papers, his joy turned to horror.

The work was translated from the Russian and stamped "Top Secret."

Working with state-of-the-art recombinant DNA techniques, Soviet scientists had inserted a bacteriophage on a bacteria, like a remora hanging on a shark. They used a streptococcus. It was a common enough germ, found just about everywhere. Most forms weren't even harmful. But several varieties, such as *streptococcus viridans* caused diseases like scarlet fever, tonsilitis, rheumatic fever. Beefed up with the bacteriophage, the scientists had made it into a super pathogen.

The bacteria was particularly active in secreting hyalouronidase, a protein which breaks down the cement that holds human cell tissue together. This allowed a rapid spread of the diseases, a ferocious attack on the respiratory system. A sudden fever of more than 104, body-wrenching spasms, coughing that can tear the diaphragm like a sheet of paper, and death.

The irony of the deadly hybrid was that a short time after being brought together, whether inside a human host or still in the air, the two killers attacked each other. The tiny virus destroyed the far bigger bacteria, but itself died in the process. Thus the disease was self-limiting and would not lead to a world-wide plague.

"We need to catch up, and fast," said the enclosed note on Benedict MacMillan's stationery. "Those knee jerkers in Congress will slow things down and leak it to the press. The Administration came to me. I went to you. The future of the free world hangs on you, Henry. I don't know when those Commie bastards plan to use BW, but it's clear they do. I want you to whip up a batch of their most effective agent forthwith for testing. We'll be shipping samples out to the CDC, Fort Detrick, Dugway Proving Grounds, and a couple of other sites. The Canadians will probably be working with us on this. It's obviously a matter of global concern. If you have any problems, our liaison with the CIA is a man named Hobbs." Under that was written a telephone number. Crenshaw recognized the Langley, Virginia exchange of the CIA. "Memorize the number and destroy this note. Needless to say, this entire operation is top secret."

Crenshaw went to the bathroom, re-read the note, committed the number to memory, and shredded the paper. He stared at the blue whirlpool in the toilet bowl as it swept the shreds away.

CHAPTER
22

"How can I help you?" Al Peters asked, devouring a heavily buttered roll.

"What can you tell me about Marshal Yuri Zabotin? KGB honcho in New York until his recent demise," Stark said.

They were sitting at a sidewalk café in Santa Monica, a short walk from the Rand Corporation. Peters worked there as a Kremlinologist, one of the leading experts in the country. His memory was as powerful as his appetite. He weighed 320 pounds, had a thick beard, and no hair on the top of his head.

Al Peters had been born Alexei Desnovitch Petrov, in Moscow, in 1945. His father was a prominent artist, but a wave of anti-Semitism under the Khruschev regime made his works unpopular. In 1962, the Petrov family moved to the United States. Peters, who changed his name when he became a citizen, used the clash of cultures within himself to become an expert. He could recite Kremlin politics the way a die-hard baseball fan offered ERAs, RBIs, and bases stolen records.

"Zabotin. A real member of the *nomenklatura, zolotaya molodyozh* made good. You understand?"

"My Russian's rusty. Golden something or other."

"Golden Youth. The children of the elite. His father was a hero in the revolution. Lots of the kids turned out to be fuck-ups, but he became a hero in the Great Patriotic War. At one point, he had a shot at the Politburo, but the shifting winds blew him away."

"How was he regarded? I mean recently."

"Very highly. Was there more to the car accident than New York insanity?"

"Can you think of any reason why the CIA would want him dead?"

Peters signaled for the waitress to refill the breadbasket.

"Oh, you do my Russian soul good," Peters said. "There's nothing like a little intrigue to work up an appetite. No, I can't think of any reason. You know how the game is played. There's no reason to rock the status quo right now."

"What about biological warfare?"

The waitress brought more bread and their salads. Peters tore into his, shreds of lettuce hanging from the corners of his mouth as he spoke.

"They've always been uptight about that. There's Marshal Zhukov's famous speech in 1956 before the Party Congress, warning about the dangers and rewarming that old canard about U.S. use of germ-infested bugs during the Korean War. Sokolvsky, in 1963, fanned the flames in the *Soviet Military Strategy* journal. Every now and then, some neo-Stalinist warmonger starts a scare."

"Would Zabotin be involved?"

"Doubtful. He was a moderate. His biggest activity was arranging art exchanges and making mutually beneficial deals. Like the pipeline stuff, and the wheat sales."

"Who'd he deal with here?"

"His big contracts were Armand Hammer at Occidental Petroleum. And Calvin MacMillan at ISS. Can you tell me what this is all about?"

"Not now, comrade, not yet. But rest assured, you've earned the meal."

"And dessert?"

"At the place of your choice."

Stark called LaGrange from a pay phone just off Ocean Boulevard. He gazed out at the water and the swaying palms that lined the shore while he waited to be put through, and exchanged pleasantries.

"I need a favor," Stark said.

"You want my wife, my car, my house, you got it," LaGrange said. "I warn you though, it needs new shock absorbers. My car, that is."

"If I brought you a Russian defector with an incredible tale, could you do something with it?"

LaGrange let out a long exhale. "Something, yes. But I couldn't guarantee anyone would pick it up. We've been burned by defectors. They all have an ax to grind; with lots of them the lights are on but nobody's home. Some are so pickled with vodka they can't see straight. Others are sent by the KGB to discredit the sane ones. Any supporting material? Pictures? Verifiable documents?"

"Unfortunately, no."

"I can assign someone to it. It'll be a quick flash, a denial from the Russkies, maybe from our side, too."

"That's what I figured. How about the name of a knowledgeable business reporter in Los Angeles?"

"In what area? Aerospace? Film? Stock market analysis?"

"I need info on a multinational."

"Hold on, lemme check the files."

The wind off the water brought the sound of the carousel on the Santa Monica pier. The boop-boop of the calliope, the shouts of children. A woman in a bikini roller-skated by. A skater wearing a Walkman followed a few feet behind her.

"Okay. Try Janet Kaye. She's the local bureau chief for the *Wall Street Journal*. Use my name."

Stark called Kaye, who agreed to see him, briefly, in a couple of hours. He dropped another couple of dimes in the phone and called the FBI. He asked for an agent he had been friendly with. The man got on the line, heard his name, and instantly hung up. He called back and asked for another agent he'd dealt with. He got the same treatment.

Stark drove over to the FBI office in Westwood. He stood by the post office, just across the plaza from the federal building where the FBI was headquartered.

FBI special agent Steve Hodel was sauntering across the plaza, heading back to the office after one of his usual long, late lunches. He was a maverick, and only his ability as an investigator had kept him from being booted out of the Bureau. When everyone else wore white socks, he wore none. Twice he had told supervisors what he thought of

173

them. He had been unceremoniously transferred after each incident.

The two men had met when an Italian industrialist was kidnapped in the United States. After a couple of initial confrontations, they had worked together. When Stark rescued the victim, he called Hodel and let him get the credit. Which was only fair, since the way Stark had operated was completely outside the law.

Hodel was a big man, nearly six feet four inches, with curly white hair and a strong jaw. He was wearing dark sunglasses and a dark blue polyester suit that had seen better days.

Stark walked toward him, not waving or signaling. He had to leave the contact up to Hodel.

Hodel took off his glasses and signaled to the left with his eyes. Stark walked in that direction. He let Hodel walk ahead of him, then followed about ten feet behind the agent.

Hodel entered the Taft office building a couple of blocks from the federal offices. He rode the elevator to the second floor and entered the bathroom. Stark followed him.

"Jesus Christ, I feel like a fag picking guys up in the street," Hodel said.

"What's going on at the Bureau?" Stark asked as they shook hands. "I called a couple of contacts and got a dial tone."

"I'm committing a fucking federal crime just by talking to you," Hodel said. "I should be giving you the Carmen Miranda rights."

"What am I accused of?"

"There's a bench warrant out for you. Defying a court order. The rumor that goes with it is that you're working for the KGB. Nothing gets my cohorts crankier."

"Damn."

"Comrade, whose dick did you step on to get this treatment?"

"I don't know. That's what I wanted to talk about."

"You're lucky the office is half-empty today. They bused a gaggle of geeks off somewhere to track a fugitive. Otherwise, there'd be someone hiding in the crapper waiting to pop us both. What're you working on?"

"I was helping this defector. A Russian doctor. She came

174

to me with allegations about germ warfare, a U.S.-Soviet conspiracy."

"She must've been cute for you to listen to that crap."

"Before I had a chance to even doubt it, Uncle Sammy came down hard. Can you see if you can find out any more on those warrants? Like where they originated, who's behind them?"

"Sure."

"You ever hear of anything special about a guy named Calvin MacMillan?"

"There was a file on him because of his dealings with the Kremlin. Nothing special, as I recall."

"Can you double-check?"

"I'll see what I can do."

"I owe you."

"I'm retiring in six months. Maybe you can take in another partner."

Kaye kept Stark waiting fifteen minutes in the outer office. Her secretary, a male model type, spent most of the time primping. Finally, a light blinked on his desk and he signaled Stark to enter.

Kaye was a sloe-eyed brunette, in a light-colored business suit that set off her olive-colored skin. She was on the phone as he entered. She was taking notes, sipping a cup of coffee, and smoking a cigarette. She asked the person at the other end of the line a few questions about an unwanted merger and the company's "poison pill" to stop it. She wasn't pleased with the answer and let the person she was talking to know it.

It was a large office that had been significantly reduced in size by the banks of file cabinets lining two of the walls. On the wall behind her desk were bookshelves loaded with titles like *Deficit Spending and the Future of the American Corporation*. A few small volumes of poetry were tucked in with the business texts. Also on the bookshelf were frames holding her MBA from Harvard Business School and a legal degree from Brandeis.

The conversation ended with her giving a throaty laugh. She hung up, made a couple more notes, and turned her attention to Stark.

"My time is limited, Mr. Stark," she said, getting up to

shake his hand. She was surprisingly petite, but her grip was strong. "Allen LaGrange did everything but hold a gun to my head to get me to see you."

"I'll be brief," Stark said. "I'm interested in Calvin MacMillan and ISS. Recent developments. I read the profiles in *Forbes, Fortune,* and *Business,* as well as the articles in your paper and the *Times.* I'd like your personal assessment, and anything that couldn't get into the paper."

She went to a file cabinet and pulled out a thick folder. She thumbed through it, reading quickly.

"Well, we're not *People* magazine. We don't generally trade in gossip."

"But there are always things that you know that you can't quite run with."

She was silent, mulling over the notepad she'd dug out of the file. "Okay. This is off the record, right?"

"Right."

"The hot rumor is that the corporate reins are about to be handed over to his son, Benedict. There're a lot more worthy successors. Calvin supposedly had a minor accident at the house. He was hospitalized; now he's in seclusion at the mansion. For someone who kept as high a profile as he did, that's probably a sign that it's fairly serious."

"What's his son like?"

"Bright, competitive. But he can't handle people the way his father did. There are reports of his assaulting people. A rumor that he killed a prostitute once during an S/M episode. No one's substantiated it, but it gives you an idea of his character that everyone believes it."

"Several corporate presidents have had kinky sex lives."

"But his attitude rubs off in the board room. He's a bully with a hair-trigger temper. I saw him being cross-examined once. He looked like he could strangle the attorney from the opposing party. A month later, that lawyer's house was torched. They never got a suspect."

"Do you have a picture of him?"

She dug a shot from the folder. "You can have it," she said.

Stark studied the picture, the bull neck, the broad shoulders, the piercing gaze. "Thanks. What about MacMillan and the Russians?"

"That's strictly his father's interest. You know he became

176

a philanthropist in his old age. He's been pushing for peace. Did you see the ads?"

Stark shook his head. She dug a newspaper page from the folder.

"Peace in our time?" the boldface print asked. He read the copy quickly. It called on the U.S. and the U.S.S.R. to make peace with each other and devote their defense monies to helping less fortunate nations.

"A noble sentiment," Stark said.

"It went over about as big as when Mrs. Kroc, the widow of the McDonald's Kroc, took out those antinuclear ads. Anyway, I've got an appointment. If you hear anything about MacMillan, a little quid pro quo would be appreciated."

"If I can, I will."

CHAPTER
23

FBI agent Jeremy Berry wiped the sweat from his forehead. He had been flashing the picture of Sultana Mirnov all afternoon and hadn't gotten anything he considered halfway productive.

He had been brought up from the Los Angeles office along with a dozen other agents. He was told Mirnov was a fugitive, but it hadn't come through the usual channels and the details were sketchy.

"Ours is not to reason why," he said.

His partner, Dave Tobin, looked at him. "Huh?"

Tobin spent many hours combing his auburn hair. He was losing it at a rapid pace. Berry was the senior man, and not impressed with his young partner's intelligence.

"What do we do now?" Tobin asked.

"Let's hit the Foodway. I could do with a juice."

They walked across the street from the gas station where they had struck out again. The air conditioner was running full blast inside the supermarket. Berry was glad there were many people to question. He hoped they could spend the rest of the afternoon inside the cool store.

"Excuse me, ma'am, FBI," Tobin said, swooping down on a pretty young woman. "I'd like to ask you a few questions."

Berry sighed. His young partner was particularly diligent

questioning pretty women. At least it would allow them to spend more time inside. The air conditioner on their Plymouth was no match for the heat.

Berry walked over to the Foodway manager's booth, identified himself, and showed the manager the picture.

"What's she wanted for?" the manager asked, fingering the picture.

"It's just routine."

"C'mon, you can tell me. I'm an auxiliary sheriff." The manager took out a brass badge and flashed it.

"Okay. She's a bank robber's girlfriend. Killed a cop in Abilene," Berry said.

"I knew it," the manager said. "You can tell by the eyes."

"Have you seen her?"

"Nope. But if you want, I'll set you up in an office in the back. You can talk to every employee you want, call 'em in in bunches. I'm supposed to get company approval, but heck, I believe in supporting law enforcement."

"The country needs more people like you," Berry said, and the manager beamed. "I'd like to take my time, question each employee individually."

"Of course. So they can't come up with an alibi. I'll get you set up."

The office was little more than a cubicle, and next to the meat department. The smell made Berry contemplate becoming a vegetarian. Berry let Tobin handle questioning the cashiers, most of whom were teenage girls. Tobin got phone numbers—in case there were any follow-up questions, he claimed—from the better-looking ones. Berry just hoped they were over eighteen.

Most of the employees were eager to please. A few were belligerent. None were indifferent. It wasn't every day they were questioned by the FBI.

"I'm going to be a cop," one of the box boys said. "My father's with the CHP."

"Very nice," Berry said, handing him the picture. "Have you ever seen this man?"

He looked at Stark's picture.

"Nope."

"How about this woman?" Berry handed over Sultana Mirnov's.

The box boy bobbed his head.

"Are you sure?"

"She's about five-eight. Brown hair, green eyes."

Despite his attitude of professional nonchalance, Berry felt his heart rate increasing.

"You are positive?"

"Yep. She came in, let's see, I guess it was yesterday, with a couple I've seen around here. They live east of town somewhere. Got a pickup truck. 'Course most folks out here got a pickup. I try to be observant but I don't know their license plate number or nothing."

"You're doing just fine. Could you describe the local residents?"

"Sure."

Berry got the manager, and the box boy described the couple.

"I think I know who you're talking about," the manager said. "Let's check my files."

An hour later, after reviewing the files for everyone authorized to cash checks in the store, the manager held up the card with Jesse and Emmy's name on it.

"This is them," the manager said.

"You're sure?" Berry asked.

"I am."

The FBI agent, the box boy, and the manager were cramped in the manager's small booth. "I'm going to swear you both to absolute secrecy. This woman and her companion are armed and dangerous. Any breach of this confidence could mean innocent lives would be lost."

"Mum's the word," the manager said.

The box boy mimicked zipping up his mouth.

The manager threw a proud, fatherly arm over the box boy as Berry hurried out to the radio in the Plymouth. Along the way, he grabbed Tobin, who was asking a busty redhead if she was married.

"I don't care about hurt pride," Hornaday was shouting into the telephone. "You tell the FBI they are not, repeat not, to bring their HRT Team in on this."

A Justice Department assistant attorney general said, "But HRT is the best-trained, best-equipped SWAT team anywhere in the—"

"I don't care if they're angels with wings and machine

guns," Hornaday said. "We needed the Bureau to do the legwork. This is too sensitive a mission for them."

"On whose orders?"

"I'm speaking for the President. You saw the finding."

Hornaday had forged a Presidential order. The finding gave the go-ahead to a covert operation, bypassing the traditional oversight procedures. It gave Hornaday virtual carte blanche and mandated absolute secrecy by anyone who read it.

"But who are you going to use?" the Justice Department official complained. Hornaday had dealt with the official before, who was usually very obliging.

"I'll handle that. You smooth the FBI's ruffled feathers."

Hornaday hung up the phone in his Washington office and breathed deeply. The forgery was the farthest out on the limb he'd gone for MacMillan, his first provable criminal act. With his old-boy network of contacts, he'd been able to gather the information Benedict had demanded without any real liability. Using friendship and the bluster of national security, he'd always been able to navigate smoothly through the tangled bureaucracy. And putting MacMillan in touch with Jefe didn't present any real problems.

But this was it. This was more than just manipulating the bureaucracy. There'd be no turning back.

Was the information substantial enough to scramble the Counter Insurgency Task Force on? he wondered.

In the aftermath of the rise of terrorist kidnappings, including the Iranian hostage crisis, various agencies of the federal government came up with hostage rescue teams. The FBI's Hostage Rescue Team (HRT) and the army's Delta Force were among the more publicized.

Little known was the State Department's Counter Insurgency Task Force (CITF). There were forty men in the unit, which was attached to the Threat Assessment Group. At any given time, two five-men squads were standing by, ready to be dispatched anywhere in the world. Headquartered at Fort Hood, midway between Dallas and San Antonio, they had trained in joint operations with the British SAS and the Israeli commandos.

Their funding came through national security channels, and everything about them, from the weapons they used, to their social security numbers, was classified. The more secret or secretive an outfit, the better chance to use its resources without word getting out.

CITF members were ex-military men, drawn from Special Forces, the SEALs, and Marine Corps counterinsurgency squads. They worked in civilian clothes, though no one seeing them together could mistake them for anything but what they were—an elite squad of superbly trained soldiers. Their bearing, haircuts, and wariness gave away their pedigree.

Their leader was Major Scott Morrigan, a tall mass of sinews who had won a Silver Star for his actions in Vietnam. Captured, he escaped from a prisoner of war camp. Along the way back to friendly territory, he came upon ten North Vietnamese regulars. He killed all but three, whom he brought back as prisoners.

They had handled a dozen jobs since they were formed. Most involved rescuing kidnap victims before terrorists got a chance to bring in the world press. Several were described as "preemptive strikes," assassinating terrorists who were planning major operations.

Hornaday hesitated. To scramble CITF from their base in Texas on an unconfirmed sighting was an iffy proposition. But it was even more risky letting anyone but the best-trained men anywhere near Mirnov and Stark. According to the dossier on Stark, he was quite a dangerous man.

Hornaday picked up the phone and called the State Department.

"Cheech" Castellano's underboss sat in front of him, not a muscle moving. Anthony Mastrangelo had the darkest black eyes of anyone Castellano knew. He had dark rings under his eyes and favored dark suits. He had been a fearsome enforcer as a young man and preserved his air of intimidation. Now he did his strong-arming in the courtroom.

Mastrangelo was able to get into the attorney visiting room because he was actually a lawyer. The conversations between him and Castellano were privileged and no judge could force either man to divulge what was said. And more important to Castellano, the thirty-five-year-old lawyer was his godson. They were bound together by God. Mastrangelo was also a made member of Castellano's crew, a full-fledged

Mafioso whom Castellano himself had inducted. Castellano trusted him more than he trusted any man, which still was not that much.

"You say you got good news for me?" Castellano asked.

"Sorta." Mastrangelo could speak perfect English in court, but when he talked to his boss, he lapsed into New York–accented slang. A peculiar quirk, since he had been raised in San Francisco.

"What do you mean, sorta?"

"Well, we didn't find that bimbo you wanted."

"Then what's the good news?"

"You know Connie?"

"Of course I know Connie. Her husband lose more on the ponies?"

Connie was a clerk in the FBI's Westwood office. Her husband was a degenerate gambler, who owed the wise guys more than thirty thousand dollars, but couldn't stop gambling. Mastrangelo had worked out a deal with her: if she tipped the wise guys off to pending investigations, details in files, things of interest, for every tidbit she provided that they deemed useful, they'd knock a thousand off her husband's debt. Since it was either that or see her husband wind up with a dozen broken bones, she chose to betray her employer. Connie had subsequently tipped them to a grand jury investigation of Castellano's meat-packing plant, a probe of a Bell poker club, beefed up federal security at the Los Angeles Airport cargo terminal, and several FBI wiretaps. Mastrangelo figured that she had saved them over a million dollars, and probably a half-dozen jail terms.

"What's new with Connie?"

"She says there's something screwy going on. She says this afternoon, they trucked a gang of Feebies to Barstow. Had 'em banging on doors looking for a guy and a broad."

"They do that all the time."

"But this was a hush-hush big deal. She checked the telexes and there was no information on it. A few hours ago, the agents come back to the office. And they are pissed. She starts talking to one of them. A guy named Tobin that's been hitting on her. Pumps him, and gets to take a look at the pictures of the people they're looking for. You know who it is?"

"This Mirnov twat and her bank-robber boyfriend."

"One and the same. Now, she finds out where they think these two are hiding. But the screwy thing is, the FBI was told to back off. What do you think it means?"

"It means you better get up to Barstow pretty quick. We snatch this broad, and I make a deal with my government friends. I walk, and I give her to them on a silver platter."

"You want me to send a few guys up there?"

"No, I want you to sit here and tell me a fucking bedtime story. Get the thumb outta your ass and get up there," Castellano snapped.

CHAPTER
24

The inside of Stark's normally neat house was chaotic. Sultana was hunched down on the floor, reading a magazine. The floor was carpeted with magazines and clippings he'd brought from the library, and sheets of paper filled with notes in Cyrillic.

"I divided data into three major areas," Mirnov explained to Stark as soon as he entered. "Soviet Union, United States, and International Sales and Service. We take the Soviet Union first.

"The dates I saw on papers at Lenin Institute indicate that work first started on project about six months ago," she said.

Stark nodded as he took off his shoes. "There's no guarantee you saw all the papers."

"I am almost sure I would have seen any papers," she insisted. "Accelerated work probably started six months ago. Tests on peoples. Transferring me. Forging my name."

"Okay. I'm bringing up these things just to play devil's advocate."

"What?"

"That's an American saying. It means I'll keep challenging you just to make sure you're on the right track."

"Fine. Then, information was sent to Zabotin in New

York. I mentioned his name to U.S. officials, Zabotin is killed by the man you call Charon."

"Right. Zabotin's a bridge between the U.S. and U.S.S.R. Also between U.S.S.R. and ISS," Stark said, pointing to an article on the floor showing wheat being loaded onto Soviet ships.

She walked to another line of papers.

"I was receiving okay treatment until I tell Hobbs about Zabotin and what I learned. He becomes nasty. And I am removed from safe house."

"Okay."

"Then Charon kills Zabotin. And visits you. Government puts pressure to shut down your business."

"The question is, how high up does involvement go?"

"What if it is like virus? A small internal obligate parasite that gets control of cell DNA and makes it do dirty work for it."

"That's quite a reach, isn't it?"

"Part of the scientific method is first dreaming up a hypothesis. Then comes proving it. Who would believe virus you cannot see can make you blind or cripple you? Or that your hair color, eye color, height, are all determined by a tiny helix?"

"Okay."

"Under the U.S. column, the only people we know are Hobbs and Charon. Others seem to be following orders. They may or may not be culpable."

Stark took out the picture of Benedict MacMillan. "Was this the man you knew as Hobbs?"

She studied it and shook her head. "Definitely no."

"It was a long shot. That's Benedict MacMillan."

She stared at it intently, then put it over on the third row of papers. "Read this," she said, pointing to a few paragraphs she had circled in a lengthy *Fortune* article on Calvin MacMillan:

> MacMillan denied that he was actively pursuing a Nobel Peace Prize.
>
> "Of course I wouldn't mind getting it," he said with a chuckle. "I just would like to see peace in my lifetime. The great powers must make peace with each other and

stop dangling the threat of nuclear holocaust over each other's heads.

"Both Americans and Russians consider themselves peace-loving people. Neither country can afford to waste so many billions on defense. Put it into building roadways, leveling slums, developing consumer products."

The elderly magnate noted that none of the dozens of international leaders he has met with ever wanted war.

"It just seems to happen that geopolitical interests conflict," he said. "And both sides have X number of generals, and troops, and munitions. The problem is, with nuclear, chemical, and biological weapons, we're no longer just talking about destroying a city. We're talking about turning the third planet from the sun into a lifeless mass. I'd hate to think that mankind has come so far only to destroy himself over a border conflict or a political dispute. I'm going to do everything in my power to make officials realize how dangerous a game they're playing. This brinkmanship cannot continue."

Asked if he had any specific ideas, MacMillan said, "Sometimes the only way to get a mule's attention is to hit it in the head with a two-by-four." Pressed further, he grew increasingly tight-lipped.

Stark lay the magazine down. "Interesting. We need to speak to him."

"I don't think that will do much good. We don't know who is on whose side."

"Charon wouldn't act without orders from higher up," Stark said. "He's like Gordon Liddy, only dangerous when programmed for God and country. How high up does it go?"

She shrugged. "We cannot tell at this stage . . ."

"Tomorrow I'll try nailing down the MacMillans," he said. "You see if you can deduce anything else."

"I will come with you tomorrow."

"No. Stay here. It's safer."

"I can help."

"You're still my client. And I operate better solo."

Mirnov woke alone. She sat up quickly, looking around for Stark. Her first reaction was that he had run off, aban-

187

doned her. How could she expect him to risk everything for her?

Then she saw his belongings scattered about the house, and a worse feeling of dread oppressed her. What if something had happened to him, he had been taken away in the night?

She reached over and took one of Stark's Brownings. She checked that it was loaded and cocked. With the gun at her side, she walked out cautiously into the dark living room.

Silence. No sign of Stark.

She found him sitting on the concrete slab that served as a porch, right near the barbecue. His legs were under him in the lotus position, his eyes half-closed, a Mona Lisa smile on his face.

He was barefoot, bare chested, wearing dungarees. She was chilled from the cold night winds blowing across the dry sand but stayed and stared at him. Watching his solitary figure under the stars was hypnotic.

"Hello," he whispered.

"How long have you been awake?"

"I don't know."

"It's five A.M."

"We used to get up at four in the monastery. The quiet helps me think. Or not to think."

"Would you like me to make breakfast?"

"Why don't you go back to sleep?"

"I'm up," she said.

"Then I would like breakfast."

She went inside and turned on the stove. She still didn't understand him. Most men were so simple to figure out. Little boys trying to impress their mommas, horny goats wanting to rut, or bullies needing a rag doll they could smack around, physically or emotionally.

"What happens today?" she asked when he came in.

"I'm going back into Los Angeles. Tap into the information nexus. I want to see what I can find out about Charon's doings. If I know where his orders are coming from, I can get an idea exactly what we are up against."

"Take me with you. I hate sitting here doing nothing. I have rights to know what is going on. Right to be with you. I can help."

188

He squeezed her hand. "At this point, I prefer to work without you."

"I am not some flimsy American woman," she said, raising her voice. "I am a scientist who knows more about biology than you. Could you diagnose one symptom? Would you be able to tell the difference between a rickettsia and a virus? Do you know proper containment procedures, how to keep a sterile field, how to deal with infectious waste?"

"No, but if you hum a few bars, I'll fake it."

"Be serious!" She smelled the butter burning and turned to flip the eggs. It was too late. *"Oh chyort!"* she cursed, and stormed away.

He made toast and invited her to the breakfast table. She stayed in the bedroom, door shut.

Before he left, he tried to talk with her. She wouldn't open up.

"When we face a biohazard situation, I promise you'll be there," he said through the door. "Do you know what to do when someone starts shooting in your direction? What's the effective range on a .380 Winchester? If someone lunges at you with a knife, do you close in, or back off? What if they have a gun?"

"Go away," she said.

"Sultana, you *have* to understand, I'm better off alone. I'll be back," he said. "Please don't go out. Turn the alarm back on after I leave."

Mirnov felt embarrassed as soon as she heard the door to his car slam. She wanted to run after him, say she was sorry, but she was too proud.

He was right, probably, but that didn't make it any easier. Sultana hated being dependent on anyone.

She reactivated the alarm and paced around the house. She looked out the window at the inhospitable desert, monochromatic in the moonlight.

The Russian scientist turned on a muted reading lamp, made herself a glass of hot tea, and sat down on the couch with pencil and paper. She had to think about what had happened scientifically, dispassionately. Within a few minutes, she was completely absorbed in her work.

CHAPTER
25

Major Scott Morrigan whispered into the microphone that was clipped to the collar of his black jumpsuit. "Baker, this is Able. Male subject just pulled away in the car."

"Roger, Able. Identity of female subject is confirmed. All indications are she's alone in premises. Do you want us to approach?"

"Negative, Baker. Foxtrot and Golf are checking for hazards. Hold your position."

"This is Echo. Do you want us to intercept the male?"

"Negative."

Morrigan knew Stark's record. He also knew that Stark was not the primary target. Stark was an obstacle, and Morrigan avoided obstacles wherever possible.

Two of the major's men were sweeping the ground with a state-of-the-art mine detector that scanned the ground six feet in front of the operator. They cautiously advanced toward the house.

Next to Morrigan, another CITF member watched the house through a night scope. The seven other members of the team were spread out in arroyos, each equipped with a walkie-talkie, and patiently awaiting orders. They had been trained to the point where they could sit motionless for a full day, in complete field gear.

Morrigan's earphone crackled. "Able, there's something underground here," Golf said.

"A pipe?"

"Negative. More likely sensors. They're spaced about fifteen feet apart. That's the optimum distance for Welltron Scanners."

"Can you deactivate?"

"It'll take a few minutes. They're not easy."

There was a glow in the east. A half hour until dawn. They could create a diversion on one side and storm the house from the other. But there were about fifty yards to the house. Fifty yards with no cover, a free fire killing zone. What if there was an automatic machine gun or hidden Claymores forming a deadly perimeter?

Morrigan peeled up the band covering his diver's watch crystal and glanced at the ticking second hand. "Golf, do it. But make it snappy."

The black Ford van pulled off the highway onto the dirt road. It had a special suspension system, and the four big men inside hardly felt the change. There was a supercharged engine under the hood, and premium radials on the wheels.

The van was ordinarily used for carrying dope down from Canada. While the feds watched the Mexican border closely, there were plenty of spots to the north where a truckload could slip in. Canadian customs was not as diligent about watching loads coming in from Southeast Asia.

The four men in the van owed their loyalty to the don. Anthony Mastrangelo, who had taken a couple of toots of coke to mute his nervousness, and Mickey No Nose—so called because he had a hooter like Jimmy Durante—were both made members of the Mafia. The other two were aspirants, around guys who hoped they'd be rewarded for doing dirty work for the don.

"That must be the place," one of them said, pointing to Stark's house. "What do we do?"

"Pull off over here. Park it by the tree," No Nose said, pointing to a couple of Joshuas. "It's dark enough still they won't be able to see it. We'll be out of here before the sun's up."

The driver pulled behind the tree and shut the engine.

"They're probably asleep in there," Mastrangelo said.

"Cops always serve warrants around this time because the body's in its deepest sleep."

Joey Fish nodded. "When they busted me on that interstate transport deal, it was about this time. One minute I'm having a sweet dream, the next I got some Feebies .357 up my nose."

The other goon nodded.

Mastrangelo said, "We peep in the windows, see where they are, then hit 'em from a couple of different sides. Be careful of the bimbo. She's worth her weight in gold. Ready?"

The men nodded.

"Party time," Mastrangelo said, and opened the door to the van.

Mirnov was so absorbed in her work she nearly missed the chirp of the alarm as the goon squad tripped the sensors. She hoped it was Stark, who had had a change of mind and was coming back to pick her up. She looked out the window, but didn't see any car. Maybe it was a coyote.

Then she saw the figures, in a half crouch, moving rapidly toward the house by the sides of the dirt road.

She ran and grabbed the shotgun. Mirnov went to kill the light, then realized that would give away that she knew. She worked the pump on the gun, the way Stark had shown her, and crouched down by the front window. Her hands trembled.

"Able, this is Delta. What's going on there?"

"Delta, this is Able. Looks like we've got competition."

"Able, this is Echo. You want us to eliminate them?"

"Negative. Let them get a little closer to the target. They can trip any other defenses for us. When I give the command, open fire. Bravo and I will take the one on the far left. Charlie, Delta, take the big one next to him. Echo, Foxtrot, take the next one over. Golf, Hotel, you've got the one on the right. India, Juliet, go to the competition's vehicle. If they get lucky, back us up. Any questions?"

"Bravo, understood."

"Charlie, understood."

Morrigan waited until all his men had acknowledged.

As the goon squad moved forward, they didn't realize they were in the sights of eight sniperscope-equipped marksmen.

As he neared the house, Joey Fish saw a faint glow in the living room window. "Someone's up," he hissed.

No Nose waved with his hand, indicating the men should spread out and approach the house from three sides. He was a Vietnam combat veteran and remembered a few tricks. He wished he had better soldiers under his command.

Mirnov could barely make out the men's faces. They looked like hooligans. She had waited, hoping for some sign that Stark had sent them, that they were coming to guard her. But there was no indication. They should've shouted something by now.

They they drew guns and spread out. She had to act quickly or she would be surrounded.

She squeezed the trigger on the shotgun. The window in front of her blew out and a hooligan's head disappeared in a shower of red.

No Nose and the others hit the ground as she worked another shell into the chamber and fired a second blast. Pellets stung Joey Fish, drawing weals, but far from a serious injury.

Mastrangelo crawled around toward the rear of the house, his thin frame hidden from Sultana's view by a ridge.

No Nose and Joey Fish gave him covering fire. A bullet from Joey Fish's .45 caught a glass fragment left in the window and sent it slicing across Sultana's arm. She cried out, but no one heard over the sound of gunfire. She fired the shotgun in the direction of the noise, then scrambled to the kitchen and grabbed a towel. She tied it around her wound.

"Able, this is Echo, we have a hostile crawling along our side."

"You may fire."

Four shots rang out. All were within a silver-dollar-sized area and ripped through Mastrangelo's heart.

"What the fuck was that?" Joey Fish asked.

"The shot came from over there," No Nose said. "We're outflanked."

No Nose hugged the ground and crawled to the dead goon who had had the Uzi. The ground was dry and rough, and his eight-hundred-dollar suit was ruined by the time he retrieved the weapon.

"You watch the house, I'll watch the perimeter," No Nose said. "We've got to get inside. Don't stick your head up for nothing."

"They're advancing toward the house," Foxtrot said.

"This is Able. Stay low but make your approach. Watch out for stray shots. We want her in one piece."

The CITF Group moved cautiously forward, their black shapes barely visible. They used every conceivable inch of cover to the maximum. The sun continued its slow ascent, providing an eerie half light.

"Fuck! What the hell is going on?" No Nose asked, as he saw the movement. He let loose a burst from the Uzi. The CITF group halted.

Joey Fish had reached the door of the house. He knew there was someone with a shotgun inside. But surrounding them was a small army with God knew what kind of firepower. By the way they crept up so professionally, he knew they weren't local yokel cops.

Fish lay with his feet against the door and kicked in hard. The door swung open and he played his gun over the room.

Empty.

"Hold your fire!" Morrigan ordered. "We can't risk hitting her."

Fish crawled in. The shotgun lay on the floor near the front window. He grabbed it, and began shooting where he guessed the men in black were. No Nose used the covering fire to crawl into the house.

"Able, this is Echo. What do we do now?"

"This is Able. Just like any other hostage situation," Morrigan said calmly. "Establish a perimeter, contain them, advance slowly."

No Nose ransacked the small house, searching for Sultana. With a gun to her head, they could bluster their way out. He found the trail of blood leading to the kitchen, then to the bedroom. There were droplets on the windowsill. The window was open.

"Fucking cunt slipped out while we were being shot up," No Nose said.

"What do we do now?" Joey Fish asked, a slight hint of a tremor in his voice.

"How the fuck do I know?"

CHAPTER
26

If MacMillan was doing something with biotechnology, it would make sense to use people and facilities in-house, Stark reasoned. He stopped at the business library and re-read the Securities and Exchange Commission 10K form which ISS and all other publicly traded corporations were required to file. He jotted down the names of any ISS company that looked like it dealt with biotechnology.

He called his secretary, Gina, and asked if he could stop by her house. She agreed.

Gina lived in a small garden apartment in Santa Monica with her daughter and two cats. The daughter was at school. The two cats were everywhere, unusually affectionate for felines.

Gina was wearing a loose robe over a string bikini. "I was on my way to the beach," she said, greeting Stark at the door with a kiss. It was not beach weather.

"Unfortunately, I'm here on business," he said, pulling back after a chaste embrace.

"How come you never made a pass at me?" she asked. "Wait. Don't bother answering. I'm sorry I asked."

"If we didn't work together . . ." He winked and let the words trail off.

She smiled. "What's the business?"

"My name is Malcolm Borden," Stark said. "I'm the

deputy director of the National Institutes of Health. I need an officious secretary. Know where I can find one?"

"I might be able to help you, but I'll have to put you on hold," she said with a clipped, biting-off-each-word, accent.

"Great." He handed her his list of companies. "Let's do it." He attached a telephone pickup coil and tape recorder to the phone.

The first two calls resulted in naught. Stark claimed to be Borden, calling on the recommendation of Benedict Mac-Millan. He got prompt and groveling response from the directors of ISS's major agribusiness lab and ISS's pharmaceutical subsidiary. Stark bluffed, pretending to know about the big, top secret ISS project. Neither director knew what he was talking about.

At the third plant, Gina was told that Dr. Henry Crenshaw was out of the country. Gina arranged for Stark to speak to the number two man, Dr. David Palermo.

"I can't believe that Crenshaw isn't there," Stark said. "There you are, right in the middle of MacMillan's pet project, and he leaves. Must be pretty damn important."

"I know," Palermo said. "I was surprised, too. Benedict MacMillan visited him personally a week ago. Henry's been agitated since then. Two days ago, he takes off, leaving a stack of paperwork for me to wade through. No instructions. No contact number. It's not like him."

"Crenshaw's name is familiar. I wonder if I ever ran across him?"

"He used to be at Fort Detrick. Doing classified work for the army."

"Biological warfare?"

"He didn't talk about it much, but that's what I gather."

"Thanks, Dr. Palermo. Can you switch me back to Crenshaw's secretary?"

Once he had her on the line, he asked, "Who handles travel arrangements for your company?"

"Five Star Travel."

He thanked her and hung up.

"You got what you wanted?" Gina asked, sharing his excitement. "What's it mean?"

"I need Crenshaw. I need you to impersonate his secretary." A cat was sitting on top of the tape recorder. Stark shooed it away, rewound the recorder, and played back

Gina's conversation with the secretary. Gina listened intently, head cocked, lips moving silently.

"One more time," she said when the conversation had finished. Stark replayed it. She nodded.

They called Five Star Travel.

"He flew into Puerta Vallerta, but we don't have a hotel for him," the woman at Five Star said.

"Of course, he did mention that," Gina said. "I forgot which hotel he was going to."

"He said he wouldn't be needing a hotel. That he was going in country from there," the woman said. "He asked about ground transportation."

"Did he say where?"

"I forgot. I don't understand why he didn't have you make the arrangements anyway."

"You know how these mad scientists are," Gina said. "You really can't recall?"

Stark grabbed an atlas off Gina's bookshelf and whispered the names of surrounding towns to her. But the woman at the travel agency didn't recall. And she began to get suspicious. Gina thanked her abruptly and hung up.

Gina stretched like one of her cats, the robe opening and showcasing her body. "Anything else I can do?" she asked.

"You were perfect."

She pouted.

Stark picked up the phone and dialed MacMillan's New York office.

"Benedict, this is Stark," he said when he finally got through.

"What do you want?"

"I know what's going on south of the border," Stark said. Stark heard the slight intake of air. That hiss, and the fact that MacMillan had taken his call, convinced him he was on the right track.

"What do you think the authorities would say about your biological warfare activities?"

"I don't know what you're talking about."

"But I'd bet you'd pay to keep my mouth shut."

"Are you blackmailing me?"

"Call it a consulting fee. I think $250,000 would be fair."

"That's outrageous."

"You've cost me time and money, Benedict."

"I won't be blackmailed."

"Okay."

There was a silence.

"You're just a cheap little crook," MacMillan said.

"If I'm cheap, maybe I should raise my price."

"How do you want the money?"

"In hundreds. Out of sequence. Unmarked."

"How do I get it to you? Where are you?"

"There's a guy named Charon who's been doing work for you. I'll meet with him."

"It'll take me a couple of days to put together that kind of cash without drawing attention to it."

"Break open your piggy bank. The day after tomorrow. At MacArthur Park. Have him by the pay phone in the northwest corner."

Stark hung up. Gina was staring at him.

"Don't be disappointed in me," he said. "It's part of the game."

"I'm not disappointed. I'm trying to figure out how to get more of a raise."

"I've got to run up your phone bill a bit more. Don't worry, I'm good for it," he said with a grin. He dialed Hodel at the FBI.

"Glad you called," Hodel whispered into the phone. "I been trying to figure a frigging way to get ahold of you."

"What's the matter?"

Gina had moved next to Stark. Her arms circled his body. She nipped at his free ear.

"That fugitive they were looking for," Hodel said. "It's you. They were in Barstow yesterday."

Stark pushed Gina away. She put her hands on her hips and frowned.

"I gather they got a righteous lead," Hodel continued. "Then they were pulled off."

"What's going on?" Gina demanded as Stark hung up.

"Trouble," he said, and ran out the door.

CHAPTER
27

"What the hell happened out there?" Hornaday demanded of Charon.

"Details are still coming in," Charon said.

"Well, what have you determined so far?"

The two men were talking on a secured scramble phone: Hornaday in his Langley, Virginia office; Charon at the El Segundo command post.

"The SWAT team was in place. They observed Stark leaving the premises. Four heavily armed white males arrived. As they approached the premises, a shot was fired. Major Morrigan neutralized them. A fire fight ensued. Two of the white males made it into the house. It took Morrigan and his team two hours to effectuate a safe entry."

"Why did it take so long?"

"Because they didn't know whether Mirnov was being held hostage or not." Charon struggled to control his anger. He spoke stiffly, staccato, spitting out each word. "They terminated the two males. They removed the bodies and cleaned up as much as they could."

"Have these males been identified yet?"

"We have reason to believe they were connected with organized crime. One is a small-time strong-arm hood. The other's a mob attorney."

"The Mafia? Is it too much to ask what reputed members of the Mafia are doing traipsing around the Mojave desert?"

"We're not really sure," Charon said. "I'm looking into it. Stark has many strange associates."

"What about the woman? Are you any closer to determining her whereabouts?"

"She wasn't there."

"Ever?"

"There are traces of her in the house. But she could've been hiding in the car when Stark drove away."

"What about the gunshot report from the house when the Mafioso first arrived?"

"One of the men was carrying a sawed-off shotgun with a hair-trigger modification. It might have been an accidental firing."

"Can't you say anything definitively?" Hornaday demanded.

"The sheriff in San Bernardino county has taken a distinctly hostile position. He detained two of my investigators and interrogated them heavily as to why there was any federal interest out there. Needless to say, the agents did not divulge the nature of the assignment. All he has to go on is bullet holes and blood traces. But he's a provincial, territorial type."

"We will simply progress a few links in the chain of command."

"We're best off letting it die down. That's why I've only authorized a limited search in the surrounding area, in case Mirnov snuck out during the fire fight."

"You're letting a podunk county sheriff get in your way?"

"We've been able to keep this thing quiet," Charon said. "What if the sheriff gets spiteful and leaks it to the press?"

The men's voices had gotten louder as their emotions rose.

"If Mirnov made her escape into the Mojave, we better locate her whereabouts forthwith," Hornaday said. "What are the temperatures running there?"

"During the day, it peaks at a hundred. At night, it goes down to the high fifties."

"I don't give a tinker's damn what that sheriff thinks. What's the nearest military facility?"

"There's Edwards Air Force Base to the west, China

201

Lake Naval Weapons Center and Fort Irwin National Training Center to the north, and Twenty-nine Palms Marine Corps Base to the south."

"I will arrange for a half-dozen helicopters from Fort Irwin to participate in reconnaissance flyovers."

"The number of people that know anything about an operation increases the—"

"I know, I know. A secret's a secret when two people know it and one of them's dead," Hornaday snapped. "The helicopters will be deployed on a routine exercise. Fort Irwin's a training facility. They're always dispatching them on unexplained assignments. A friend at DIA owes me a big one. He'll inform them they're practicing searching for a terrorist encampment in the Arabian desert. They won't find it, but maybe they'll find Mirnov."

"Whatever you say."

"I want hourly updates on this crisis."

"Yes, sir," Charon said, gritting his teeth.

Charon hated working under tight supervision. He hated Hornaday's supercilious manner. Most of all, he hated Stark, the traitor causing these problems.

Hornaday drummed his fingers on his desk. Why hadn't he taken that offer last year to become a professor at Georgetown University, his alma mater?

Academia offered some of the rewards of politics. There were the same power plays and struggles to gain control. There were the vast masses underneath, content to obey orders. But the ultimate outcome was so insignificant compared to what he could achieve in government. No one could compare flunking a sophomore to destabilizing a government.

His desk was cluttered with the symbols of his significance. He had three computer terminals, all protected with TEMPEST level security, the highest available. They allowed him access to the major news service wires, the PROFS interoffice computer network, the mainframe that handled all diplomatic cable traffic, and the National Security Agency's counterterrorism ops center. The counterterrorism computer beeped any time there was noteworthy activity reported.

When he'd first been caught in MacMillan's trap, he had

tried to figure a way out. There was no question the photo would ruin his career. No man with a top secret clearance could ever explain a photo of himself meeting in an underground garage with a known KGB agent. Powerful as Hornaday was, he knew that MacMillan had numerous friends in every branch of government. And with every action, Hornaday had dug himself in a little deeper.

Hornaday paced around the office. A report to Congress on international terrorism was due, and everyone believed he was conscientiously burning the midnight oil to get it out on time. No one realized what he was really working on. He hoped.

He walked out into his secretary's office. She had nearly as high a clearance as he did. The office safe, the KL-43 encryption machine, and the shredder were near her desk. Keeping word of MacMillan's project from her was one of the hardest parts of his collaboration.

She had seen a few hints of the operation, mainly calls being returned when Hornaday was arranging things. At first she'd given him questioning glances. But when he'd refused to answer, she hadn't persisted. She was a good little trooper, not that bright, but very loyal and efficient. She'd make an ideal wife, Hornaday thought. He realized he didn't even know if she was married.

He stroked the shredder idlely. It was always on, and the fan motor made it purr.

He no longer wondered about backing out. He had convinced himself that the success of MacMillan's mission was vital to the national defense. If he stopped cooperating, MacMillan would rely heavily on the Russians. They might be able to sway him or gain control of MacMillan's project. The consequences were mind-boggling.

So Hornaday would continue to risk all for the good of the American people. And they probably would never even know. That was the price of being a front-line cold warrior.

His hand was caressing the shredder, and the purring seemed to grow stronger.

"What were your people doing at the house in Daggett?" Charon demanded of "Cheech" Castellano.

The Mafia boss shrugged. He had thrown a temper tantrum when Charon first told him his men had been killed.

Yet Charon had the feeling that somehow through the incredible prison grapevine that operates more effectively than most intelligence services, Castellano already knew.

"Don't give me that shrug shit," Charon growled, rapping the counter in the Terminal Island attorney meeting room. "What were they doing out there?"

Castellano's mouth twisted into a smile that would do a Great White Shark justice. "Scusa me, us guineas, we talk with our bodies. We're just a simple people."

"Are you going to get cute with me?"

"I don't put up with backtalk from no one. Not no cops, not no judge, not no politician. Not you. You start getting smart-mouth with me, our relationship is through."

Charon wanted someone to take apart, but he needed Castellano. When this deal was done it would be a different matter. At the very least, he would arrange to have the don transferred from sunny Southern California to Sandstone in Minnesota. Get him a nice outdoor assignment for the winter. Charon forced a conciliatory smile to his face.

"I'm under a great deal of pressure," Charon said soothingly.

Cheech unfolded his arms and waved his hands in a gesture of dismissal. "You work hard. We all do. Let's not let that get in the way of our partnership."

"Can you tell me what they were doing out there?"

"If you tell me what happened?"

"They got in the way of a top secret military exercise from the Twenty-nine Palms base. They accidentally sparked a shootout with a squad of Marines. The whole matter has to be kept hushed up."

"What about their bodies? Their wives and families need to be assured they get a proper burial."

"I'm afraid the bodies have already been disposed of. A Catholic priest was in attendance."

"I wanna talk to this priest."

"I'll see what I can do. You tell me, why were they there?"

"That's simple. I sent them to see if these people were the ones you wanted. I was going to deliver this couple to you on a silver platter."

"I see. They were heavily armed for a reconnaissance

patrol. The army found chloroform and handcuffs in their van."

"You never know what you'll run into."

Both men looked at each other, neither believing what the other one was saying.

"I'm glad we got this settled, Don Castellano," Charon said. "This need not go any further. I appreciate your efforts and will speak to the proper authorities about your cooperation."

"Thanks."

As Charon left, Castellano was thinking, "Fuck you, you asshole son-of-a-bitch. I know you're going to double-cross me. I ain't backing out now."

Castellano had tried, through numerous corrupted government channels, to find out who the man and the woman in the picture were, and why they were wanted. He had gotten zip. Charon was no entry-level flunkie. His eagerness in finding the couple made Castellano sure they'd be a worthwhile bargaining chip.

Now that fucking gray-suited son-of-a-*puta* was trying to ace him out, Castellano decided. After costing him four good men. Including his godson and top attorney. Castellano resolved to double his efforts. If he could get his hands on those two, he could write his own ticket. A Get-Out-of-Jail-Free card.

CHAPTER
28

With the accelerator to the floor, Stark chewed away at the miles to his hideaway. He rode Interstate 10 west through the bloat of the Los Angeles megapolis. In Ontario, he switched to I-15 heading north, and after ten minutes, the number of houses cluttering the landscape began to lessen.

He lowered the windows, letting the hot, dry desert air blow across his face. Every now and then the smell of horses reached his nostrils. The road was traveled by leathery westerners in pickups, flashy urbanites on their way to Las Vegas, and truckers trying to make time between major cities.

He tuned the radio to the Barstow local station. It played country-and-western music, which was appropriate with all the cactus and scrub brush around. Barstow was just 130 miles east of Bakersfield, the West's country-and-western capital. Shucks, it was even the birthplace of Merle Haggard.

As a song about yet another love gone bad came on, he thought about Sultana. Her value system, her frame of reference, had been shot out from underneath her. She was brave. Bright. Beautiful. He realized that it wasn't just concern over the conspiracy she uncovered that made him obsessed with the case.

The folksy newscaster was talking about weather conditions. A heat wave was rolling across the area. Which was about as welcome as a cold snap in Antarctica. The National Weather Service was predicting it would last a week.

"Here's one out of Daggett," the announcer said, and Stark raised the volume on the radio. "There was a shoot 'em up there this morning. The sheriff says it was just a bunch of plinkers had too many beers too early; but we hear a house on the edge of town was turned into the O.K. Corral."

Stark pressed harder on the accelerator.

In the parking lot of a bar on the outskirts of Barstow, he spotted a light-colored, four-wheel drive vehicle. It took him less than a minute to open it up. He transferred his belongings to the Ford Blazer and drove off.

He passed by his house without stopping. A San Bernardino County sheriff's black-and-white was parked off to one side, partially hidden by the trees. He might have missed it if he had raced up the driveway.

He continued a half mile up the dirt road. He parked the Blazer between a low hill and a clump of Joshua trees. It would be difficult to spot from anything more than fifty feet. Using an arroyo to stay out of sight, he made his way cautiously toward the house. His eyes were just above ground level as he moved in the gully in a half crouch.

He had explored the area surrounding his property for several miles. That, coupled with training he had received while on liaison assignment with Israel's Mossad, made him unafraid of the desert.

But how long could Sultana last? There had been no news of her. Of course the authorities could be hushing it up. But he was convinced she was alive and refused to consider that it could be just wishful thinking on his part.

He crawled across a stretch of ground on his belly, sand and pebbles scraping him. He had to cross in that spot. It was the only place he had gapped the sensors wide enough so he could sneak in or out if need be.

The lone cop got out of the squad car, walked to a tree, and urinated. Stark kept crawling. He reached the side of the house furthest from the sheriff's car and peered in through a window. Empty. He pried open the window and climbed in. There were a dozen bullet holes on the walls and in the floor. A forensic technician had circled them in red.

White chalk marks outlined a faint stain on the floor. Dried blood. The flecks led toward the kitchen counter, then stopped.

He sat in the middle of the floor and tried to visualize it exactly as it had been that morning. He could feel Sultana's presence. He studied the sink, the cabinets, the counters.

The towel. It was missing from the handle of the hook where it always hung. A cop could've taken it to wipe his face, but Stark doubted it. The San Bernardino sheriff had a reputation for professionalism, and keeping a crime scene intact was basic to good police work.

Someone had been bleeding and taken the towel. He retraced the steps. Then what? He scanned the small house.

His camping gear had been disturbed. He went through it. What was missing? The topographic map. He took it as a sign she was alive. He let out his breath.

He went over the house like a white-gloved drill sergeant out to give his boot camp recruits a hard time. He found droplets of blood on the bedroom window sill.

Okay, she grabbed the map and took off out the back window. Whoever had been there had probably been where the cop was now. It limited the number of directions she could've taken.

What had he told her during their discussion of the area? Could she have remembered what he had said about the desert? He thought of the depth in her gray green eyes.

He grabbed supplies—a compass, two pairs of sunglasses, a survival knife, a bag of pretzels, a tan sheet—and stuffed them in a knapsack. He took a few apples. He wasn't sure, but it seemed like a couple were missing.

Stark filled a five-quart, prospector-style canteen, and grabbed his Japanese parasol. He climbed back out the window, careful to keep the house between him and the cop.

He headed in the direction that made the most sense. Southwest. He had told her of the dangers in other directions, the vast tracks of unbroken, scorched landscape known as the Devil's Playground; jagged mountains, pushed upward by the volcanos and shifting of the continental and Pacific plates; and the military bases and testing ranges.

Barstow, the nearest city, would be watched. Her only hope was Victorville, about thirty miles southwest. If she made it there, she could hitch a ride anywhere.

He wished he could've taken the four-wheel-drive vehicle with him, but he knew even the most rugged jeep couldn't hold up. The ground was split by deep, unfordable arroyos and wadis.

When he was over a ridge away from the sheriff's car, he opened the parasol. He draped the sheet around himself like an Arab's robe. The sunglasses protected his eyes, but the heat shimmered off the ground, blurring his vision. The soles of his feet felt singed.

He made sure to drink a pint of water and eat a pretzel for every two miles covered. Thirst was not a safe indicator of the body's need for water in the desert. Heat exhaustion could creep up on a traveler, leading to confusion, irrational behavior, nausea, headache. Heat stroke had the same symptoms, only worse, as well as seizures and death. The pretzels kept his salt level balanced.

He was alone with low hills and hot sand. There were clumps of yellow-green creosote brush, and an occasional Joshua tree. In the distance, he could see the mountains, their image quivering as heat waves bounced off the sand.

How far could an untrained, unequipped, wounded woman get? And there were Manson-type freaks living there, who had come to bake what remained of their brains in the desert.

"Sultana! Sultana!" he yelled. At times his voice echoed off low hills. Other times it too died in the hot, still air. He felt small, insignificant, as out of place in the vast expanse of hostile environment as a shipwreck survivor bobbing in the midst of the ocean.

Stark had traveled about eight miles. Even considering that Sultana had been fleeing before the sun had a chance to warm up, this was near the limits of endurance.

Could he have missed her? The Mojave desert was fifteen thousand square miles. Ridges and arroyos could hide someone just a few yards away. He could have passed right by her.

He thought of his training in the Negev, the unforgiving brutality of the desert. With a gallon of water, traveling at night, expect to go no more than twenty miles. During the day, half that. Remember to keep drinking, even if you aren't that thirsty. At temperatures above ninety degrees Farenheit, more than a twelve percent dehydration weight loss was dangerous.

He kept telling himself "just one more ridge, one more hill." How long would he keep looking? Just one more ridge, one more hill. He scanned the sky for buzzards and crows, scavengers that could enjoy an aerial view.

He saw a flock circling to the east and hurried in that direction, dreading what he would find. He saw the birds descending and increased his pace. There was a swarm of them over a shape on the sand.

He bellowed "shoo" and ran toward the still figure. The birds reluctantly gave up their prize.

It was a dead burro, body half picked by the birds. Stark took a gulp of water, checked the compass, and got back on track. The birds returned to their meal.

He made a serpentine shape, a giant sidewinder, as he made his way across the desert. He saw no one. He heard nothing but his own labored breathing. The heat beat on him. He had to face it. She was probably dead.

He turned and looked back where he had come from. Bleak desert, as conducive to life as a hotplate. The walk back would be harder, knowing he had failed.

One more hill, it could be as much as a mile away. It was hard to gauge distance on the shimmering sands. Multiply distance estimates by three in the desert. The hill was a big one, a mini-mountain.

He'd call it quits there. On the way back, he'd try another route. Maybe he'd find her. He had to find her.

Dr. Sultana Mirnov lay wedged in the cave. It wasn't much of a cave—only two feet high and eight feet deep. It was a couple of feet wide at the opening, rapidly tapering down to a hole, which stretched off into blackness. Her face, near the mouth, felt like it was inches from a blast furnace. She had finished the apples she'd brought, chewing everything down to the seeds.

She slipped in and out of consciousness, and in and out of reality. A half-dozen times, she had seen Stark coming for her. Twice he'd been done up like Lawrence of Arabia, white robe flowing as he walked. Another time, he had been astride a stallion, galloping like a desert sheik to sweep her up in his arms.

210

If only she'd grabbed fluids. The thought of a sip of water made her move her parched, cracked lips, begging the empty air for fluid. *"Vah-dee, vah-dee,"* she repeated.

She closed her eyes and thought back to Vladivostock. The cold winters seemed inviting. She shivered. A snowball to suck on, cold and numbing. Her father punished her by washing her face in the snow. It hurt so much. Now she wished for it. Cold and wet, cold and wet.

She thought back to the lab and the way her slow plummet toward death had begun. If only she hadn't been curious. But she had to know. She always had to know. To know what?

She thought about the Zen stories she had read. What did it mean to know. Before studying Zen, a mountain was a mountain, a river a river. While studying Zen, a mountain was not a mountain, a river not a river. After enlightenment, a mountain was a mountain, a river was a river.

Could something change, or just an individual's perception of it? Did the pond know how it reflected the moon?

"Stop thinking this is mine, this is not mine," the Patriarch said. "Tell me, what was your face before you were born?"

She heard a scraping noise.

She nearly screamed. A rattlesnake had crawled into the mouth of the cave. It sensed her, an intruder in its shady haven, and raised its head. Tongue flicking, tail shaking.

The five-foot-long snake had retired to beat the heat of the day. It crawled forward. She pressed against the back wall of the cave.

She watched, breathless, as it advanced slowly, still sluggish from the heat. The nervous quivers of its tail subsided, and it dozed off.

Impossible to crawl past it without disturbing its slumber.

She shifted position, trying to get up on her hands and knees. The snake roused, gave a nervous rattle, then calmed as she froze in position.

If she could lie still long enough, the night-hunting reptile would crawl off in search of prey. Unless it sensed her mammalian body and decided she was prey.

She glanced around, moving only her eyes. There wasn't even a rock in the cave that she could bash its head in with. How many hours until dark?

She had an itch by the nape of her neck. It felt like an insect burrowing into her. A scorpion? A spider? Another snake? Afraid to move in the cramped space, there was no way to get relief.

The snake dozed fitfully, eyes hooded, head bulged by the pits for the venom sacs.

She played with formulas in her mind, envisioning double helixes, endoplasmic reticulum, mycotoxin compounds. What she had seen and heard in Russia came back to her, startlingly clear. As well as her experiences in the United States. It was, she imagined, similar to one's life flashing before one's eyes.

The rattlesnake rested.

She looked out at the desert. Because of the twist in the small cave, she could barely see through the mouth of the cave.

A figure was coming closer. Stark! But her mind had boiled over. He carried an umbrella, a sheet draped over his head and body. She enjoyed the silly-looking illusion, watching it come closer. Then she closed her eyes to erase it, and reopened them.

Still there. She blinked again.

The mirage was closer. She inhaled deeply, to shout as best she could with the dry throat.

As she moved, the snake awoke. It swayed its head from side to side and shook its rattles, angrily seeking the one who had disturbed it.

Stark walked toward the hill. She couldn't move. She prayed that he would climb up and look into the hole.

With a flash of horror, she realized that from the desert floor, the mouth of the cave was blocked by several large rocks and she was too far back in the cave for him to ever see her.

She watched helplessly as Stark came closer. He was walking off now, nearly out of her view.

She concentrated on him.

"Look over here, look over here," she kept thinking. "Look over here. Look over here. Look over here. Look over here." If she had any extra fluids left in her, tears of frustration would've run down her face.

She thought of a deadly way to attract his attention.

* * *

Pushing onward was foolish, Stark decided. No one could have made it further. He turned and started back, angling over a few hundred feet to cover new ground.

Her eyes had been so full of life and fun and promise. Were they staring now at a scorching sky while crows picked at her bones?

One more hill. He'd climb to the top and see what was on the horizon.

He clambered up the hillside. A couple of times he had to grab rock as sand and shale slid under him. The rock burned his hand.

The hill was weathered in spots, with cracks and crevices from baking and erosion. He peered into a shaded gap. It was cooler, maybe only in the high eighties inside.

He skiddled along the side of the hill, peering into cracks. He was about to give up when he heard the rattle. He thought he had disturbed a snake. But the rattle was coming from further up the hill. It could just be a couple of rattlesnakes having a territorial dispute. But maybe . . .

He found her. She didn't move, didn't say a thing, staring at him. Between them was the coiled, venomous creature.

She had deliberately riled it, hoping that the rattle would be loud enough to attract Stark. She had taunted it, getting it mad enough to make noise, but not mad enough to strike.

But when she saw Stark coming, she had moved. Now the snake was getting ready to lunge. He couldn't shoot it. The bullet could easily ricochet inside the small, rocky place.

"Lie absolutely still," he said. Her terror was building as she realized a confrontation was imminent. "Close your eyes," he said. "Relax every muscle."

He stepped back, deliberately scraping his boot on the ground, and the snake turned. He set down his pack and parasol. The full heat hit him.

The snake watched his slow movements, its rattles getting louder and louder. He was just out of striking distance. He took the parasol in his left hand, the knife in his right.

He repeated soothing words to Sultana. Her eyes were shut. The snake edged toward him.

Stark stepped back. The snake advanced. Its tongue flicked, sensing the heat, feeling the presence of the intruder.

Stark shoved the umbrella forward.

The snake lunged, sinking its fangs into the fabric. Stark

swooshed the knife through the air, decapitating it. The fangs continued to pump venom. The milky poison dripped down the parasol. The body thrashed. Sultana screamed.

Stark dropped the parasol, grabbed the thrashing body, and threw it down the hill.

He reached into the crevice and took her in his arms. She pressed her face against him and sobbed.

CHAPTER
29

"Stark wants money," MacMillan said over the scrambled line to Hornaday. "A quarter million. Delivered by your man Charon."

"I'll arrange it."

"I don't care about the money. If Stark doesn't live to spend it, Charon can keep it. Or you."

Hornaday was silent.

"I'm going to be heading down south soon, to oversee the facility."

"What facility?"

"The plant. It's near Mazatlán. You should come down and see it."

"Some day."

"Soon."

MacMillan hung up and bounded upstairs to his father's room.

"Dad, Dad, Dad," Benedict MacMillan said, his hand running along his father's cheek. "It's so wonderful to call you that. You know what I would've loved? If you would've called me Benny. No one ever called me Benny."

Benedict MacMillan stood up from his father's bed. "But enough of that. It's the amphetamines. I haven't been getting much sleep. There's too much to do. The best never rest you always said. Nice thing about the amphetamines. I'm

215

stronger than ever. I did five hundred push-ups yesterday on the plane. No sweat." Benedict rolled up his shirt-sleeve and flexed his muscles. "Look at those biceps. Oh, I'm sorry, here you are sick and I'm showing how healthy I am. But I owe it to you, Dad. You made me what I am.

"I'm doing this for you. It's great having unlimited funds. Like, look what we did here," Benedict said, his hand gesturing to take in the room.

It had cost nearly two million dollars to set up the sound-proof, filtered, room-inside-a-room. It was stainless steel, sterile, outfitted with high-tech monitors, oxygen equipment, a hospital bed. Cabinets held the latest medical gear, as well as fundamentals like bedpans and clean sheets.

A doctor and four nurses, all with impeccable credentials, slept on twenty-four-hour call in adjacent bedrooms. The doctor, who examined Calvin MacMillan every couple of hours, had advised Benedict that his father would be better off in a hospital. MacMillan had told him to shut up and do his job. The doctor was getting so much money that he did.

A nurse sat by Calvin's bedside at all times, except when Benedict was in with him.

"That flea Stark that was snooping around, I bought him off," Benedict said. "I just got off the phone with Hornaday. A worker of his will handle the delivery. A quarter of a million, he wanted. Actually, I don't think he'll live to enjoy it." Benedict stopped himself in the middle of a long laugh. "I remember when I was a kid, one of the first lessons you taught me. Every man has his price. Remember? There was that idealistic senator who was against your offshore drilling. I really believed he'd stand up to you. But he buckled under. You never did tell me how you got to him. Oh, I wish we could talk.

"Dad, I have some bad news," Benedict said, shifting gears suddenly. "Yuri Zabotin died in New York a few days ago. He was hit by a car. I was too busy to go, but I sent a thousand dollars worth of flowers to his funeral. I thought you'd be pleased.

"It's falling into place. The data's come in. Crenshaw's setting up the plant in South America. I've got good news. We'll be ready to run a test real soon. If it goes well, the project will go into effect even sooner than we planned. The

Russian idea was brilliant. Let me tell you about it." He sat on the bed again and lowered his voice conspiratorially.

"There's a thing called bacteriophage. Phage for short. It's a virus that preys on bacteria. But when it attacks the bacteria, it makes it more virulent. Like you take a harmless strain of diphtheria, sic the phage on it, and it becomes lethal.

"The phage also kills the bacteria after a twenty-four hour period. It's limited, you don't have to worry about spreading a plague. It's easy to handle, has long shelf life, and can be disseminated by air. The bacteria it reacts with is a streptococcus, which is found just about everywhere.

"Here's something I know you'll be happy about. Death is quick and painless. Aren't you pleased? Oh, I wish we could talk. I love you, Dad. I know now you love me, too."

From the moment he'd gotten the stroke, Calvin MacMillan had been able to do nothing but watch. He had created two monsters. First, there was his plan to bluff the governments at high-stakes poker. The ultimate high stakes. Then, there was his son.

MacMillan prayed for his son to die, for the plan to fail. It was all he thought about. His frustration burned inward. He willed himself to die. Even at that, he failed. He had no control, even over his own body.

Now, as his son rattled on and on, the horror again overwhelmed MacMillan. He felt a shooting pain race through his left arm.

The pain worsened. A tight band across his chest, getting tighter.

Please, don't let it show on the monitor, don't let them get to me in time, he silently begged.

Benedict heard the high-pitched beep, then a sound like a muted siren. The doctor and two nurses raced in.

"What's happening?" Benedict demanded.

"Infarction. Heart attack. Get the defibrillator," the doctor barked, though one of the nurses was already rushing the crash cart in.

"Save him, save him," Benedict shouted.

The defibrillator didn't help.

217

"A hundred milligrams lidocaine! I.V. push," the doctor said.

A nurse had anticipated him and was prepared to pump the antiarrhythmic into his system. The doctor climbed on the bed, straddled Calvin and did chest compressions.

A nurse put an ambu bag over MacMillan's nose and mouth and pushed oxygen into his lungs. The medical trio worked with feverish intensity.

After fifteen minutes, the doctor stopped. "He's dead," he pronounced. "I'm sorry."

Benedict MacMillan nodded and walked from the room without another word. He went to his bedroom and took the Uzi out of its canvas carrying case. He screwed an eight-inch-long silencer onto the end.

He returned to the room, where a nurse was putting the sheet over Calvin MacMillan's face. The other nurse was the first to see the gun. She screamed. The doctor grabbed the gun, and tried to wrestle it from MacMillan's hand.

MacMillan smashed him, a crashing blow that sent him flying across the room. The doctor fell in the corner.

Benedict sprayed him with the Uzi. One nurse stood frozen. He shot her. The second ran for the door. He killed her too. MacMillan took out the empty clip and put in a fresh one.

The two other nurses were still sleeping in a bedroom at the end of the hall. They hadn't heard the slaughter by Calvin's deathbed. MacMillan opened the door to the room, the gun held behind his back.

One of the nurses groggily raised herself up on the bed. The slut probably figured he was there to make a pass at her, that he was holding flowers behind his back. "You miserable failures," he growled.

"Huh?"

The second nurse blinked her eyes open.

"He's dead," MacMillan said. He opened fire with the Uzi.

On his way downstairs, he shot and killed the butler and maid. They wouldn't understand what had happened, the kind of petty people who'd run to the authorities, interfere with his plans.

The servants had been with his father for as long as

Benedict could remember. As he gazed at their lifeless forms he thought about times they had reprimanded him.

"Who got the last laugh?" he muttered.

It had long been a tradition when the king died for his retainers to be sacrificed with him. The king was dead. Long live the king.

He snapped out of his reverie. The only person who had died was his father. Half of the medical staff, and the servants, were staring at him.

"Are you all right?" the doctor asked. "Perhaps you'd like a sedative?"

"No. You're all dismissed. Your checks will be mailed. Get off my property."

He strutted to his bedroom and called his pilot. "We're leaving for Mexico. I want the plane ready immediately."

"Yes sir."

"I'll be at the airport in a half hour." He hung up and packed his suitcase, muttering continuously under his breath.

His father would never get to see the outcome of his glorious project. Our project, Benedict thought. No, now it's my project.

CHAPTER
30

Spike Ramsey disliked his passenger from the moment he saw the man walking on the tarmac. He had seen that kind in 'Nam. Spooks. Ghoulies. They came along to play mind games, and death games, with the VC.

Ramsey didn't mind killing gooks. He hated them. They hated him. That was what war was about. But the CIA men who came along on covert ops, they got under his skin. Human scabies. They were stone cold. They didn't care about the VC. They didn't care about the Americans either. They came in, played their games, and withdrew.

Sometimes it was psy ops, dropping weird things on VC loyal villages, like rubber bats or fake blood. Sometimes it meant taking suspected North Vietnamese spies up a few thousand feet, interrogating them, and sending them down the quick way. Sometimes it was transporting a half-dozen Meo tribesmen—who had freshly bloodied human ears on a string around their neck—from a hot LZ in VC territory.

Ramsey had spent several lifetimes in Vietnam. 307th Combat Aviation Battalion. It was his commander who had coined the slogan "search and destroy." He had planned to leave after his latest tour. But there just didn't seem to be anyplace else to go. He knew he'd probably re-enlist.

The spook got into the Black Hawk, ducking his head only slightly as he came under the whirring big blade. The spook was wearing dark aviator glasses, even though it was twilight. Ramsey wondered if they gave out those glasses at CIA graduation.

Of course he hadn't been told the man was CIA. Just a "civilian observer" along to watch the training exercise. Why would a civilian observer be on such a bullshit exercise? Search the desert at night for a mock Arab encampment.

Ramsey presumed there was something else involved. Maybe they were going to pick up Somoza's bodyguards in the Mojave. Or retrieve a gold cache for a corrupt South Vietnamese general. He wouldn't put anything past those CIA motherfuckers.

"Welcome aboard," he said, giving the spook his best smile. In a synthetic pilot voice he announced, "Army Airlines flight 102 will be leaving shortly."

The spook didn't smile, shake hands, or give his name. A confirmed asshole. Ramsey turned his back and began adjusting the controls, getting the engine up to speed. Unlike the light plane he flew for pleasure on weekends, the chopper was an unstable platform, constantly capable of plunging to earth. He checked the torque on the tail rotor, the autothrottle, and the collective control.

The Black Hawk was replacing the Huey, and he missed the heavy hogs. But flying the Black Hawk was still a novel enough experience, and a challenge. He could almost get the passenger out of his mind.

He made radio contact with the five other helos in his squadron, established a band for general communication and emergency, and arranged for takeoff.

The confirmed asshole sat behind Ramsey, in the gunner's seat, looking over his shoulder out the window. Ramsey deliberately made a sudden, rough takeoff. The passenger kept his balance, and his unreadable expression.

Charon removed his dark glasses as they reached cruising altitude. The humming roar of the helicopter brought back many memories. The players seemed familiar. The Okie copter pilot, probably barely literate, but able to make the chopper do everything but hum "The Star-spangled Banner." His two crew members, observer/copilot, crew chief, obedient, relying on his abilities, knowing their lives de-

221

pended on him. The weapons pods on the side—eight Hell-fire missiles, 40mm grenade launchers, a couple of Side-winder missiles.

But it was the two thousand pounds of electronic gear Charon was counting on this night. And out there in the night, five other similarly equipped Black Hawks, swooping over the desert like devil bats.

The chopper pilot followed the course Charon had given to the army general. The general had wanted to know what it was about. Charon had fended him off with the ever reliable words, "national security."

They passed over the freeway, where head- and taillights made steady streams of white and red. The helicopters were silenced, and with the traffic noise, barely audible. They flew in "flight regime," the tight formation used in darkness that demands skillful communication, handling, and direction.

Then they were over Stark's Daggett house, and they began moving in big lazy spirals, covering larger and larger areas.

"You have ARGUS?" Charon asked.

Ramsey nodded. ARGUS stood for Aerial Reconnaissance, Ground Unit Support, a sophisticated detection system that worked on a variety of sound and light frequencies, including subsonic and infrared.

"Why don't you use it?"

"Too early. Different rocks and things heat up different during the day," Ramsey said. "You can't much tell anything until things cool off."

"Turn it on anyway."

The copilot looked at Ramsey. The pilot gave a "I'd-love-to-rip-his-heart-out, but-orders-is-orders grin," and nodded. The copilot switched on a six-inch TV at the front of the cockpit. The black-and-white monitor showed the ground. Black objects were the hottest—white the coolest. A computer-linked display console lit up with a confusing array of colors.

They passed over a man outside a small store getting into his pickup. The man and the front of the car were black forms. The middle of the pickup was white, with a black cloud near the exhaust pipe.

"Let's go up higher," Charon said. "And tell the others to turn on their monitors."

Ramsey did as he was told. The grin was locked on his face. The copilot knew there'd be some hard drinking after the mission.

All day Stark nursed Sultana. Gently pouring sips of water down her parched throat, wiping her brow, breaking bits of fruit into pieces that she could chew. Her lips were cracked and dry.

Her feet were badly blistered. Her thin-soled shoes were not meant for desert wear. The wound on her arm was superficial, but blood loss coupled with dehydration had weakened her. It was impossible to tell if she had a fever. Everything was so hot there was no valid frame of reference. After a few hours she stopped slipping in and out of consciousness and no longer mumbled to herself.

He had set his sheet up as a shade over the little burrow. He couldn't quite fit in next to her. Periodically, he had to get up and walk around. For a while, he sat in the shade of a nearby crevice.

When he returned, she was awake, and her eyes were clear.

"*Bolshoye spasibo*. I mean, thank you very much."

"My pleasure. Quite a stroll you took. Can you tell me what happened at the house?"

"The alarm went off. Four hooligans. I got gun and shot one. It was first time I ever kill a man." She shivered. Her words came out breathlessly, and she was weak after each sentence. He gave her a sip of water. Although he had only taken a couple of sips himself, their supply was nearly gone.

"Someone else shot one of them. Then lots of shots. I hit by glass. I escape. This looked like shortest, safest way." She pointed to her route on the topographic map. "I use map to protect my head from sun. But it was too hot."

"We'll travel tonight," he said. "You just rest now."

"But I remembered things." Despite her enthusiasm, her voice had grown weaker. "About Russia."

"You won't forget. Relax, get your strength back."

Within seconds, she was asleep.

She awoke again as the sun was setting. The yellow turned

to orange, and long shadows spread from the rocks and sparse trees on the desert floor. And the heat began to lessen.

She asked for more water, but he withheld it.

"There's only about a cup left. You can have a swig after a mile, the rest two miles after that."

"Any food?"

He took out an orange and gave her half.

"What about you?" she asked.

"I can hold off." He put the other half back in the bag. His stomach grumbled, seeming to echo off the walls of their little cave.

"You're hungry," she said, offering him some of her orange.

He pushed her hand back. "Finish, and let's head out."

It was painful for her to put any weight on her feet. She leaned heavily on him as they made their way across the desert. There was a full moon, and they could see clearly on the bleak landscape.

Several times they heard coyotes howl and sounds of animals prowling in the darkness. As the floor cooled, air whipped across the surface, chilling and stinging them with sand.

Stark took off his shirt and wrapped it around the shivering doctor. She was too weak to refuse.

It took them an hour and a half to go a mile, walking on flat ground. Sultana was exhausted, heaving. They leaned against a tree and took a fifteen-minute break. He gave her the water. His throat was so dry, he could barely speak.

She got a second wind, and they made the next two miles in as many hours. She insisted he take some of the water during their next fifteen-minute rest break.

"If you pass out, I cannot carry you," she said. "If you do not drink it, I will not either."

He took the canteen and let a few wonderful droplets trickle down his throat.

He handed it back, and she finished it.

"We go now," she said, and they did.

They had traveled five miles when he stopped suddenly.

"Is something the matter?" she asked.

He motioned for her to be silent, and listened carefully. He scanned the sky, and then the landscape.

"Quick, over there." He just about carried her until they were underneath a Joshua tree. The branches and scant foliage provided little cover.

"What is it?" she asked.

Before he could answer, the six ominous shapes came over a ridge.

"You think they look for us?" she asked.

He watched the helicopters divide an area up, and then slowly sweep back and forth. Periodically, one would turn on a Xenon light, and a cone of white as bright as the sun would light up the desert floor.

"They do not use visible spectrum of lights most of time," Mirnov said. "Must be some other sensor."

"Infrared," Stark said. He began digging in the soft sand like a dog about to bury a bone. Dirt kept caving in. Finally, he had an indentation about three feet deep.

"Get in," he told her.

When she did, legs against her chest, he shoved the sand back down so only her head stuck out above the surface. He set the parasol up to cover her head.

The choppers were nearly overhead. Even with their silenced engines, the slap-slapping of the blades in the air was overwhelming. The blades stirred up dust devils on the desert floor.

He burrowed frantically and dove in. Stuck in a fetal position, he wiggled a little, until the sand around him collapsed and covered him.

The choppers were nearly overhead. He hoped the sand could conceal them and muffle their body heat. If not, the Browning in his bag—which was buried next to him—would be his only defense against six helicopters and their crews.

Charon had moved to the helicopter's door, and was scanning the desert floor with a high-tech Night Scope, a piece of equipment Ramsey knew was still classified.

Civilian observer, my ass, he thought. When Charon wasn't looking, he turned down the gain on the infrared scanner up front and gave his copilot a wink. Bullshit night exercise wasn't worth a damn anyhow.

He shifted the joystick suddenly, nearly dumping Charon out the door. If the CIA man hadn't had a tight grip on the gunner's seat he would've been dropped to the desert floor.

Charon turned to smile at Ramsey. Ramsey was sure that smile was the last thing many men had seen. He kept the helicopter on an even keel and continued to fly. He couldn't wait to get to the bar.

Charon kept the smile on his face. He wanted to go over and rip the Okie son-of-a-bitch's throat out. He knew that maneuver had been deliberate. The pilot was a typical cowboy, the kind who'd run you off the road in the woods if he didn't like your license plate. The bastard had tried to frag him. Charon would have to be careful.

He strapped himself into the seat and resumed scanning.

The dust devil swirled over Stark, tugging at his hair and abrading his face like a sandblaster going at a sooty wall. He held his breath as sand clogged his nostrils, scraped his eyelids, coated his lips.

The sand covering his body began to be sucked away. The tops of his shoulders were just about clear. He could hold his breath no longer. He began exhaling, blowing the particles away from his nose.

The dust devil moved on. He inhaled a deep lungful of clean night air. Cold and fresh.

He gazed over at Sultana. The umbrella had been swirled away, and the top of her head was clearly visible. The helicopters were sweeping the ground barely twenty feet away. As long as they continued on their path . . .

The light caught a dozen furtive shapes.

Coyotes. They were staring at Stark and Sultana's heads, wondering what strange sort of food it was. They would never attack a full-grown man. But the scrawny, hungry beasts might take a bite of a head. It was about the size of a plump jackrabbit, their main food.

Stark could do nothing as the pack came in closer. If he scared them away, the observers in the copters above might notice and re-examine the area.

"You see that down there," the copilot said to Ramsey over the radio, so Charon couldn't hear.

"Looks like a fuckin' umbrella. Them coyohts sure is interested in it."

226

"Wanna go in closer?"

Ramsey looked back at Charon. "Fuck no. Scraggly little mothas, ain't they?"

"Sure are."

"Let's put 'em out of their misery."

The copilot activated the 7.62mm M60C flexibly mounted machine guns on either side of the copter.

"How wide a spread you want?" the copilot asked.

"Suit yourself."

"Fire when ready," the copilot said, making a final adjustment through the reflex sight.

Ramsey squeezed the pistol grip control. The copter shook and there was a howling, spitting sound.

Charon, who had flown on combat missions in Vietnam, knew what it meant. He ran to the front of the copter, fearful that his quarry had been killed. He grabbed the pilot's shoulder.

"What did you do?" he growled.

"Killed a few coyohts is all," Ramsey answered coldly.

Charon peered down at the ground. The copilot had focused the spread in tight. There was no way to tell what had been shot. There were just pieces of red meat scattered on the ground.

"If our targets were around here, they're gone now," Charon said. "Move on."

"Whatever you say, boss," Ramsey said in an exaggerated black accent.

The bullets had come much closer to Sultana than to Stark, within two feet of her body.

She had a dazed expression, but no signs of fear. She was beyond that now. What she had been through would catch up with her later.

As the copters moved off, Stark helped her out of the hole, and retrieved his pack.

She draped an arm over his shoulder. The combination of rest and adrenaline from their near slaughter helped her press on with renewed energy.

They reached his Ford Blazer while it was still dark. He circled the vehicle for ten minutes before approaching it, making sure no one was waiting for them. Then he spent another ten minutes checking it for booby traps or alarms. Apparently it had not been discovered.

"We'll have to drive a ways," Stark said. "They've probably got every motel in the area staked out."

But Sultana didn't care. She was already asleep.

CHAPTER
31

Stark stole a late-model Pontiac station wagon, very All-American family looking, with wooden panels on the side and a roof rack on top. In back, under a light blanket, he concealed Sultana Mirnov.

He stopped at a large drugstore—bought Betadine, sterile wipes, aspirin, and bottled water—and cleaned up her arm wound and her feet as best as he could.

Sultana thrashed around in the back of the station wagon. He pulled into a roadside rest stop and brushed her fevered brow with the alcohol. He wondered about brain damage from a high temperature, kidney damage from lack of water, infection from the wound.

He went to the pay phone and called his assistant, Pedro Quesada. They spoke in Spanish.

"Pedro, know who this is?" Stark asked.

"Of course."

"You know that big picture you helped me carry to my apartment?"

"Yeah. That picture of a pretty lady."

"Right. Well, I broke the frame. I know Carmen's good with that sort of thing. Do you think she'd be willing to look at the picture?"

"Of course."

Quesada's wife was a registered nurse who worked in the

emergency room at County-USC Medical Center, one of the largest and busiest facilities in the country.

"Do you have any company?"

"Haven't had any today," Quesada answered, and Stark knew he was not under surveillance. "Carmen isn't due to leave for several hours."

"Do you want to check with her?"

"Carmen will do it. Hurry over."

Pedro lived in a single-story orange stucco house in East Los Angeles, the Mexican barrio. His home was well kept, with yuccas growing all around, and a six-foot chain-link fence enclosing a neatly trimmed lawn. Like Stark, he had spent several thousand dollars on an alarm system.

Stark drove right into the garage. The door shut behind him. The inside door to the house opened and Pedro stepped forward, followed by his wife. Pedro was carrying his Ingram machine pistol.

Carmen, a petite woman with a deferential manner and a steel core, nodded to Stark and rushed right to the patient. She lifted Sultana surprisingly easily and carried her into the house before the men could say or do anything.

"You look like hell," Pedro said to his boss. "Go in and get some sleep. Two of my cousins are coming by. They are brave men. We will watch over you and your lady."

"I've got errands to run. We'll be out of your hair as soon as possible."

"You stay as long as you like. You are safe here."

Stark nodded and slapped Pedro's shoulder.

At a bank of pay phones in a downtown Los Angeles office building, Stark called Halliwell in New York.

"This is Adam Dawson, remember me?" Stark asked in a husky voice.

"Sure, the Secret Service Academy. It's been years, hasn't it?"

"I'd say twenty if it was a day. I hear you got a business going that gives retired cops a way to make money."

"Things are slow right now, but I'm always looking for good men. You can make anywhere from twenty to thirty thousand your first year. By your third year, guaranteed fifty."

"Sounds fair. When do I give you a call?"

"In a week, I should know better. Say, Thursday afternoon?"

"I'll speak to you then."

Stark hung up. Early on in their relationship, he and Halliwell had worked out a plain language code, designed to be used if they suspected someone was listening in.

What they had just arranged was to call prearranged pay phone numbers at a given time. The phone booth was two miles from Halliwell's house. He was supposed to be waiting there in fifty minutes.

Stark headed to the garment district at the other side of downtown. There were signs in Spanish, Arabic, Chinese, Vietnamese, Japanese, and even English. Mannequins in front of stores grinned at him insincerely. Sweating youths humped carts of clothing onto trucks. From second-floor windows the hum of sewing machines could be heard.

Every style was available, from custom designed high fashion to cheesy Hong Kong knockoffs that wouldn't survive their first washing. Stark shopped for clothes and accessories that would help Sultana and him disguise themselves.

At the appointed time, he called the pay phone booth in New York. Halliwell answered on the second ring.

"I've been waiting for you to call," Les said. "A couple of the operatives damn near slit my throat when they thought I'd backed out on you."

"Sorry. But don't tell anyone we're still partners," Stark said. "File papers to get rid of me. While you're at it, file suits against our clients who breached their contracts with us."

"You know what our legal bills are going to be?" Les asked. He sighed deeply. "I've arranged to bail out our people who got busted. The charges are bogus and the lawyers can clear them, but we're eating into our Christmas savings. Are you almost done ruining my life?"

Stark chuckled. "I need some very, very discrete reconnoitering in Washington. A man named Hobbs, high up. He appears to be involved. Also Calvin and Benedict MacMillan of ISS."

Stark convinced Les that it was indeed worth their time and trouble. Halliwell, complaining about the cost, grudgingly agreed to sniff around.

"I heard through the grapevine there's an outstanding warrant for you," the ex–Secret Serviceman said. "Mail fraud and unlawful flight to avoid prosecution. I tried getting information, but everything's sealed. Doesn't add up."

"What do you mean?"

"There's stuff planted here and there, but when my contacts look into it, there's nothing behind it."

"That's reassuring."

"But why did this bogus bull crop up all over? It didn't come through channels. It just seems to have floated down from Mount Olympus."

"Any idea from who on Mount Olympus?"

"No luck. No one covers their butt better than a bureaucrat. Do you know what this is all about?"

"Not yet."

She awoke in a strange bed, with a dark-haired woman wiping her down with a damp rag. She cried out. The door opened, and a stocky man with a drawn gun ran in.

"It's okay, Miguel," the woman tending Sultana said.

Miguel politely averted his eyes, and Sultana realized she was naked. She pulled the covers up over herself. Miguel glanced around the room, saw there was no danger, and stepped back outside.

Carmen introduced herself and told Sultana what had happened. "You looked half-dead when your boyfriend brought you here," Carmen said. "But all we needed to do was break that fever."

"Where's Robert?"

"He had to go out. But Pedro and his cousins are here. They get a chance to walk around the house with guns. It makes them feel like big men." Carmen shared a you-know-how-men-are smile with Sultana. "Would you like something to eat?"

"I'm starving."

Carmen helped Sultana get out of bed and get dressed. Sultana insisted on walking by herself into the kitchen. Her feet hurt, and her wounded arm throbbed, but otherwise, she felt good.

She recognized Pedro from the New York office and gave him a warm hello. Pedro was digging into a tostada.

He stood until Sultana was seated at the formica-topped

232

kitchen table. He refused to continue eating until Carmen had served her, and Sultana began her meal.

"You are lucky lady," Pedro said. "You had the best protector in the world. And now the best nurse."

He patted Carmen on the bottom. She gave him an annoyed look and busied herself around the kitchen.

"My boss, he is one in a million," Pedro said. "A man of courage. And honor."

"Like yourself," Sultana said.

"I try to be," Pedro said. "But no one can be like him. He will make some woman quite a catch."

"My husband wants Stark to settle down, have children," Carmen said.

"You saw the way he looked. He is getting too old to run around," Pedro said.

"What about you?" Carmen asked. "You have three sons and two daughters, and still you run around with him. Flying here, flying there. Coming back with big secrets. Sometimes with cuts and bullet holes."

"He needs me," Pedro said.

"How long have you known Robert?" Sultana asked, after interrupting their bickering by commenting how good the salsa was.

"Seven years. I would die for him."

"Maybe someday you will," Carmen said bitterly.

"How did you meet?" Sultana asked.

"I was a working as a truckdriver in Mexico City. There was an accident. I went to help the people. He was passing by and stopped to do the same. It was in a part of the city where gringos don't go, and certainly don't stop. I saw by the way he handled himself that he had *huevos*."

Carmen slammed a pot down in the sink. "You men are like bulls. You have to show off how tough you are, how brave, how strong. You know how many *cholos* I see every night in the ER?"

"I am not a gang punk," Pedro said indignantly.

"But you live by the same codes. Loyalty to the gang. Violence. Honor! It is the women who become widows, who take care of the children with no fathers."

"That is no way to talk in front of our guest," Pedro snapped.

Carmen returned to savagely scrubbing a pan.

*　*　*

Quesada didn't want them to leave. When they insisted, he wanted to come along. Only after Stark vowed to include him in any operations did Pedro allow their departure.

Stark and Mirnov drove to a motel at the eastern edge of Los Angeles. After assuring himself that the room was secure, Stark promptly lay down and fell asleep.

Mirnov sat by the bedside, the shotgun by her side. She watched him doze. His chest rose and fell slowly. She took his shoes and socks off and tucked him in.

She didn't know how to describe how she felt about him. It was an emotion she had never experienced. She could not imagine how she would cope without him.

After an hour, she climbed into bed and pulled him to her. He was wide awake instantly, saw what had happened, and relaxed.

"If we market this as an alarm clock, we'll be rich and famous," he said.

She pressed her fingers to his lips. He took her hand, and kissed his way up her arm, to her neck.

Her breath quickened. His hand traveled between her legs, and she ground her hips against it.

For a short while, there was no thought of anything.

They lay in bed afterward, communicating with silence.

"That was perfect," she said.

"Mmmmm."

"I think of the Zen story about the man trapped hanging on to a vine on the edge of a cliff. With a mouse nibbling vine. Tigers above and below him."

"He picks a strawberry, and it's delicious," Stark said.

She nodded.

He took her in his arms. "How about another strawberry?"

She watched him get dressed, and only reluctantly came out from under the covers and began pulling on her own clothing.

"Do you feel comfortable with the gun?" he asked.

She regarded him quizzically.

"After what happened at the house," he added.

"I did what had to be done."

He gave her a peck on the lips. "You're one tough broad, you know that?"

She grabbed him and drew him in for a deeper embrace. They separated reluctantly.

"What do we do now?" she asked.

CHAPTER
32

Benedict MacMillan's pilot, a silver-haired former 747 jockey with the melodious name of Hogan Stimson, made a perfect landing at the airport in Mazatlán.

"There'll be a runway at our plant soon enough," MacMillan said. "Until then, you and the great bird wait here."

Stimson nodded. The great bird? Benedict, always a strange one, had begun talking even weirder more recently. Sort of macho tough guy. And the glaze in his eye had gotten brighter. Stimson made it a point of staying out of Benedict's way.

Before he deplaned, MacMillan dressed in an Abercrombie and Fitch safari jacket and bush pants. He strapped a .45 automatic on his hip. To Stimson, the big man looked like a parody of the great white hunter. All that was missing was a pith helmet. But the look on Benedict MacMillan's face was nothing to laugh at.

MacMillan took his suitcase and the attaché case he had guarded and strode from the plane.

The lab was located in the Mexican state of Sinaloa, less than two hundred kilometers south of Mazatlán. That city provided an international airport for the many gringo tourists flying in and out.

The nearest city was San Pedro, a town of ruined haciendas, thatched homes and shanties, sleazy cantinas and particularly vicious gnats. It had been a pirate base at one point, and the harbor featured a view of the Tres Marias penal islands.

The lab was located on two hundred acres near the mouth of the Rio del Muerte, which flowed down from the jagged peaks of the Sierra Madre Oriental. The area, at the southern tip of Sinaloa province, was densely overgrown, a mangrove jungle in some parts. Marijuana was a major cash crop, and natives knew better than to snoop around other people's property.

The compound was ringed by a ribbon wire fence. When people saw the dozen *pistoleros* appear, they merely nodded and accepted the change. Perhaps they'd bring prosperity to the area.

On the property were two large Quonset huts. One was the living quarters, which lacked even the charm of a Marine Corps barracks. The lab was housed in the second hut, nearly invisible from the air, covered by banyan tree leaves and camouflage netting.

It was a completely self-contained, state-of-the-art microbiology facility. Better than a million dollars had been invested in the rusty-looking tin hut. Most of the money had gone for biological security. The windows on the lab were sealed, the air conditioning equipped with special double filters. A revolving door, with negative air pressure, protected the entrance. Only three of Jefe's men had permission to enter.

There was a heavy-duty generator, necessary to power the voltage-gobbling high-heat autoclave. A centrifuge, cages for the numerous white mice, oil immersion lens microscopes, work benches, refrigerator, tanks of oxygen and ether, as well as the basic scalpels, tweezers, clamps, and chemicals needed to run a lab.

Crenshaw had been working through the night, reproducing the results of the Russian study. The killer phage could only live for a few hours outside laboratory conditions.

The streptococci were kept in the refrigerator. They reproduced rapidly in the warm tropical air. For the phage, Crenshaw needed living bacteria.

Crenshaw had been aided by three of Jefe's men. None had a biological background, but one had been a machinist,

237

another a gunsmith. They were used to precision work. Since titrations and scrapings had to be accurately repeated over and over, their help was necessary.

Another one of the men had a metalworking background, mainly learned in prison. He was kept busy customizing the hundred fifty-five-gallon steel drums. Each drum had a cradle which supported an oversize metal Thermos. Around the Thermos was foam which served as both an insulator and cushion. The entire package was put inside the drum.

Why did he have to go ahead with this? What did MacMillan want it for?

The questions occasionally surfaced, but Crenshaw pushed them from his mind. He kept himself focused on his task.

He had found several mistakes in the Russian data, minor things, but alarming. Perhaps there were mistakes he was missing. He wished he had back-up, a support team to review his work. Then again, it was exciting to be out on the high wire. MacMillan had chosen him. The U.S. government was depending on him.

After this, it would be hard to go back to the routine. Perhaps MacMillan would have another special government project.

Crenshaw heard the hiss of the revolving door. He looked up as Benedict MacMillan strode in.

"How goes it?" MacMillan boomed.

"Very well, very well."

"How much do you have?"

"More than enough."

"How much is that?"

"Another day, and we'll have about two hundred million doses, depending on weather conditions," Crenshaw said with a grin. "It's simple repetitive work from here out. Anyone can do it."

"Excellent. It's time for a test."

"The mice die right on schedule."

"I was thinking of a more accurate test. A lab animal is not the same as a human."

Crenshaw looked at him in disbelief.

"You can't, you couldn't. I won't let you."

MacMillan smiled. "Just kidding, Doctor. C'mon outside, you need a breath of fresh air." MacMillan put his arm over

Crenshaw's shoulder and waved for the lab assistants to follow him outside.

Jefe and the rest of his men were standing at ease just outside the lab. They were a motley crew, but well disciplined. They ranged in age from early twenties to late fifties. Most were Hispanic, but there were three Anglos and two blacks.

Jefe saluted MacMillan, who returned the salute. The men snapped to attention.

"We are nearing the time," MacMillan said in his booming voice. "You will all be a part of history."

Crenshaw stood next to him, bobbing his head, wondering what he had gotten into. Standing in the compound in the heart of a Mexican jungle. Somehow, it all made much more sense when he was safe inside the lab.

". . . leaders will not listen. We will make them listen," MacMillan was saying. "The Communist oppressors will be brought to their knees . . ."

Crenshaw had missed a part of MacMillan's speech. What was the big man saying?

". . . right to the walls of the Kremlin." MacMillan lifted the attaché case and opened it. It looked empty. Only a careful inspection would reveal the secret compartment on top. He demonstrated the sprayer mechanism, depressing the microswitch built into the handle. There was water with red dye in the hidden container. The men jumped when they saw the crimson spray. MacMillan laughed.

"This is no exploding cigar or depilatory," MacMillan said. "Death to our enemies. Castro will fall."

The men broke ranks and cheered.

"Attention!" Jefe growled, and they returned to order. But Jefe was grinning broadly.

"What are you saying?" Crenshaw demanded of MacMillan.

"We are warriors," MacMillan shouted, raising his arms, fists clenched. "Some of you will go to major American cities. You will be given a harmless dose. But it will show our power."

"What the hell are you talking about?" Crenshaw demanded.

MacMillan pointed to him. "Dr. Crenshaw is a brilliant man. He has helped us greatly. But he is not a warrior."

The men grumbled.

"He doesn't understand. He wants us to give up. Do you want to give up?"

"No!" they shouted.

"The vote is in," MacMillan said to Crenshaw.

Crenshaw turned and walked toward the helicopter. Mac-Millan drew his .45.

"Crenshaw!"

Crenshaw turned back and saw the gun. His face was expressionless. He didn't believe it was happening.

"Thanks," MacMillan said, and blew the doctor's head off. "Quitters don't win. Winners don't quit." He turned to Jefe and his men. "We need volunteers to test this out on a village."

All the men stepped forward.

"I'm proud, very proud," MacMillan said sincerely.

CHAPTER
33

Pedro Quesada drove past the telephone booth meeting site. "Crab to Big Fish. No one," Quesada said, his voice crackly.

Stark drove to the far side of MacArthur Park. He sat in the car with Sultana.

"We can make out while we're waiting," he said, though he kept scanning the street.

She looked at him, momentarily taking him seriously.

"What happens if we are not successful?"

"At making out?"

"Please be serious."

"I go to New York and get a hold of MacMillan."

"What then?"

"I hang him out of a building until he cries uncle."

She couldn't tell if Stark was kidding.

Quesada had parked his car across and diagonally up the street from the phone booth. He'd bought a Coke and a couple of chili dogs from a street vendor—that was true courage in itself—and wandered over to a park bench twenty feet from the phone. He had a navy watch cap pulled low on his head and a long-sleeved T-shirt saying L.A. Raiders.

At the exact time, Stark dialed the number of the pay phone. He kept a list of over a hundred pay phone numbers around major cities. He knew to be careful not to keep using the same pay phone. A sloppy KGB agent, for example, had repeatedly used a pay phone near the Soviet Mission on East Sixty-seventh Street in New York. The FBI had bugged it and recorded unguarded conversations that led to three major cases.

Stark dialed the pay phone number from another pay phone. It was picked up before the second ring. "Hello, Charon."

"Stark? You want to talk?"

"Who told you that?"

"That's irrelevant. Where do we meet?"

"You know the routine," Stark said.

"Dry-cleaning time. I presume you won't just take my word I'm alone?"

"Hah! Your next stop will be the phone booth near the John Anson Ford Theatre. Know where that is?"

"Just off the Hollywood Freeway. In the Cahuenga Pass. Clever. That means radio transmission, if I'm wearing a long-distance transmitter, will be impaired. Cute."

"Shucks."

"You think you're smart. I know you're right around here. The traffic noise I'm hearing through the phone is the same as I'm hearing with my other ear. If I blanketed the area, I'd find you. I didn't think you'd be so stupid or I would have a search team with me."

"Touché."

"We'd probably find you in the park. I remember the operation you ran in Hibiya Park. That was clever, too."

Stark realized he had used a similar method of operation back during his CIA days in Tokyo. Charon must've studied the file carefully to remember it.

"I'll see you at the theater," Stark said, and hung up.

Round one had gone to Charon, Stark thought, as he waited for Pedro to check in. He couldn't allow himself to make mistakes.

"You look in turmoil," Sultana said, reaching over and stroking along his clenched jaw as he settled into the car seat next to her. She had waited in the vehicle, engine running, while he was on the phone. "Everything okay?"

"Fine. Charon's as sharp as ever. A most worthy adversary." The phrase came from an MI6 man he had chummed around with. You only improve yourself, whether at cricket or espionage, when faced with a most worthy adversary.

The walkie-talkie crackled. "Joker didn't seem to talk to anyone after your chat. No body contact. Drove away, heading north on Alvarado. Do you copy?"

"Roger, Crab. You know the next stop."

"Roger Wilco."

It seemed Charon wasn't wired. Unless he waited until he was in the car. Maybe he had swallowed a transmitter. Or was wearing a tap switch, a radio transmitter similar to a Morse code key, that he could signal a back-up team with.

Quesada watched with binoculars from a hill near the theater as Stark called the booth and sent Charon out to the Santa Monica pier.

After two hours of ping-ponging, Stark felt pretty confident he had handled Charon well.

"By the way, you can tell the Mex with the big arm he's doing a good job," Charon said, as he picked up the pay phone near the corner of Pico and Sepulveda. "He must've changed his shirt about a half-dozen times. And he's got quite a hat collection. I didn't notice him until about two meets ago."

Stark was silent.

"Let's get on with this, Stark. It's coming up on evening rush hour. I don't want to get stuck in traffic."

"Life is tough. American Airlines departure lounge. Buy a ticket for the flight to Las Vegas. Be at the phone bank nearest the men's room."

"Why the airport?" Sultana asked as they drove there.

"High transient population. Possibility of a quick escape to just about anywhere in the world. Lots of entrances and exits. He'll have to pass through a metal detector to get to me. Makes it a little harder for him to get a gun, a tape recorder, or a transmitter through."

"Isn't there some other way to do this?"

"Maybe. But I don't know what it is."

The sun was setting, a huge fireball in the sky over the Pacific. They got to the airport fifteen minutes before Charon was due. Stark bought a Las Vegas ticket and positioned himself so he could watch the metal detector. Sultana drove off.

Charon entered the terminal. Carrying a thin gray attaché case, he stood in line at the metal detector and passed through. The case slid along the conveyor through the X-ray machine. It too passed muster. The CIA man hadn't shown any ID or received special treatment.

Charon sauntered toward the departure lounge. Stark watched the crowd behind him for any of the characteristic swirls or eddies that would indicate a back-up team. He saw none.

If Sultana's "virus theory" was correct it would reduce the possibility of additional agents. The people behind the plot would want as few agents aware of the payoff as possible.

Stark followed Charon down the long passageway to the departure lounge. Passengers were already boarding. The plane was leaving in fifteen minutes.

Stark went into the men's room, into a stall, and peeled off his suit. Underneath he was wearing a blue jumpsuit similar to the kind the American Airlines maintenance workers wore. He waited until the restroom was empty and threw his suit in the garbage. He walked back out into the terminal. Charon was waiting by the phone bank.

Stark breezed up to him. "Let's take a ride to Vegas." Stark held his hand in his pocket like he had a gun.

"It's not necessary to launder the money at the gambling tables," Charon said. "It's clean."

"So's Bill Colby's conscience. C'mon. We have lots of old times to talk about."

Over the loudspeaker the announcer gave the last call for the Las Vegas flight. "You disgust me, Stark. The sooner we get this over with, the better. There's nothing worse than a traitor."

"Really? Have you ever tried tuna salad that's been left in the sun too long?"

Stark walked toward the jetway to the plane. Just before he reached it, he made a sharp turn. At a door marked "Restricted Access—Authorized Personnel Only," he paused to make sure no one was watching. Using the plastic "Do Not Disturb" sign he had taken from the motel, he slipped the lock.

He stepped through. Charon was right behind him.

"I knew the CIA class in locks and picks would come in

244

handy someday," Stark said cheerily as they walked down the metal stairs to the tarmac.

Charon's response was lost as a nearby 747 began revving its engines. The sneer on his face made his feelings clear.

"You're not carrying any weapons, right?" Stark asked.

"Of course."

Stark suddenly shoved Charon into the recession near the baggage pit. He grabbed Charon and pulled his jacket down over his arms. He reached in and took out a pistol from a shoulder holster.

"A Glock-17. One of those new 9mm Austrian Army guns," Stark said. "Steel barrel and firing pin. Plastic polymer body. Nice, lightweight. Great for smuggling past metal detectors. Is it any good for killing people?"

"Screw you."

Stark took the pen out of Charon's pocket. He pointed it at Charon and toyed with the clip.

"Be careful!" Charon said.

"Afraid of getting ink on you?"

"A .22 cartridge. With a neurotoxin."

"The pen is mightier than the sword, eh? Any other goodies? Rosa Kleb shoes with garrote laces?"

"That's it."

"Now why don't I believe you? Take off your right shoe."

Charon bent, eyeing Stark, calculating distances. Stark sensed it and stepped back. He cocked the Glock. Charon took off his shoe and tossed it to Stark.

"Basic Florsheim," Stark said, turning it over in his hands. He handed it back to Charon. After Charon slipped it on, they stepped out of the recession. Stark kept the gun in his pocket.

The DC-10 heading for Las Vegas made its pullback from the terminal. The few personnel near enough to see Stark and Charon were too busy with the jet to pay much attention. In the gloom, Stark's outfit looked official. Charon, in his suit and with an arrogant manner, looked like an executive on his way to chew out a maintenance crew member.

"Where are we going?" Charon asked.

"I want to talk."

The air was thick with the smell of jet fuel. The myriad airport vehicles—pickups, vans, fuel trucks, firefighting vehicles, conveyor belt jeeps, Hobart external power generators, baggage tractors—scurried about the field like determined insects.

Stark led Charon to the side of the terminal near the baggage pit. A Cyclone fence separated them from the loading and unloading area, where a catering truck was parked. They stood in the shadow of the building. The next flight was not due in for thirty minutes. There was no one within two hundred feet.

"Take the money and let's be done with this," Charon said.

"If you really care about the country, you'd better listen."

"There's nothing you can say."

"You're being used. You're not working for the Company. You're working for a group that has corrupted it, that's working inside."

Charon looked bored. He extended the case. They waited until a 747 rolled by, its engines making any conversation impossible.

"Who told you to come here?" Stark asked, ignoring the gesture.

"That's classified."

"It's important. The only way we can crack this."

"We? Is that you and the Reds? Have you sold out completely?"

"We, meaning me and you. The Russians are part of the conspiracy. I know about MacMillan and Hobbs."

"I never heard those names. You've gone over the edge, Stark. You're a rabid dog."

"You've got to believe me, Charon. Who is your contact?"

Charon shoved the case at Stark.

"Listen, there's a quarter million in there," Stark said. "I know, because I told that to a businessman named MacMillan. He's the civilian behind it. But I need to know who's working for him in the government."

Stark took the tape recorder out of his pocket, and played the tape of his conversation with Benedict MacMillan.

A flicker of doubt shown in Charon's eyes. His resolute look quickly returned. "I'm as good at turning agents as you are. I can dummy a tape or forge a picture as well."

"I don't have access to that technology. I'm on my own."

"Bull. The Reds are pulling your strings."

"If I was working for them, why wouldn't I have given them back their doctor?"

"It's a clever ploy."

Charon shoved the case at him again. Stark accepted it.

"Count the money," Charon said.

"I don't need to."

"I need you to count the money. Agency rules."

Stark felt the hairs on the back of his neck stiffen. He passed the case back to Charon. "You open it."

Charon gave a Cheshire cat grin, took the case and unsnapped it. Inside were stacks of one hundred dollar bills. He handed the case, still open, to Stark. "Take your coins, Judas."

"What would it take to convince you? Would your keeping the money do it?" Stark asked.

"No."

"How about if I gave you back your gun?"

Charon narrowed his eyes.

"I want us to be on the same side."

"Okay." Charon extended his hand. They shook hands.

Stark took out the gun and gave it to him.

Charon pointed the weapon at him. "You really got soft, didn't you? Do you want to confess?"

"There's nothing to confess. I told the truth."

"You're trying to make me doubt a man who is above suspicion. Peter Hornaday's as much a patriot as I am. He's got the President's ear," Charon said proudly. "Set the case down. Let's make this quick and painless. That's more than you deserve."

Stark set the case on the ground. Charon aimed and pulled the trigger.

Click.

Stark took the bullets out of his pocket. "I'm disappointed in you, Charon."

Charon whipped a pencil-thin plastic dagger from a sheath behind his neck. He lunged. Stark threw the bullets in his face. The 9mm slugs stung. Stark grabbed Charon's wrist and twisted, but the CIA man held on to the knife.

They struggled on the ground, rolling and flailing, punching and clawing, the knife in Charon's hand the ultimate prize.

247

Charon tried biting Stark's nose. Stark butted him with his forehead, catching Charon squarely on the jaw. Stark got control of the knife and twisted. He pushed the blade into Charon's thigh.

Charon pulled back, and Stark let him. Charon got up and ran.

"Wait!" Stark shouted.

Charon sprinted across the grass barrier separating the taxiing part of the field from the takeoff runway. Lights set in the grass blinked, marking the field.

He reached under his coat for the ampule. The poison on the dagger tip was already taking effect. His leg felt numb. He got the ampule out. The numbness had spread to his lower abdomen. He wobbled back and forth. He cracked the ampule under his nose and breathed deeply. The numbness rose no higher.

The air was filled with the roar of an L1011. Charon saw the plane bearing down on him. He turned to run. But his legs refused to obey. He stumbled, fell to his knees.

Stark raced to help him. But the plane was coming in too fast. Stark dove, trying to knock Charon to safety.

The landing gear missed Stark by inches. It caught Charon head on, throwing him several hundred feet.

Even before the plane had completely touched down, Stark scooped up the attaché case and ran back toward the loading area.

He found the cut portion of the fence and slipped through. Sultana was waiting in a nearby parking area, the bolt-cutter still on the seat next to her.

"Let's get out of here," Stark said.

"You okay?"

He leaned against the seat. He wanted the stench of jet fuel out of his nose, and the ringing in his ears to stop. He could still feel the raw power of the jet as it narrowly missed him.

"Fine. Let's go, we've got a plane to catch."

PART
III

CHAPTER
34

Mexico

Jefe and his men returned from their attack on the village and Jefe reported to MacMillan on what he had seen.

"You killed those who weren't affected?" MacMillan asked at the end of the briefing.

"Yes."

"Good. Your men looked unhappy when they came back."

"It is one thing to kill Communists, other soldiers. It is another to kill innocent women and children."

"When the going gets tough, the tough get going," MacMillan said jovially, slapping Jefe on the back.

Benedict didn't notice Jefe's contemptuous look, the look of a military man around a civilian who had no idea of what it meant to take lives on a wholesale basis.

"We've loaded the first few drums," MacMillan said. "They should be transported to the airport by helicopter. Have a crew take them to the shed at the airport. Leave a couple of men to stand guard. I'll be in the lab."

"Yes, sir." Jefe had made a pact with the devil. The least he could do was make sure that Castro and the other Communist pigs would go to hell with him.

"It's fucking mind-boggling," Les Halliwell said as he and his former partner sipped cups of coffee. They were seated in a diner in Hicksville, on Long Island, about five miles from Halliwell's home.

"I had LaGrange send me a picture over the AP wire," Stark said. "Sultana ID'd the number two man at the NSC as the one who had visited her at the safe house. He used the name Hobbs. His real name is Peter Hornaday. I want to know everything I can about him. Could you use your contacts in the personnel departments?"

"This is bona fide? She's not disinforming you?"

"She's legit."

Shaking his head in disbelief, Halliwell said, "A conspiracy, headed by MacMillan, involving key elements in the U.S. and Russian governments. You don't know how many people. You don't know what the purpose is, only that it involves germ warfare."

Stark nodded and slid Charon's attaché case under the table to Halliwell. "There's about $240,000 in there. I've taken some out for my own use. Before I spend it, can you check to see if it's marked?"

The money appeased Les. "Piece of cake. Can I use my old Secret Service buddies?"

"I wouldn't. Never know who works for who," Stark said. "There's a copy in there of a tape I made of my chat with MacMillan. If anything happens to me, make sure it gets to LaGrange. Send a dupe to Kaye at the *Wall Street Journal*."

"Where's the lady that caused all of this?"

"I have her tucked away."

"I bet you do, you devil you."

After each undergoing a half hour dry-cleaning routine, Stark met Halliwell the following day on a Manhattan street corner. Assured that neither had been followed, they went to the Midtown Motel on the West Side. It was far from deluxe but not quite a by-the-hour joint. Stark rapped three times, waited a second, rapped twice, waited another second, then rapped once. Sultana, the gun at her side, let him and Les in.

Les eyed her. "You're looking none the worse for wear."

Sultana smiled.

"This is a copy of Hornaday's personnel file," Halliwell said. "Interesting guy. Fletcher School of Diplomacy. Harvard. Dartmouth law school. He's survived a half-dozen administrations.''

"He's in New York right now," Halliwell continued as Stark and Mirnov thumbed through the folder. "He left a number at the hotel he's at. According to his expense vouchers, he's up here frequently. Always on official business that sounds kind of dubious. Of course, most of those bureaucrats live for the perks. He could just have a New York girlfriend.''

Stark riffled a page. "Interesting. He doesn't have a bodyguard when he's here.''

"No one really knows where he goes," Halliwell said.

"No one will know where he's going," Stark said.

"What are you talking about?" Sultana asked.

Peter Hornaday walked down Second Avenue, the coffee shop breakfast he had just eaten sitting uneasily in his belly. It was the first decent meal he had had since he got the bad news about Charon.

He had thought of Charon as invulnerable. Hornaday realized he was in way over his head. He tried to look at the bright side—Charon's death meant one less person who knew of Hornaday's machinations.

"Excuse me, don't I know you?''

Hornaday looked over. A well-dressed man was standing uncomfortably close. He had a trenchcoat draped over his arm.

"I don't think we've met," Hornaday said.

"But I do, Hornaday," Stark said. He shifted the coat, revealing the barrel of a gun. "There is a van up ahead. Step inside. You won't get hurt if you obey.''

"This is outrageous," Hornaday said, his head turning from face to face as people walked by him. "You'll never get away with this.''

"If you act up, you won't be around to find out.''

Hornaday took a few steps forward and looked around again. No one seemed to be noticing his predicament. Could he count on passersby?

Fearful, he complied with the orders. In all his bureaucratic in-fighting, he'd been a hardball player, a self described tough cookie. He always thought he'd choose death before dishonor. Now he knew the truth about himself, and it shamed him.

Just before the van, he got his courage up. The man beside him saw the change in his demeanor. He squeezed the trigger. A dart pricked Hornaday's neck. He opened his mouth to yell. Instead, he buckled at the knees.

"Knew you shouldn'ta had that fifth martini, Pete," Stark slurred loudly, his arm slipping under Hornaday's.

Several passersby gazed at them contemptuously. A few looked sympathetic.

They reached the van and the door opened. Powerful arms pulled Hornaday in. There was a driver, with a hat pulled low on his face, and the man who had helped him in. Hornaday was blindfolded, his hands bound. He could hear the kidnapper climb in.

The van started up and pulled away.

The kidnappers spoke very little, and when they did, it was in Chinese. One voice predominated, the others uttered monosyllabic responses.

Barely conscious, Hornaday kept listening for familiar noises, trying to guess where they were going. No one asked him any questions. The drug made his muscles rebellious. He tried to move his fingers and they refused to respond.

The men began to argue in Chinese, their sing-song voices getting louder. He heard his name repeated several times in the midst of angry sentences.

Hornaday gasped for air. He thought of the stereotyped images of the cruel Oriental, the Chinese water torture, Fu Manchu.

The van pulled into a garage and stopped.

He was helped out and into a house. He was regaining his equilibrium as the muscle relaxer began to wear off.

"We're going to give you a drug to help you speak truthfully," the voice said. "Don't fight it."

"I'm allergic to many drugs," Hornaday lied.

"Don't worry, a doctor will be present," the voice said.

Halliwell took off the hat that had covered his face.

"If you're wrong, boy, are we fucked," Les said, shaking his head. "Kidnapping a national security advisor." He wiped the sheen of sweat from his brow.

"We didn't have the manpower to follow him for a prolonged period of time," Stark said.

The third man removed his ski mask. He was a grayhaired, supremely dignified looking Oriental.

"Ready?" Stark asked him.

The man nodded.

Stark strode in to where Hornaday sat, eyes a trifle glazed, tied to a chair. Stark had made a big show of injecting him with a harmless saline solution.

"We know about your involvement with MacMillan," Stark said.

Hornaday gulped. "Water, please."

Sultana came in with a glass and gave him a sip.

"This is Mr. Hsu," Stark said, and the Chinese man gave a slight bow. "He's with the Central External Liaison Department of the People's Republic of China."

"What's he doing here?" Hornaday asked.

"When I learned that you and the Russians, with MacMillan's help, were planning germ warfare against the Chinese, I felt it my obligation to inform them."

"What? That's crazy."

"Then why were you doing it?"

"MacMillan wanted to help us. He was going to do germ warfare research covertly. But now I don't know."

"How many people in the U.S. government know about this?"

"I don't know." Hornaday was bug-eyed, staring at Hsu.

"Who gives you orders?"

"I—I acted on my own initiative."

Stark turned to the man he'd introduced as "Mr. Hsu."

"Do you believe him?" Stark asked.

"Mr. Hsu" shook his head.

"It's the truth, honestly," Hornaday said shrilly. "I was blackmailed into it. There's no one else. It's not government policy. I swear." His gaze swerved from Hsu to Stark and back again. "Please, we don't want a war. It's a mistake. I didn't mean anything. Please."

Hsu bobbed his head and walked out.

"Did he believe me?" Hornaday asked. "Did he believe me?"

"Where's MacMillan?"

"He went to Mexico. The plant there, a hundred miles from Mazatlán."

"What's he doing there?"

"I don't know. You've got to understand, if his father was handling this, it would be different. But he's crazy. A kid still pulling wings off flies."

"Nice guy to trust with germ warfare info."

"I didn't know, I just didn't know."

CHAPTER
35

Stark stepped outside with the man he had introduced as "Mr. Hsu."

"Christ!" Chuckie Lee said. "How'd a bozo like that get so high up in government? I can't believe what I just heard."

"You can't tell anyone," Stark emphasized.

"Hey, don't forget, it was my people who brought meaning to the word inscrutable," the restaurateur said.

"Thank you, Mr. Lee," Stark said.

"Thank you, Robert. I haven't had this much excitement since I knocked out Santiago in the fifth."

Stark went back inside.

"Hornaday wants to make amends," Halliwell said cynically. "He's our buddy now. Creep's hoping to save his pension."

"It's a lot more than his pension he should be worrying about," Stark said. "Where's Sultana?"

"She's in with him now. Seeing what he actually knows about the biological details."

She came out in a few minutes, white-faced.

"He only read pieces of report when he had it translated from Russian," she said. "But it is dangerous, very dangerous."

257

"You don't think MacMillan would try to save the world by destroying it, do you?" Halliwell asked.

"I didn't think anyone would be stupid enough to play around with BW," Stark said.

When a cold-eyed Stark entered, Hornaday asked nervously, "Did Hsu believe me?"

"I hope so. You're going to get busy cleaning up the mess you made."

A half-dozen phone calls by Hornaday and the remaining federal obstacles—the warrants and alerts planted against Stark in the bureaucracy—were knocked down.

"You think about how you're going to persuade MacMillan to shut down the operation," Stark said, striding from the room.

Mirnov and Halliwell were sipping coffee at the kitchen table.

"We're going to need firepower, just in case," Stark said. "Automatic weapons. A LAW rocket or two."

"And white phospherus or napalm," Sultana said.

Halliwell regarded her quizzically.

"Conventional explosives will spread germs," she explained. "We need high heat."

"I'll arrange for Pedro to meet us in Mexico," Stark said. "Les, speak to our munitions people. I'll handle getting the plane ready. Sultana, you stay with Hornaday, see if you can get anything more out of him. Let's move."

In less than two hours they had a fueled Lear Jet waiting at the airport. The plane had an Inertial Navigation System, the NASA-developed guidance system used on commercial aircraft. A platform stabilized with gyroscopes measured the earth-rate precession, pinpointing the exact longitude and latitude even when traveling through the magnetic turbulence at the North Pole. Linked to a computer, it was able to find the shortest Great Circle route and automatically compensate for wind and atmospheric conditions.

The docile Hornaday was led into the plane by a gun-toting Sultana. Halliwell was the last to arrive. Behind him came a baggage tractor, loaded with two crates of weaponry. He had paid premium prices to get the rush order through.

There was a crate of TH grenades, thermite filled and each capable of burning to 4330 degrees Fahrenheit. Another

258

container held several thousand rounds of ammo and white phospherous grenades. The third held a carbine, two Uzis, a pump shotgun, flak vests, and assorted gear, including high-filtration gas masks.

As the baggage handler moved the heavy crates off the cart, he glanced up and saw Mirnov standing in the doorway. In the hubbub and hurry, no one noticed the flash of recognition in his eyes.

Hornaday, only too eager to cooperate, used his clout to get priority clearance for takeoff. Even as the plane taxied down the runway, the baggage handler was at a phone.

"This is Tony at JFK. You know that doll you was looking for, I just saw her. That guy you wanted was with her. Plus a couple others. They're on their way to Mazatlán."

Mirnov, Halliwell, and Hornaday sat at the small table in the passenger compartment of the Lear Jet. Stark was in the cockpit, keeping one ear on the conversation, and both eyes on the sophisticated guidance system.

"Do you think MacMillan will cooperate?" Mirnov asked Hornaday.

"I can't predict," Hornaday said, stroking his chin. "He is a bully. If we confront him with enough force, make it evident that he has no viable options, perhaps." Hornaday was regaining his confidence.

"What about the Mexican authorities?" Halliwell asked.

"We can't get them to help on this," Hornaday said.

"I was thinking about their reaction to the firepower we're bringing in," Halliwell said. "You can't tell them we're planning to use LAW rockets for deer hunting."

"I can smooth things over at the airport," Hornaday said. "I've dealt with the local head of Mexican Customs on a drug interdiction matter. It might require a small donation."

"How much *mordida* will he want?" Halliwell asked.

"He'll initially demand ten thousand dollars, but chances are we can get him down to five," Hornaday said.

Halliwell looked pained.

"There is not time to bargain," Mirnov said. "Pay whatever they demand."

"That's easy for you to say," Halliwell snapped. "You know how much you've cost us already?"

Stark stepped into the cabin. "It's for a good cause,"

Stark said. To Sultana he explained, "Whenever you negotiate, you shouldn't give in to the first demand. Otherwise the other person thinks they didn't quote you a high enough price, and they'll screw up the deal." He turned to Hornaday and pointed to the attaché case with the money he had taken from Charon and said, "Whatever you need. Call him now, start working on the deal."

The plane gave a jolt, the wheels screeched, and the Lear Jet shuddered to a halt on the tarmac at the edge of Mazatlán *aeropuerto*.

Hornaday had arranged for safe passage into the country for a five thousand dollar bribe. Customs Chief Miguel Guzman had arranged for them to land at the edge of the airport.

Guzman and three men strode toward the plane.

"Miguel, *cómo está Usted?*" Hornaday said cheerfully.

"*Muy bien, amigo*. Your Spanish is much improved."

Hornaday smiled as he and the others walked down the plane's stairs. The national security advisor was carrying a flight bag with five thousand in it.

"Why the welcoming committee?" Hornaday asked the Mexican.

"We can help you unload," Miguel said, grinning and throwing an arm around Hornaday. "I want to talk to you about another matter as well. Is everyone off the plane?"

"Yes," Hornaday said.

The question made the hairs on Stark's neck tingle.

"*Bueno.*" Miguel drew his gun. Simultaneously, the men with him bristled with Mauser machine pistols.

"What's going on?" Hornaday demanded.

"There is a gentleman in Los Angeles named Castellano who wants your companions. You are all under arrest."

"We're here under your protection representing the United States government," an outraged Hornaday shouted.

"I must insist that the lady and the one named Stark come with me. The rest of you will be searched and taken to a safe place." He extended his hand in a gentlemanly manner, beckoning Sultana.

Her eyes met Stark's. He knew what was going to happen.

She rushed to Miguel. "Please, don't let them take me back. Don't let them hurt me."

She pressed against his chest. Guzman grinned, stroking her blond hair, his gun still aimed at the men.

The other gunmen made puckering noises.

"Can't you just say I got away?" she pleaded. "We have more money."

"I will compromise," Guzman said. "I'll accept your gracious offer of more money, and turn you over to my northern friends."

She lifted her knee between his legs with all her strength, cutting him off in mid-smirk. She got her hand on his gun as he screamed.

Stark charged—the last thing the men with the guns expected. He smashed down on the bridge of one man's nose. His follow-up blow with the heel of his hand shoved the bone fragments into the gunman's skull.

Another man aimed at Stark. Stark snapped a knife-edge hand into his throat and sent him spinning. He grabbed the man's gun and returned fire at the welcoming committee.

Guzman tried to wrestle his gun back from Sultana. He pulled it from her hands, then a stray round caught him in the neck. She jerked the gun back.

Fifty shots were fired in the furious thirty-second fire fight.

Two of the three gunmen lay dead. Halliwell always wore a bulletproof vest. The front of his suit was shredded where bullets had stitched. He was stunned, but essentially unharmed.

Guzman lay dead, still clutching the cash-filled flight bag. Hornaday lay next to him, an ugly moist sound coming from the widening red patch on his chest. Mirnov was already tending him.

Stark raced to the plane and retrieved their first aid kit.

Stark stood over Hornaday as Sultana cleaned his sucking chest wound and placed a thick sterile gauze pad over the red hole. They exchanged one look and Stark knew Hornaday wouldn't make it. He turned from the carnage.

"Les, are you up to getting Pedro from the terminal?" Stark said. Les nodded and stumbled off.

The two survivors of the welcoming committee, both suffering minor wounds, sat on the tarmac, nervously watching Stark's every move.

Stark walked briskly to the survivors, his face full of cold menace. *"Su nombre?"*

"We don't know that spic talk," one of the wounded men said.

"All right, who are you? Where are you from?"

The man hesitated, weighing the pros and cons of hanging tough. Stark produced a K-bar knife and nonchalantly flipped it in his hand. He stepped toward the wounded man.

"We was just doing a job. For Castellano," the man blurted. "We don't know why he wanted you. I hear he's got a soft touch with a fed, doing him a favor."

Stark sidled over to Dr. Mirnov, still keeping an eye on the two survivors.

"I'm sorry," Hornaday said, and died.

Mirnov got up slowly. "What do we do now?"

Stark scanned the airport. "Assuming this is the nearest major air facility, MacMillan may have left some clue. We might have to interview every cabdriver, or . . ."

Sultana followed Stark's gaze. The MacMillan Lear Jet, with ISS logo on the tail, was sitting like a well-fed bird on the tarmac.

A few minutes later, a cleaned-up and composed Stark strode up the steps into the Lear Jet. The pilot, who had been reading a copy of *Aviation Week,* glanced up.

"Well, if this don't take the cake," Stark said. "My name's Jerry Miller. Of Miller Technical. Tech and Elec, we call it. You must be Cal's pilot."

"Yes."

"Is that old coot around?"

"No."

"Don't tell me you hijacked his jet?"

"I'm here with Benedict."

"How is that boy? Still crazy as a bull-goose loony?"

The pilot smiled.

Stark looked over the controls. "You know, I fly my own baby. 'Course it's not as big as this one."

"What kind do you have?" the pilot asked.

The two men began discussing the relative merits of various fixed-wing crafts. Hogan Stimson was grateful for the break in the boredom. He had strict orders during his travels not to talk to strangers. But that was as far as divulging business secrets, like where MacMillan had been or who he met with. This was different. Besides, Benedict wasn't someone to respect like the old man was.

"Where is Benedict?" Stark asked. "I guess I ought to say hello. Find out if they need any more insulators. Ours are top notch, you know."

"Benedict went off somewhere into the bush. Dressed like big bwana."

Both men laughed.

"No idea where?"

"Afraid not."

"They might be able to help you there," the pilot said, pointing to the last shed in a row of metal buildings on the edge of the field.

"Much obliged," Stark said. "Hey, maybe you got a radio to contact him with?"

Stimson shook his head.

"Ah, well." Stark deplaned and hurried to where Halliwell, Quesada, and Sultana were waiting.

"I need someone to serve as a distraction," Stark said.

"I can do it," Quesada volunteered.

Sultana unbuttoned the top two buttons on her shirt.

"She's got a pair of aces to your busted flush," Halliwell said.

Sánchez, who had been with Major Ortega at the Indian village, stood in the doorway of the shed, a carbine in a sling over his shoulder. An Oakland Raiders baseball cap drooped over his forehead.

Sultana walked slowly toward him, languidly, sensually.

"Buenos días, señor," she said, stretching her arms up. It showed she was unarmed and lifted her breasts. He didn't notice that her index finger was extended.

Halliwell was watching from the distance, through the scope of Pedro Quesada's sniper rifle.

"She only sees one guard," he hissed to Stark.

"Got it."

Halliwell shifted the scope until the crosshairs were centered on the chest of the man in the doorway.

"I'm looking for Señor MacMillan," Sultana said.

"He's not here."

"Can I come in and cool off?"

"Sure," Sánchez said eagerly.

Sultana was just a few yards away when he noticed the baggage tractor pulling a luggage cart coming toward him. He unhitched his carbine.

"Restricted area, get out," Sánchez yelled when the driver was twenty yards away.

The driver cocked a hand to his ear as if he couldn't hear.

"Get out of here, *cabron*," Sánchez yelled. The tractor was only ten yards off now.

The man stopped the tractor. "What did you say?" the driver asked.

"Get the fuck out of here, pronto!" Sánchez yelled.

Sultana began hurrying away.

"Not you," Sánchez shouted, taking a step after her.

The tractor driver, Pedro Quesada, dove behind the tractor. Stark popped out of the luggage cart.

As Sánchez lifted his gun, Stark shot his legs out from under him. Sultana ran to him and applied direct pressure to his wounds.

"Pedro, debrief him, find out where the base is, the layout, the number of hostiles," Stark barked.

Sultana worked on patching the man's wounds while Quesada questioned him.

Stark stepped inside the dark shed. A bare bulb hung from the ceiling. There were a couple of chairs, a picnic cooler with beer, and men's magazines on the dirt floor.

Behind him were six steel drums, painted red. Black letters warned "FRAGILE—KEEP FROM HEAT."

Sultana entered. "Man is dead. Shock. He said MacMillan is nearly ready to go."

She knelt by the drums and inspected them for leaks.

"Looks okay. We put thermite grenades here," she said. "Hurry. Man said helicopter from base is due here in ten minutes with more cans."

Stark found Sánchez's cap lying on the floor and pulled on Sánchez's shirt and pants, which were blood-spattered and a couple of sizes too small. They had just finished cleaning up the area outside the shed when they heard the chopper.

A few moments after it landed, they heard, "Hey, lazy bones, get out here!"

Stark, head tilted down so the cap covered his face, walked out briskly.

"That's right, get a move on," the chopper pilot said. He was one of the two blacks in Jefe's team. "Lucky bastard siestas in the shade all day playing with your pecker."

Stark was fifteen feet from the pilot when the man noticed how poorly the clothes fit. He reached for his pistol, but Stark was already aiming at him.

"Don't," Stark ordered.

The man obeyed.

"Drop your gun. Tell me your exact course for the base. Don't make any trouble and you get to live," Stark said.

The man nodded. "No trouble."

"No trouble."

A few minutes later, Stark, Sultana, Halliwell, and Quesada were ready to climb onboard. The chopper pilot, hands and legs bound, was sitting in the shed. He stared nervously at the red drums. Now there were eight of them.

Quesada had questioned him, using what they had learned from the dying Sánchez. The details they'd been given jibed.

Stark borrowed Quesada's rifle. He aimed at MacMillan's Lear Jet, several hundred yards away. Two shots, and two of the tires were useless.

Halliwell loaded the armaments into the helicopter while Stark and Sultana gazed at the deadly drums.

"You're a brave lady," Stark said. He took her in his arms and they kissed.

"You don't have to come with us," Stark said.

"If there is a biohazard, I am the most experienced to deal with it," she said. "I come. No argument."

"No argument."

She smiled. "You know what you are?"

"What?"

"A delicious strawberry."

CHAPTER
36

Benedict MacMillan—in the midst of harvesting the deadly bacteriophages—heard the helicopter returning and moved quicker. After a dozen cans were at the shed, he would go to the airport and instruct his pilot to transport the load, with the mercenaries, to the selected cities.

In those cities, he had arranged for skywriting the words PEACE—MacMillan.

For the more restricted Soviet Union and the People's Republic of China, he'd have to use the attaché cases. He already had several volunteers among the mercenaries. He had told them he'd be providing a vaccine that would protect them. They believed him.

The helicopter didn't land. He was used to hearing a certain rhythm, after its four trips to Mazatlán. The copter seemed to pause at the edge of the compound.

He continued scraping the semisolid agar solution, each movement the same precise sweep. Then he heard the loudspeakers on the helicopter. The voice was speaking Spanish. He couldn't make out what was being said.

MacMillan set the microbes he was working with aside and peered out through the thick, double-paneled window. His men were scrambling around, waving their guns and shouting. He ripped off his anticontamination suit, grabbed his .45, and rushed out.

The vintage Huey hovered in the sky, noisy, dark, menacing, as its wash kicked up dust in the compound. Sánchez's body was thrown from the chopper. The troops on the ground were instantly demoralized as the corpse made an ugly thump. The body lay with limbs and neck twisted in grotesque angles.

Stark was piloting the craft. As soon as the body was dumped, the Huey gained in maneuverability.

The mercenaries fired. The armor plate on the helicopter shrugged the bullets off.

Jefe ran to the surplus M60 machine gun at the edge of the small field, near the helicopter landing pad. It was a fortified machine gun nest, with a three-foot-high wall of sandbags all around. Fifty-five gallon drums were waiting to be loaded.

"We have taken your helicopter, and your germs," Stark said in English. "In five minutes, we will be spraying the area with the microbe solution. Throw down your guns and run to the east and we will not hurt you." He repeated the message in Spanish.

Three rifles hit the ground simultaneously. Two more soldiers hesitated, saw their buddies deserting, and they too dropped their guns and ran.

"Pick up your weapons," Jefe shouted, halting at the belt fed, 7.62mm tripod mounted machine gun. He fired into the pack of fleeing men. Two deserters fell dead. It made the survivors run quicker.

MacMillan ran out of the lab in time to see the desertion. He counted four mercenaries left, including Jefe.

Jefe barked orders at his remaining men. They found cover and began winging shots at the helicopter. Halliwell, in the doorgunner position, fired back a spray of automatic fire from the front gun. Mirnov emptied the clip in the carbine.

They aimed wide of the buildings, fearful of piercing any containers. The ammo for their small arms was soft-nosed lead, dum dums, which would not penetrate metal. But the ammo from the Huey's guns was copper-jacketed, military issue, and could lead to a catastrophe if it hit a biohazard area.

The pause MacMillan had initially heard was the chopper dropping Quesada, from a ten-foot height, into a pond at the edge of the compound. He cut through the barbed wire and hustled to high ground position on a foliage-covered hillock. He had a .380 Winchester with a Bushnell scope.

Quesada opened fire. The soldiers began shooting back at him.

Jefe loaded armor-piercing rounds into the M60 and swung the machine gun into play against the Huey. The tracers it fired streamed bright, even under the hot Mexican sun. One of the rounds hit the tail rotor. There was an explosion. The chopper shook like a marionette with its strings cut.

Hot metal flew through the compartment. Halliwell screamed in pain. Stark wrestled with the controls, cutting the engine, and trying to autorotate it down. The copter pinwheeled.

"Jump!" Stark said to Sultana. "Head for the Quonset hut."

"What about you?" she asked, grabbing a knapsack with ten thermite grenades.

"Just jump!" He moved the helicopter to block her flight from the soldiers on the ground.

Quesada was within twenty yards of the sandbagged circle where MacMillan, Jefe, and two soldiers were crouched.

Quesada tossed a white phos; herus grenade. It fell inside the circle. One of the soldiers picked it up to throw it out. Quesada shot him dead. The grenade exploded. There was a cloud of smoke and the screams of burning men. But the body of the soldier who had tried to toss it absorbed most of the blast. MacMillan and Jefe were only dazed.

The chopper was barely six feet off the ground. Mirnov jumped, the wash from the chopper rolling her in the dirt. She got up, limping, an ankle twisted, and hobbled as quickly as she could toward the camouflaged Quonset hut.

Stark, still wrestling with the controls, managed to touch the crippled copter down. Even before it had settled, he was diving from it and zigzagging toward shelter, his movements slowed by his carrying Halliwell.

The defenders had been distracted by Quesada's assault on the sandbag fortification. By the time they redirected their fire, Stark and his partner were safe behind the barracks.

The chopper slowly turned over. The rotor blades hit the

ground, and the flying beast ripped itself apart. Metal fragments, some as big as motorcycles, flew through the air.

Then it was quiet.

Stark, breathing hard, checked Halliwell and found his partner was still alive. Stark ripped off his sleeve and used it to bind up an ugly wound on Halliwell's shoulder. He took out a gas mask and put it over Halliwell's face.

Stark had trouble moving. He didn't understand it until he saw the red seeping through the shirt on his right side. He tore open his own shirt. There was a two-inch gash, but it didn't appear to have pierced the rib cage. There wasn't time to dress the wound. He pulled on a gas mask and checked that he had a full clip in his Uzi.

Stark peered out from behind the barracks. Jefe and one other man were in the sandbagged circle.

Had any of the shots hit the steel drums?

Dr. Mirnov pulled on a gas mask as she hurried through the safety airlock into the Quonset hut lab. There was only one file cabinet. Locked. She found a tool kit and used a screwdriver to pop it open.

She skimmed files, dumping them on the floor as she finished. There were occasional popping noises in the background as shots were exchanged by the men outside.

At last she found the Russian report on bacteriophage in germ warfare. The research was meticulous, brilliant, a clever extrapolation of previously done work. She flipped to the final page to see who had signed it.

Dr. Dorokhov. Her mentor.

Suddenly someone ripped the gas mask from her face, taking clumps of hair from her scalp that made her cry out.

"Enjoying your reading, bitch?" MacMillan asked, the .45 steady in his hand.

CHAPTER
37

The hot air was acrid with fumes from the burning helicopter and the gunplay. The cordite smell seeped through the Whetherlite filter on his gas mask.

Stark crept forward on his belly, out of view of the defenders in the sandbag circle.

Sporadic gunfire. Pedro would wing a shot at the two men, Jefe would fire back a half dozen.

Stark was near the circle when a mercenary, who had hidden by MacMillan's jeep, saw him. Stark heard the man's movement and rolled even before he fired. Bullets stitched the ground where Stark had been.

Jefe and the other soldier spun in his direction. Stark jumped up and ran, broken-field style, toward the jeep. It hurt when he breathed in deeply, a stabbing pain in his side. Stark's Uzi stopped its reassuring song midway through his sprint. Jammed. Stark threw the gun aside. No time to draw his Browning.

The mercenary in the jeep was trying to reload when Stark hit him, nearly knocking him out of the vehicle. The man swung his gun butt, catching Stark's ear. Vision blurred from the pain, Stark grabbed the man's arm. The mercenary clawed at Stark's face.

Jefe opened fire. Bullets smashed into the jeep's body, making whining thumps. The slugs hit the windshield of the jeep, and the mercenary was battered with glass shards. Stark twisted the man upward, directly into Jefe's deadly spray. The mercenary was shredded by the 7.62mm slugs spewing out at nine rounds per second.

While Jefe's attention had been drawn by the struggle, his remaining ally had run off, arms waving wildly so Quesada wouldn't shoot him.

"Give it up!" Stark shouted to Jefe.

Jefe spat. "I'm not afraid to die." He fired in Stark's direction.

Stark started the engine on the jeep. It turned over, though it made a sickly grinding sound and leaked pungent antifreeze. Stark revved the engine and sent the jeep hurtling toward the sandbag fortification. Jefe pumped bullets into the car. They tore out what was left of the radiator and much of the engine, but the car's momentum kept it going.

Stark was crouched down behind the dash, the solid metal of the firewall keeping him safe. At the last second, just before the jeep hit the bags, and possibly the steel drums, Stark swerved it away. At the same moment, he leaped from the jeep, landing inside the sandbag circle.

Jefe had a K-bar knife in his hands instantly. Held low, darting forward like a snake's tongue. Stark didn't have a chance to draw his gun. Too busy dodging the weapon.

Jefe lunged, Stark grabbed his arm and tried to twist, but Jefe spun away.

The wounds made Stark weak. Jefe lunged again. The knife grazed Stark's side. Jefe grinned as his blade came back painted red.

Jefe feinted and charged for the *coup de grâce*. Stark grabbed his arms, pinning them to his side. The men struggled and fell, rolling in the dirt. The gas mask was torn from Stark's face. He got a mouthful of dry dust.

Jefe had a ferocious, wiry strength. He edged the blade nearer and nearer to Stark's throat.

Then suddenly his head bobbed. He stopped and his eyes rolled. Stark shoved him away.

Pedro stood over him. His rifle butt had crushed the back of Jefe's skull.

Stark stood up and gave Pedro a silent glance of thanks.

"Les is by the barracks," Stark said. "He needs help."

"You do, too."

"You gave me all the help I need," Stark said, drawing his gun.

"I'll go for the girl. You take care of Les," Pedro said.

But Stark was already springing toward the lab. There was no logical way to explain that he had to do it, that he could trust her life to no one else. He was in a state of *munen muso*, not thinking. Not not thinking. Ecstasy.

"Why—why you doing this?" Sultana asked.

"To show the leaders of the world," Macmillan said. "My father knows. He knows them all. But I'm better than any of them."

"It is over," she said. "Put the gun down. We will get you help."

"Over? No way. It's just beginning. The operation will go ahead. You can't stop it."

"What was your plan?" she asked, stalling for time.

He didn't answer. He lifted the gun, about to fire. She grabbed a vial of the microbe solution from the counter and held it aloft.

"If you shoot, I throw this down."

"Put that back."

"You know what it is like to die from this?"

"Put that down, I said!"

"Give me gun."

"You wouldn't drop that. You'd die, too."

He saw in her eyes that she would indeed break the glass. She saw in his eyes the manic insanity. They stared at each other, a mongoose and a cobra.

Her arms grew weak, quivery, exhausted. Still she held the vial high like a grim parody of the Statue of Liberty.

When there was a hiss at the door to the entrance, Benedict made his move. He plunged forward. His big hand closed around the tube and wrenched it from Sultana's grip. At the same time, his other hand grabbed her throat. MacMillan set the vial down in a wooden holder and turned his murderous attention to Sultana.

Stark came through the biosafety door, crouching low, expecting a shot.

Instead he saw Mirnov in Benedict's stranglehold grip.

MacMillan twisted her to block Stark from shooting. She

272

kicked and struggled, but he held her like she was a helpless child.

"Lay the gun down on the table or I break her neck," MacMillan said.

"Let her go," Stark responded.

Benedict tightened his grip. "I'll kill the bitch. Drop the gun."

About an inch of MacMillan's shoulder protruded behind Sultana's smaller frame. Stark was twenty feet from him, holding the pistol at his hip. An impossible shot.

Stark stared into Sultana's face. "Kill him," she mouthed, and renewed her fruitless struggles.

"In weakness, there is strength," Stark said, locking eyes on Sultana.

"What're you talking about?" MacMillan demanded.

Mirnov tried twisting and turning, but Benedict's massive arms held her nearly immobile.

"A baby is soft and weak, a corpse is stiff and strong," Stark said. "In weakness, there is strength. And life."

"Only a weakling would say that," MacMillan said.

Mirnov stopped her struggles and went limp, dead weight in MacMillan's arms, dropping lower. About two inches of his shoulder were visible.

The arrow and the target are one. The archer mustn't aim.

Stark lifted the gun and fired.

The bullet grazed Benedict's shoulder. His grip loosened momentarily. Sultana fell to the floor.

Stark pulled the trigger again.

The bullet entered MacMillan's right eye. It didn't have enough momentum left to exit his skull. It spun round and round, coring his brain like an apple.

Stark ran to Sultana and helped her over to a counter. She leaned against it, swaying weakly from her ordeal. There were dark red thumbprints on her neck.

He took her knapsack and removed the grenades. He planted them every few feet around the perimeter of the room, putting extra ones near the tanks marked "Flammable."

He hoisted the wobbly Mirnov over his shoulder. She held the papers with the results on the germ warfare. Just before they stepped through the doorway, she deliberately dropped the papers to the floor.

He helped her to where Pedro was tending Halliwell, set her down, and hurried back to the lab.

He raced around the room, pulling pins, and then ran from the building. He had just thrown himself down when the Quonset hut lab seemed to glow, the light preceding the sound. Then there was a whump, a whoosh, and a loud bang, and the building turned into a giant ball of flame.

The guard at the American consulate in Mazatlán had seen all kinds. Usually it was stoned smart asses, trying to mooch a loan to get back to the States. Their stories were as threadbare as their clothes. They claimed to be innocent tourists waylaid by bandits. Most were dope dealers ripped off by their Mexican connections.

But the four people before him were standouts. They said they'd been in a car accident, but he didn't believe it. He'd seen survivors after the bombing in Lebanon that looked in better shape.

The leader was a guy with killer eyes, no doubt about it. The guy, who said his name was Stark, was insisting the local CIA man punch a cryptonym into the computer. Official policy was to deny that there even was a local CIA man.

"We can't help you here," the guard said. "Go back to your hotel, take a hot bath, and you'll feel better."

"Just tell the station chief that I have a message from Peter Hornaday," Stark said.

The guard blocked the doorway. "Station chief? You looking for a fire station?"

Stark smiled disarmingly and hit the guard once on the carotid artery. He dropped like he'd been poleaxed.

Stark stepped over the body, pressed the buzzer on the desk, and they strode into the inner sanctum of the embassy.

They found the CIA chief of station's office. Like most embassies, it was the most modern office without a name on the door.

They walked in and the chief of station, a portly man in a sweat-stained white shirt, jumped up. A woman clerk stared. A young man reached for his desk drawer.

"Don't do it," Stark growled, and the young man, a codebreaker by trade who liked to fantasize about the exciting world he was in, froze.

"My name is Robert Stark. My cryptonym used to be Terrier. Punch it up, and see what you get."

The young man looked at the station chief, who nodded.

The codebreaker went to the computer, which was linked to the Octopus at Langley, and typed in his access code. Then he typed in Terrier.

The screen filled with words describing Stark's time with the Agency and his work as a private security consultant. The last entry was one of Hornaday's final acts, canceling the all-stations alert for Stark.

The station chief read the entire account and grumbled. He prided himself on running a quiet station that generated just enough intelligence to justify its existence. He had a year to go before retirement. His passion was deep sea fishing and doing as little work as possible. "What can we do for you?"

"I need to send an 'eyes only' cable to the DCI," Stark said. "My friends need clothes, medical attention."

"Well, okay. Just make it clear I wasn't informed of any activities you may or may not have been involved in," the station chief said.

"Good. There's a guard outside who's probably going to come to soon and call for the *federales*. Better go calm him. I need someone to show me how to work this thing," Stark said, indicating the secure transmitting computer. "There's been some changes since I last was a civil servant."

EPILOGUE

Stark reclined on the couch, sipping his freshly squeezed orange juice.

He had spent the morning on the phone with security clients eager to come back into the fold. Making up for their lack of loyalty had been the higher figures in their renegotiated contracts.

Stark had not wanted to get back to business so soon. It was only a week after the assault on MacMillan's base in Mexico. Halliwell was still in the hospital, due to be discharged in a couple of days. He had thrown out his back and one of his wounds had gotten infected, but he was expected to suffer no permanent damage.

Stark knew the best way to aid Les in his recovery was to get the business going again.

Pedro Quesada had returned to his family in Los Angeles. His wife had gotten him to promise he would retire. Stark wired him a substantial severance pay check.

The next day, Stark had gotten a call. Quesada wanted to return the check, to go back on active duty. He couldn't take sitting around the house. Stark laughed and got him to promise to try it for a month.

"I'm not hiring anyone to take your place, amigo," Stark said.

Stark had checked out of the hospital, against the doctor's

advice, after just four days. He had two broken ribs, a dislocated shoulder, and numerous cuts of various depth and severity.

He picked up the phone to return another call.

"No more," said Sultana Mirnov, coming out of the kitchen with a steaming pot of *chifir,* the thick Russian tea. "You've done enough work for the day."

All she wore was one of his shirts, which covered her to a few inches above the knee. She opened his robe and inspected his wounds, changing a dressing, pleased at the lack of any fresh bleeding.

"Were you able to make the arrangements?" she asked.

"Your federal grant comes through in a few weeks," he said.

"How did you do it?"

"Even though Hornaday was acting on his own, it would be a major scandal if what he did were to get out."

"You blackmailed the government?"

"Let's just say grateful authorities are repaying us for our silence."

"I am nervous about working for government again," she said.

"They've promised you your own project. Choose whatever you want."

She clapped her hands, leaned over, and kissed him.

They touched each other tenderly.

She took his hand and tugged. He got up. She pulled him toward the bedroom.

"Is time to start physical therapy. Under doctor's supervision."

"What did you have in mind?" he asked, grinning as they reached the doorway.

She began unbuttoning her shirt.

"Let's pick strawberries."